Brazen

Brazen

CHRISTINA FARLEY

SKYSCAPE

SKYSCAPE

Text copyright © 2015 by Christina Farley

Published by Skyscape, New York

www.apub.com

Amazon, the Amazon logo, and Skyscape are trademarks of Amazon.com, Inc., or its affiliates.

ISBN-13 (hardcover): 9781503945081
ISBN-10 (hardcover): 1503945081
ISBN-13 (paperback): 9781503945104
ISBN-10 (paperback): 1503945103

Cover design by Cliff Nielsen
Printed in the United States of America

For David, brother and friend.

למרות שאני אלך בגיא צל מוות
אני מפחד לא רע, כי אתה עימי

(Even though I walk through the valley of the shadow of death,
I will fear no evil, for you are with me.)
Psalm 23:4

CHAPTER 1

Darkness will eat you alive, piece by piece, until there is nothing left except emptiness and loneliness.

It's eating away at me, chunk by chunk, ripping out the person I was. The person I'm meant to be. It's a daily struggle to resist its pull. Its power. I don't know how much longer I can hold it off, how much longer I'll last before it wraps its cold, icy fingers around me and I no longer feel or even care.

That's the scariest part.

But tonight the darkness serves its purpose for what I'm about to do. A warm wind whispers across my face as I crouch in the shadows of the Korean National Intelligence Service. The massive four-story building looms before me, its walls pocked with small square windows that glint as spotlights roam past. The building curves inward, centering on a glass-faced entrance with a dome cupped over its top. The buzz of the city is muted behind the stone walls that I just slipped over, and the soft grass beneath my boots creates a deceptively calm atmosphere, masking the building's true purpose: intrigue and espionage.

I'm about to commit my first of a billion crimes. Not that it matters. I'm dead to my friends and family anyway. From their perspectives, I died with my best friend, Michelle, two weeks ago. The remains discovered in a car wreck were claimed to be Michelle's and mine. The god of darkness, Kud, made sure his cronies scattered our DNA within the wreckage. It was his terrible way of making sure I suffer as much as possible. A scream claws at my throat as I remember how Michelle's blood pooled at my feet after Kud murdered her.

I shut my eyes and inhale deep breaths, shoving that scream far down within my chest. There it must stay buried, or I will lose control. And that must never happen. Instead I run my hands along my crossbow and recheck the equipment attached to my belt: cable, clamps, leather pouch, and dagger. I slip my mask over my face. Dressed in a black bodysuit with this mask, I'm hoping my outfit will allow my form to blend with the shadows.

Tonight is my first step toward avenging Michelle's death, and if everything goes as planned, I will be on my way to implementing my own insane scheme.

With these tortured thoughts, I take off in a sprint across the courtyard. The surveillance camera will pick me up in . . .

One.

Two.

Three seconds.

The alarms blare. I jab my fists into my pouch and pull out two glass vials filled with red vapor. I smash them to the ground on either side. The vapors rise and contort over the grass. With a blast of crimson light, they erupt into wild hounds spinning through the air, all claws and snarling and drool.

Kud's bloodhounds.

"Remember your orders," I tell the hounds. "You are to keep the guards at bay. Do not attack."

Just as I expected, two guards race across the grounds and aim their guns at my forehead, their red lasers blinding me. One yells a warning in Korean to stop. I freeze, unsure of my next move. The hound on my left leaps through the air with white poison frothing from its mouth. The poison will kill its victim, which is why Kud promised me they wouldn't attack. As the hound's claws reach for the guard, anger rises through my core. The hounds are not obeying my orders, which Kud also promised me they would.

Liar.

I whip out my crossbow, notch an arrow, and release it within a few seconds. It sinks into the hound's grungy fur moments before the hound's razor-sharp teeth can clamp on to the guard's shoulder. Even still, the two sprawl to the ground as the hound falls on top of the guard. The other hound howls and charges at the second guard, who begins shooting useless bullets at it. I sink another arrow into the second hound's body as it leaps to attack. Both guards take off screaming, and the hounds vanish in puffs of gray smoke.

The spotlight searches back and forth across the courtyard, hungry for me, so I tuck myself into the shadows. I shudder, thinking about what I just unleashed. I'm ready to turn around and give up, but then my dad's face flashes before my eyes. Clenching my crossbow, I steel myself. I know I must continue if there is any hope for me to break free of Kud's hold and return to my family.

I duck out of the shadows and pump my legs, throwing every bit of my power into my run. At the building's base, I crouch behind a bush and aim the crossbow again. I shoot an arrow, casting a cable up into the darkness. A clinking sound above and a tug on the line tell me the hook is in place. I toss the crossbow into the bushes and clip the cable to my belt. Bullets skitter across the grass, one nicking my calf. I wonder if they are shooting to injure or to kill.

I press my watch timer and begin scaling the building. If my calculations are correct, I have approximately twenty seconds to reach the top floor before the guards find their way there. Tonight I'm racing against time.

Beams of light crisscross the building's surface and converge on my body as I zip up toward my target window. I press the dagger Kud gave me against the glass just as a bullet pings off the concrete centimeters from me. *Perfect.* I've become target practice for a sniper. The knife's power shatters the glass into a million shards, and I dive through the window, tumbling into a somersault across the floor.

Emergency lights pulse in the room, and footsteps clatter down the hallway. Maybe twenty seconds was generous. These guards are far too efficient. I unclip from the cable and dig back into the pouch, this time grabbing a handful of Kud's bugs. After the hounds, I don't want to do this, but there is too much at stake here to fail.

I will not fail.

The door directly in front of me slams open. Red pinpricks of light hit my chest. I lift my arms up as if to surrender. They don't know I'm holding hell itself.

"If I let this handful drop," I warn the guards, "a thousand man-eating cockroaches will be released. Lower your guns now."

The guards hesitate, glancing at each other. From their looks, I gather that they think I'm crazy. If I'm to gain time and come out of here alive, I need to unleash the monsters in my palms. I try to tell myself this is a small sacrifice to save the greater good, a means to an end, because this isn't about me or even my family. It's about stopping the madness of Kud's campaign to rule all of Korea. Yet should the deaths of innocent guards be part of the price?

I wish I could use them, but I can't.

I throw myself into an aerial, tucking the cockroaches into my pockets. Shots ricochet off the floor, trailing after me as I backflip onto the top of a desk and then kick off the side of a bookcase. By the time I've landed back on the floor, they're gaping in shock.

I snap-kick the closest guard in the chest, which sends him reeling backward and knocks him out, and I snatch the other's gun before he can recover.

"Don't move." I point the gun at the guard.

I don't bother to mention that I have no idea how to use this gun, but from his wide eyes and raised arms, I see he's finally taking me seriously. I smile beneath my mask. If he only knew I'm just a sixteen-year-old girl. In the distance, the pounding of footsteps floods the hallways. I have a few seconds left at most. I smack the side of the gun against the guard's head, sending him crumbling to the floor. He'll have a bad headache, but he'll live.

I slide my hands across the wall's surface, searching for the hidden panel I know exists. Finally my fingers snag on it. With the tip of my dagger, I flip open what looks to be a concrete block, revealing a keypad.

I punch in the code: X52YZ98.

The keypad slides inside the wall, revealing a small compartment. A leather pouch rests within. My heart catches in my throat and I recognize that feeling. Hope. It's been so long since I felt that emotion, I'd almost forgotten it existed.

"Dong-gyeol!" A man calls from behind me to freeze.

As my palm wraps around the pouch, I hate myself for every moment of this mission. It's crazy how since signing a contract with Kud I've become the bad girl. Intruder. Thief. Deserter. I have so many names now. Too many. I should never have trusted the god of darkness, but I'd been so desperate to save Marc from being killed by Kud that I'd believed I could live like this.

When I turn to face the guard, there's actually a group of four, hovering by the entrance and gaping in shock over the revealed compartment and the knocked-out guards.

I'm so annoyed with myself for trusting Kud to offer me protection without the consequence of killing others. If only I had access to weaponry of my own choosing. It would definitely make all of this easier. I tuck the pouch into my belt as I consider my alternatives.

I run toward the first man, leap up, and front-kick him. He crashes against the wall. I spin a three-sixty and kick the next guard, sending him stumbling backward. Bullets fly all around me, but I'm spinning and moving so fast that I manage to only get grazed across the shoulder. At the door, I snap a front-punch at the next guard, knocking his gun to the floor, and then kick the gun off the last guard. I race past him as he writhes on the ground, yelling into his walkie-talkie for reinforcements.

Slipping across the marble floor, I career around a corner only to be met by bars descending from the ceiling to block off my escape route. I sprint even faster and fall into a baseball slide. The bars slice my arm, but I make it through. Ignoring the rush of blood trailing down my arm, I scramble back to my feet and bolt to the stairwell, slamming open the metal door so that it bounces against the concrete wall. Below, I spot guards racing up the stairs toward me, their boots thundering, and I jerk back to stop myself from heading down.

I turn and run up the stairs, taking two at a time, but when I reach the roof, the door is locked. I whip out my dagger and jam it into the lock. Steam sizzles from the door's handle, and it shatters. I wrench open the door and stumble out onto the roof.

I blink, waiting for my eyes to adjust to the semidarkness of the lights of Seoul. As I regain my vision, I realize a group of figures blocks my way. There's something different about these guards. Perhaps it's their stance: feet spread apart, arms at their sides. Then I realize what the problem is. They are too calm. It's almost as if they've been expecting me.

The guard directly in front of me reaches behind his back and pulls out a sword. It gleams silver in the city lights. Following his lead, the others also draw their swords and hold them before their bodies, waiting.

My heart stops as if it has decided to refuse to beat. I spin in a circle, my breath coming out in heavy gasps.

I'm surrounded by the Guardians of Shinshi.

No ordinary guards would know that in order to defeat me, they must use weapons created in the Spirit World. And I can feel that power flowing off these swords.

No. No, no, no.

The first Guardian steps closer, and moonlight falls across his face. Marc. My knees weaken, and suddenly my heart is beating again. Wildly. Frantically.

I want to tell him I'm doing all of this for him. That I've stolen the pouch and unleashed the creatures of darkness, hoping to save us. To save what we had.

But in this moment, in this now, I know how foolish I've been. I ruined everything the moment I signed that contract with Kud. I can't go back to who I once was.

"Put down the object you stole," Marc calls in Korean.

When I don't obey, Marc cries out and charges at me. I stumble backward, barely avoiding the blade. One plunge of his sacred sword could kill me because I'm a slave of Kud now, whether I like it or not. The bronze contract branded onto my forearm burns with every breathing moment, a continual reminder of the agreement between Kud and me.

I duck away from a blow behind me and then another that slices the air just above my head. I roll and dive, back-flipping, until they finally corner me against the wall of the stairwell.

There's no way I'm going to die without Marc knowing who I am. I rip off the black mask I've been using to cloak my identity. My hair tumbles over my shoulders and down my back as my disguise flutters from my fingers. The wind cuts across my cheeks as if it's slapping me.

Marc's eyes widen in shock, and then their beautiful green churns in stormy anger. His face scrunches, and he staggers back as if he's been punched by some unseen hand. But I know the truth. He loathes what he sees. My insides crumble at his disgust.

"Jae?" Marc's voice catches.

"Marc." I hold up my hands. "I had to. I'm trying to do the right thing."

"I don't understand. I thought you weren't able to leave Kud's land."

Behind him, the other Guardians murmur in confusion. Now I can see them better. I recognize Jung, and I think the guy just to his left is Kumar. I knew he'd been recruited to work for the Guardians of Shinshi, but I hadn't realized he'd made it to Guardian status.

A girl strides up next to Marc, placing a hand on his shoulder. "You know the orders. Any creature under his rule must die. She's a slave of the dark lord now, and our enemy. God knows how many she has already killed."

"We don't know that." Marc shifts uneasily on his feet. "The Council hasn't heard her side of the story."

My eyes flick between Marc and the girl. Who does she think she is? And if she's one of the Guardians, then why haven't I seen her before? It's petty, but I don't like how comfortable she seems around Marc. It's as if—no. I can't even think it.

I open my mouth to plead my innocence, but I'm everything the girl says I am. I think about how Kud killed Michelle to hurt me, how Komo died trying to save me, and how I couldn't save either of them. Maybe she's right. Maybe all I bring is death.

"I have a plan," I say. "You have to trust me."

"A plan?" Marc scoffs. "To break in, hurt people, and steal? There are better ways to execute a plan. The Council is waiting for any excuse to kill you. They say you can't resist Kud's power no matter how strong you are."

"You have to understand. I don't want to hurt anyone. Besides, didn't we do this very same thing when we broke into the museum to steal the *samjoko* amulet?" I glance over at the girl and then back to him. "Or have you so quickly forgotten what we had together?"

"We may have stolen the amulet," Marc says. "But no one was hurt."

Across the roof, the air stretches and twists into a crimson glow. My forearm burns from the tug of Kud's call, and the power of the Spirit World rushes through me. He has opened a portal for me, and there's no doubt in my mind that he's watching us right now, waiting to see what I'll do. I can't have Kud knowing the truth, yet I can't leave Marc without him knowing how I feel.

"Don't ever forget that I love you," I tell Marc.

And then I run at them. Surprise lights their faces, and as I expected, the Guardians reach to grab me. But I'm already spinning through the air above their heads, using the Spirit World's power rushing out of the portal to propel me. I drop down into a crouch on the other side of them.

Disorganized, they turn and rush at me again, but Marc cries out, "Stop! Don't hurt her."

"Are you crazy, man?" Jung shouts.

Before they change their minds, I race across the roof and leap over the edge, diving into the swirling, twisted madness of my own living hell.

Away from the living. Away from those I love.

CHAPTER 2

I land on both feet, my boots slamming onto the stone walkway, but I still have to hold out my hands to gain balance. It always takes me a moment to adjust to the Spirit World. The burn in my arm where the contract blazes lessens when I'm in Kud's realm, but I still find myself rubbing it, as if that will soothe the pain.

Blood gushes from where the bars cut across my arm, dripping down to the tips of my fingers before splattering onto the stone floor. I rip off a portion of my shirt and wrap it around my arm to stop the bleeding.

Once recovered, I start down the corridor. I've been living in Kud's realm for two weeks now, but even still, I can't shake the feeling of dread this place gives me. Fire burns within the shapes carved into the walls, making the symbols appear to twist and flicker as if they are alive. I should feel hot, but I don't. Only a perpetual chill that drains every inch of me.

I halt at the top of the stairs to Kud's throne room. Below is the massive hall where he loves to display his recent kills. It's beyond revolting and makes my stomach twist every time I enter it, which is why I avoid the throne room at all costs.

When the side doors open, I expect to see Kud strolling through them, but they're only opening to allow the lead hound, Bae, and his sidekick to enter. Bae is the leader of Kud's Bulgae, bloodhounds sworn to protect and fight for Kud, and just the sight of him makes me clench my fists until my knuckles practically pop.

How dare you kill two from my pack? Bae says in my mind. He licks his lips, and his ears slip forward.

"The orders were to hold the guards back, not kill them," I say from the top of the stairs. "Obviously you have no control over your pack."

I have complete control, Bae snaps back. *It is you who is under suspicion.*

The gleam in his red eyes tells me he's taunting me for a reaction. Both Bae and his sidekick have been itching for me to break Kud's rules so they'll be allowed to sink their teeth into my neck.

But there's no way I'm giving them the satisfaction. I lift my chin and glare down at Bae. "One of these days I'm going to slice your mangy body into pieces and then feed them to the pit, one by one. Trust me, you'll pay for allowing your hounds to attack those men."

He snarls and leaps up the stone stairs to me in three bounds, lashing out his paw and jutting his muzzle into my face so close I can smell his reeking breath and count each jagged, rotting tooth. I brace myself, unwilling to flinch.

We stare at each other. Eventually he growls, *The master awaits your presence.* And then he trots away, head held high.

Sucking in a deep breath, I turn away from the stairs, unable to face Kud just yet. Instead I squeeze into an alcove, safe from the dripping flames of the candles that rain fire drops from the ceiling, and sag against the wall. Anger courses through me, and I take deep breaths to release the tension in my chest. Kud thrives on anger, and I can't stop thinking about how it continually threatens to overtake me, too. Every day I'm stuck in this death trap with the feeling that my humanity is ebbing away and being replaced with anger, pain, and emptiness. This is the magic of his realm.

Closing my eyes, I focus on Marc's face, wishing I could have reached out and touched him, if only for a second. I can't wipe away the image of the disappointment and shock flashing across his face after I ripped off my mask and he realized who his enemy was.

Me.

I'm the one he now hunts.

I press my fingers against my lips. My body aches for his touch, for his lips to be pressed against mine. I groan, wrapping my arms around my stomach.

I'll never forget when he told me he loved me or how he was willing to sacrifice everything to save me when he left and entered Kud's realm on his own. I cling to the memory of the two of us riding on the train to Busan. It's one of the longest periods of time when it was just the two of us, no Guardians or mythological creatures. Just me curled up against him, the rocking of the train lulling us to sleep. I want to go back to that moment and never get off that train, just keep riding away forever. Away from what lay before us.

But that's impossible. He's a Guardian, a protector of Korea, sworn to defend it against those like me. I pull back my sleeve and study the agreement that blazes in aqueous bronze across my skin. It's written in ancient Chinese, so I'm not sure of its exact meaning, but my guess is that it says something along the lines of *Jae Hwa is now bound to the most horrible god of darkness and will live in complete misery forever.*

Then I hear my dad's voice: *Endurance is the difference between the impossible and the possible.* Memories flicker across my mind. My aunt, Komo, who sacrificed everything to train me to stand up to these mythological creatures. A smile creeps across my face as I see her in my mind, pacing before me as she lectures me about how we choose our destinies and destiny never chooses us. Haraboji, my grandfather, holding out the Blue Dragon bow and telling me this was my purpose. And Marc, who believed in me when I didn't.

The pouch I stole from the agency is soft between my palms. Pulling at the drawstrings, I open it. A small mahogany box printed with gold Chinese characters is tucked inside. It's so intricate and petite that it must have been created as a gift for royalty. I flip back the brass clasp to open the box and pull out yet another silk pouch. Inside rests a gold turtle sitting on top of a golden box. A crimson braided cord is looped around the figure's end to make a handle. The turtle is about six inches long and three inches high. I flip it over and find an imprint and grooves on the bottom. My guess is that it's an ancient seal.

I have no inkling why this object is supposed to be a clue to the location of the Black Turtle orb. When I show this to Kud, he'll be angry because I'm not any closer to finding this orb than I was before.

Below, the hounds both break into a howl, pulling me from my reverie. Kud is restless. If I don't hurry, he'll throw himself into a full fit. Inwardly I groan as I push myself up, bracing myself to face the dark lord.

I slip down the stairs, darting around the fire drops, and walk down into the throne room. Two hounds trot up next to me and flank my sides. At first glance one might think they were my escorts or even pets, but the hound to my right snaps his jaws and grinds his teeth. He's desperate to sink his fangs into my human skin after I killed two from his pack. The only thing keeping him at bay is Kud's command not to eat me. Yet.

We pass by the latest bodies pinned to the wall, which have joined a long line of skeletons. I straighten my back and refuse to look at them as I hurry by, but the stench of their rotting flesh won't allow me to pretend them away. Skirting around one of the massive pillars that stretches to the arched ceiling above, I come to stand in front of another door leading to Kud's hate-infested control room.

The door is inlaid with a silver snake that moves in a never-ending figure eight over the door's surface. The snake's unblinking eyes inspect me.

Then, as if I've passed its test, the doors swing open, revealing the dark god's inner sanctuary. I've only been in this room twice: once when Kud pulled me here through the mirror in my aunt's hospital room, and another time when Kud decided it was time to use "my gifts," as he called them. I can't decide whether or not it's good that he doesn't trust me enough to allow me into his inner sanctuary.

The walls are filled with screens. They remind me of television screens, but each screen can watch whomever Kud chooses. It's how he keeps track of people he wants to observe. A blanket of mist floats over the floor, and above, the ceiling is open to a sky of endless darkness sprinkled with stars that feel an eternity away. Kud's presence permeates the room as he stands before me, his black robe trailing to the floor, the ends becoming long tendrils that snake across the cold stone. His face remains shrouded beneath his hood, but I can see his silver eyes studying me. Standing there, I feel as if a hundred snakes are crawling over my skin.

"My dear princess," Kud says. "You have returned. Were you successful?"

He knows I was. He was watching my every move. It's beyond creepy.

"Of course," I say airily. "Did you expect otherwise?"

"Bae tells me you killed two of our trusted hounds. Was this necessary?"

"Absolutely. I hardly see him being capable of breaking into buildings and stealing valuable artifacts. Who is he to say what is necessary or not?" "Indeed." Kud rubs his chin, thoughtful. His thick silver ring sparkles in the darkness. The coils of silver rope form a tornado around his finger, a constant reminder of his love of calamity and chaos. "Come, then. Show me."

I hesitate, half my body screaming to run from the horror that he is while the other half demands to spit on him and sink my dagger into his nonexistent heart. But I don't do either. Instead, I swallow the lump of fear in my throat and straighten my shoulders as I step inside the rotunda. The door slams shut the moment I cross the threshold. The turtle in my palm digs into my skin as I tighten my fist around it. I don't want to let go of it and hand it over to Kud. It has become my connection to the real world. The world I want to belong to again.

"This, my friends," Kud says to the two figures standing on my right, hovering in the shadows, "is Princess Jae Hwa, my personal assassin. She has sacrificed everything to be with me. Is this not true, my dear?"

"I'm not your *dear*," I say through clenched teeth. I know I should indulge him. It would make my life easier, but he makes it just too impossible. He ruined my life. It's my goal now to ruin his. That thought perks me up, though, and I grin. "But yes, I sacrificed everything to be with you. That's okay, though. My family doesn't matter to me anymore. They are nothing but a forgotten memory."

This is pretty much how our conversations go every time we meet. I tell him I don't care about my family in the hope that he won't use them as leverage against me. He tells me to do something he wants me to do or he'll kill them or send one of his creatures to torture them. It depends on his mood. All of this only makes me detest him more, which he probably loves.

The fact that my dad, my grandfather, and Marc mean everything to me is my greatest weakness. Kud knows he can use them against me, and that eats at me.

"Really?" Kud points a gnarled finger at one of the screens. It shows me on top of the National Intelligence Service, running. I hear my voice yell out to Marc, "I love you!" And then the screen goes blank. "Care to explain that?"

"I had to trick him." My heart beats wildly against my rib-cage as I realize my usefulness might be at its end. I still haven't found the location of the final orb, and I'm holding a clue that doesn't make sense. There are two somethings beside him—humans maybe?—that I wonder if he's planning to use to do the rest of the legwork so he can get rid of me. Which would make it impossible for me to destroy him.

Crap.

"If I hadn't said that, he wouldn't have let me go. You heard him." I point to the screen. "He told the other Guardians not to hurt me. I wouldn't have made it back to you alive if he hadn't stopped them, and then they would have the clue to the resting place of the final orb."

Kud remains quiet, assessing me. The tentacles of his robe scuttle about my ankles as if they're itching to crawl up my body and strangle me.

"Perhaps," Kud finally says. "Perhaps."

He holds out his palm, and a pedestal rises from the center of the rotunda. "Show us what you have found."

I place the turtle on the pedestal, but I hold my hand over the top of it. I nod toward the two figures hovering in the shad-ows. "How do I know I can trust them?"

The creatures move from the shadows to peer at my hand, and I get a better view of them. They are both definitely men, or at least they were at one time. The taller one has long hair, which falls down over his shoulders, and his face is long and nar-row with a short nose. The skin on one side of his face appears shriveled, as if it is diseased. The other man has a rounder face with a smooth, shiny bald head. He's got a pointed black beard that reaches just past his chin. A jagged scar runs the full length of the right side of his face, and his mouth is curled into a snarl.

But it's their eyes that startle me the most. They are more like glassy marbles, and they look exactly like the eyes of the assassin who appeared at my Tae Kwon Do second-degree black belt test and tried to kill me. Lovely.

"These two?" Kud laughs. "Oh yes, you can trust them completely. I have given back their lives, so they owe me their very existence. They will follow my bidding to their second deaths. Just like you will."

"Second deaths? Are they alive?" I ask, and then I scrunch up my nose because there's a horrible stench coming off them.

"It really is all about perspective, do you not think?" Kud says. "They walk, talk, and think. That should be suitable to meet our needs."

I bite my lip. The longer I'm here in Kud's lair, the more I realize living is about feeling and believing and loving. None of those emotions belong in Kud's realm. I think back to how I acted at the intelligence service and the things I nearly allowed to happen. How far have I fallen from humanity? Perhaps I'm no different from Kud's two resurrected man-creatures. I pull my hand away from the turtle.

"This is what I found." I can't look at him, afraid the artifact won't be enough to please him, especially since I don't know what it means. I cringe, waiting for his anger to fill every crevice of the room.

"This is excellent work." Kud snatches up the turtle and begins pacing, his voice full of excitement.

"Excellent?" My head snaps up. This reaction from Kud is not what I'd been expecting.

"Come hither, my princess."

I clench my fists at his use of that nickname. It's the same one Haemosu used on me, and it would send me into a fiery fit every freaking time. Perhaps that's the very reason why Kud loves to use it, too. Still, I can't lose my cool, so I press my lips together and join him to look into one of his disturbing mirrors.

His finger points to the Blue House where President Lee lives. Standing at the end of a wide green lawn, it's a traditional-style Korean building with a fluted blue roof. Puffy clouds drift by above, and a light wind rustles the leaves on the cherry trees. Rising up behind the president's house is Bukak Mountain. I've never actually been on the grounds, but since Marc's house isn't far from there, I have passed by the gates often.

The whole scene makes my insides ache. It takes every ounce of control not to throw myself into the mirror and land back in Seoul.

If only I knew exactly how the mirrors work. It was through one of these that Kud pulled me into his realm to talk to me the first time. I escaped back through the mirror, but Marc had been on the other side, guiding me back to Seoul. I'm not sure what would happen if I dove into one. But now I see why Kud has been reluctant to allow me into this room. The mirrors could be the key to my communication with the Guardians.

"I don't understand," I say. "Why are you showing me this place?"

"Beneath the Blue House is a secret room containing many of the treasures of Korea," Kud says. "In the center of this room is this very turtle statue."

"How do you know this place exists?"

"Because I was there when they created the room, dearest." Kud curses and slams his fist onto the stone pedestal, causing a jagged crack to streak across the stone. "I should have seen this. I have been the idiot."

Then he turns to me, and I can see his face. There's something there that reminds me of Kang-dae, the human he once impersonated to trick me into finding the White Tiger orb. But this face is alabaster smooth, with streaks of red pouring out of its silver eyes. Kud's pale lips stretch up into a bizarre grin as calm slides over his features. I can't decide which is more terrifying, his anger or his complete stillness.

"We are so close," he continues. "Once we gain this orb, there will be a balance of power between Palk and me. Then we can storm Palk's realm and gain access to the final three orbs. When I have all six, I will finally have enough power for phase three."

"Three?"

"One can't be content with small, attainable goals," he says. "A true goal, one of consequence, will stretch you and allow you to grow."

"You don't just want to rule Korea." Everything now makes sense. He's obsessed with the orbs because he thinks they will give him power over everything and beyond. "You want to rule the world. Is that even possible?"

"Try living in a single land for all of eternity and being limited to one country. It gets rather boring after a thousand years. There are no other immortals who possess all of their country's power. When I have accumulated all of Korea's, they will be unable to stop me. What greater goal could one have?"

"I can think of a few."

"And should I accomplish it, think of what we could achieve together. So much more than what we can do now."

"Together?" I don't like any of this, but he's sharing his deepest secrets and I'm not about to stop him.

He reaches out a gloved hand and runs a finger along the side of my face. "And Jae Hwa, without you, I would not have this. I have waited for a millennium for the right one to rule by my side. Finally I have found you."

"Don't touch me," I say in a growl, batting his hand away. When he says things like this, it's impossible for me to pretend I want to be here with him.

He chuckles and touches the mirror beside the one showing the Blue House. A stream of pictures flashes across it until it settles on one image in particular. It's an invitation written in English and Korean.

The South Korean government cordially invites you to
Lee's Second Annual
Presidential Ball
Saturday, June 23rd
6:30 p.m. V.I.P. Reception
7:00 p.m. to 11:00 p.m. Evening Ball
The Blue House
1 Sejongno, Jongno-gu, Seoul, South Korea
~Black Tie Event~

"We will go to the Blue House, the two of us, and find this statue. The Black Turtle orb should be hiding somewhere inside or nearby," Kud says. "I have yet to take you out on a date. This ball would be the perfect opportunity."

My heart sinks. All this time I've been feeding and enabling a monster in the hope of eventually destroying him, but now I'm second-guessing whether I'm strong enough to do this task alone. If there was a way to contact Grandfather or Marc without Kud knowing, then perhaps I could convince them to help me get the Black Turtle orb before Kud does. Together we could put it into Palk's hands and stop this all from happening.

I reach for the White Tiger orb hanging on my chest beneath my jumpsuit. It's only a matter of time before Kud's devious mind figures out a way to use me so that I will command the orb to do his bidding. Until now, I've been able to block him from using the orb's power, and I've been strong enough to resist his commands for me to use it against my will.

I grind my teeth and push my lips into a smile. "Yes, your greatness." Kud's head whips around to face me. I've never called him "great" without my words dripping with sarcasm. It takes pretty much every bit of my willpower to do so. "After completing this past mission, I feel as if I've become even closer to you. With the final orb, you'll have power no other immortal could possibly dream of."

"Indeed." I can't ignore how his eyes linger on my chest where the orb is tucked safely away. It's always on the forefront of his mind, especially since he can't touch it. I still remember him trying to pick it up on the hotel roof in North Korea and the orb burning his hand, causing him horrible pain.

He turns from me and begins pacing. "Prepare yourself. We will leave tomorrow at seven p.m., Seoul time. I have not spoken to the president for a while. It will be good to meet again."

I practically race out the door, eager to leave his presence. My steps are lighter, filled with hope as a plan unfurls before my eyes. Hope. It's a foreign emotion in this world of Kud's because it implies a future, a purpose, and a beginning. Do I have a right to those? I don't know the answer. And that's what scares me the most.

CHAPTER 3

Once I leave the rotunda, the hounds slip in beside me and one of the shadows hands me a traditional square lantern. The lantern's glow fills the void as we enter the first corridor in the long hike to my chamber. Without the lantern, I'd be lost in the darkness because the walls in this wing of the palace aren't filled with fire to light the way.

Even though the barrier between my room and the hall is only tight latticework, not a solid wall, I still feel better when I close the door to my chamber and leave the hounds behind. They'll guard my door, which is ridiculous because there's no way I could escape without Kud knowing. Still, not having their jaws snapping, eager to eat me, is something of a relief.

My chamber is lavish, with dark blue and silver silks streaming across the walls. Statues carved out of marble are planted around the room. Every bowl, every brush, and even my mirror are inlaid with silver. My *yo* is massive. I could do a somersault across it and still have room. A shimmering, silky spread lies over the top, black as night. There's no doubt that Kud has gone to extremes to make me feel comfortable in his land, and the thought of why makes me uneasy.

The ceiling is painted with horned monsters and scaly demons, their eyes always watching me and their sharp-toothed mouths open wide as if desperate to consume me. It's disturbing and the reason I always sleep under my blanket. I haven't decided if Kud painted the ceiling this way because he thinks it's a work of art or just to torture me. Probably both.

A floor-length silver dress hangs beside my yo, sparkling in the candlelight. This must be the dress Kud intends me to wear. It's the most beautiful thing I've ever seen, strapless with sequins sewn across the bodice like an ocean wave.

I set my lantern on the traditional step chest and gaze at myself in the oval silver mirror edged with dragons. It's still me in there, but the brown eyes staring back at me look haunted, confused. Dark half-moons hang below my eyes from never being able to sleep. And the silvery glow that Marc and Bari, the guider of the dead, had once warned me about seems stronger today. Bari's words haunt me as I remember the ghostly glow of her form.

It's the fading that's the hardest, she had said.

It's only a matter of time before I fade just like her and lose all of my humanity. I grip the sides of the dresser, wondering how much time I have left.

Now that I'm alone, I can finally unleash the emotions tumbling through me, battering at my heart like a raging storm. What exactly happened tonight? Obviously the Guardians of Shinshi believe I'm their enemy. But what about Marc? Does he believe in me, in us? Snapshots of the night flash before my eyes. The hounds. Guns. Guards. Guardian swords. Marc's face. Kud's silvery eyes glowing, eager with anticipation.

What am I becoming? A killer? A deceiver? A hunter for evil? Or am I saving and protecting those I love? The line feels too thin, too fragile.

The images won't stop, whirling through my mind, terrorizing me, and suddenly I wonder if that line has snapped. My breathing intensifies until I'm gasping for air, but I can't seem to get enough oxygen. My chest seizes up, and I know I need to pull myself together or I'll become a mess of tears and wails. I can't have that. Kud must never know how much he has hurt me. Still, I'm desperate for my punching bag or *something* to vent my anger on. I pick up the silver hairbrush and smash its end into the mirror. The glass cracks, splintering into webs.

I freeze, staring at this new reflection. This new me. Broken, unconnected, unrestrained.

Alone.

And I hate myself.

My eyes land on the origami creations wedged in the cracks between the silver and glass around the mirror's edges. These are the only real pieces of Dad I have left. The only reason Kud lets me keep them is so he can threaten to take them from me. Through my internal agony, my fingers reach up and touch the fish.

The fish is supposed to represent happiness, determination, and strength, Dad had said as he handed it to me. I close my eyes, visualizing his face. His voice feels warm, rich, and full of life in my memories. *All of these are needed for the fish to swim upstream.*

I trail my finger around the fish's edges. I have no happiness. I left that behind the moment I signed Kud's contract. As for determination and strength, tonight my actions have gutted even those from me. How am I supposed to go on this next mission with Kud?

I pull out the picture of Marc and me standing on Seoraksan Mountain. I stole it from his room the night I realized he'd gone to turn himself in to Kud. While his mom was lighting the candles and sending up prayers, I'd slipped it into my pocket.

Tonight I stare at his face: the strong jaw, the dimpled smile, and those twinkling, beautiful eyes that have always warmed my soul, telling me he still loved me.

Until today.

I grasp hold of his image in my mind as I lay the picture on the dresser, my hand shaking. Once again that spark I felt leaving Kud's throne room explodes in my chest. Mom told me in the last days before she died of cancer that through suffering we gain perseverance and through perseverance we gain hope. I had never understood how she could say those words days before her death, but there's something in her words that resonates with me now.

Whatever it is, it has ignited a flame inside me. Somehow I must be strong enough to continue pretending to go along with Kud's plan. Then I'll strike Kud when he least expects it.

CHAPTER 4

The limo rolls past the blue guardhouse and enters the circular drive up to the Blue House's entrance, following a long stream of cars. South Korean flags swish back and forth in the evening winds as guards patrol along the stone walls.

Gingko trees line the front of the two-story building and the two smaller houses on either side. All three structures are crowned with the distinctive fluted blue tile that gives the Blue House its name. The second floor of the main building has a balcony that stretches the entire length of the house, and tonight it's lit with spotlights streaming upward from the ground, illuminating the house in a pale blue. Behind the house, the outlines of the mountains rise up like guardians themselves, and the final embers of sunlight slip through the clouds, creating waves of burnt reds and oranges. Tall lanterns hang from bamboo posts that line a path from the road to the Blue House's doors. Boxes of flowers placed between each bamboo post make it appear as if we're entering a garden rather than a house.

I feast on the beauty, the color, and the smiles of each person exiting the vehicles and strolling into the building. They all look so festive.

So alive.

"You look stunning tonight," Kud says, breaking the silence of the limo. His eyes follow the line of my dress from my bare shoulders to where my ankles peek out from beneath the hem.

His statement startles me, and I'm momentarily at a loss for words. He reaches up and lightly touches my hair. I push his hand away.

"The statue is in the basement." Kud's smiling mischievously now. "If all goes as planned, we shall find the piece with no issues. Hopefully the Black Turtle orb is tucked somewhere within the statue."

It's hard to think of Kud as the god of darkness with him wearing his human form, and that throws off my game of deception. I haven't seen him like this since he was impersonating one of the Guardians of Shinshi and trying to get the White Tiger orb for himself.

What I see now is the old Kang-dae, a college student dressed up to impress the President of Korea, with slicked-back hair and a tuxedo. A light scruff of hair runs along his jaw, making him look sexy enough to be a model. As I study him, his thick eyebrows rise slightly.

"Why are you looking at me like that? Do I not look human enough?"

The uncertainty of his tone, the vulnerability in his expression, and his need for my approval nearly undo me. I wonder if, in taking on this disguise, he also takes on humanity. The moment brings back too many memories of standing beside him before as a friend, an ally in the fight against evil.

But I was a fool then. I won't be fooled twice.

"Where did you get the model for your disguise? Don't tell me you killed someone for it."

"Now you are being ridiculous." He leans forward, his elbows on his knees. "If this is to work, you will need to at least appear to be attracted to me. You are my date, after all."

I clench my teeth together but manage a pressed-lipped grin. Why couldn't I have been born a better actress? It certainly would make everything easier. I reapply my lipstick as if that alone could conceal my true intentions.

"Let's get this over with," I say as someone opens the limo door.

I step out, careful not to let my heels snag on my dress. I'm momentarily overcome by the smell of fresh-cut grass and flowers. They smell of life and newness and the hope of things to come. So often I had taken those smells for granted, but now my whole being craves them. I consider the task before me: to get this orb tonight and to escape Kud's clutches to return the orb to the Heavenly Chest. The impossibility of it all freezes me, and suddenly I become unsure of myself and what I'm about to do.

But then Kud's hand presses against my lower back, shoving my senses into check. My skin responds to his touch, and I'm propelled forward. I may fail in this task, but at least I'm trying.

"Jae Hwa," Kud says, gazing down at me with warm eyes. Surprised that he used my real name, I stop in my tracks. He never calls me by my name. Only "princess" and "dearest" and other ridiculous nicknames that he knows I hate. My world is confusion again.

Kud holds out his arm and cocks his eyebrows. With a shake of my head, I slide my arm through his and walk the red carpet up to the large main doors of the Blue House.

Guards line the entrance. I can't ignore the guns tucked in the holsters at their hips. After Kud hands over our forged invitations, we stroll into the main hall, a stunning room with rich wood paneling and a massive staircase lined with crimson carpet. It's so wide, ten people could fit across it standing side by side. The entire back wall of the first landing is a map of Korea.

To the right, a massive circular bronze crest hangs from the ceiling. It's the yin yang. The white shimmers like it's made from diamonds, and the dark glows with black onyx. A man is telling a group of foreigners how the yin yang works.

"This represents two complementary forces," the man explains. "When they touch, they form a dynamic system where the whole is greater than the parts."

I can't get those words out of my mind as I think about North and South Korea. If the two would join, they would be complete and stronger for it.

After we are introduced to various ambassadors and leaders of state that Kud somehow knows, we enter the ballroom. Traditional Korean music plays while servers move about, passing out champagne and hors d'oeuvres.

The last time I'd been surrounded by so much wealth was at the museum event with Dad and Grandfather when Dad's company sponsored the *Illumination* exhibit. Even the air smells expensive due to the perfumed guests, and I stand there unsure what to do with myself. I may be dressed in a shimmery silver gown and wearing a string of diamonds around my neck, but as I eye the guards scattered about the room, I'm jealous of their jobs. Holding a weapon in my hand seems far easier than playing the part of some rich donor with Kud.

People chatter around us, discussing the imminent war between North and South Korea. Kud grabs a glass of champagne from one of the waiters and joins a small group discussion on politics. I sidle next to him.

"There is no way the North Koreans have a chance," one of the men is saying. "If they attack the South, it would be suicide. The allied countries would come to our aid and counterattack within minutes."

"North Korea should not be underestimated," Kud says. "Their powers are more far-reaching than the allied countries could fathom."

The members of the group gape at Kud in shock, but before they have a chance to recover and respond, Kud lifts his champagne glass and turns away.

"What did you mean by North Korea's powers?" I ask Kud, hurrying after him.

"All in good time," Kud says, finishing off his glass.

We cut our way through the party to the back of the room. A guard stands beside a back door, but he doesn't make eye contact with us. Kud nods at me to open the door.

"Right in front of everyone?" I ask.

"They can't see us." Kud checks his watch. "I've got both of us cloaked for at least ten minutes."

I slip off my shoe and press the indent in the section where my heel rests. A sharp knife shoots out of the heel. I press the tip of the blade into the lock, and the door opens. We slip inside, unnoticed.

A long hallway yawns before us. It's such a contrast to the opulence and ancient atmosphere of the ballroom. The walls are solid white, the floor is smooth black tile, and can lights shine from the ceiling every so many feet. I feel like I'm in a high-tech lab rather than an old house.

I have to practically run after Kud to keep up, my silver heels clicking across the tile. A guard at the end of the hall turns from his post and eyes the hallway. He whips out his gun and points it at me. From his lack of focus on a particular target, he obviously can't see us approaching, but my guess is that my heels are acting like little alarms clicking down the hall.

"Take those damn shoes off," Kud snaps. "You're waking the dead."

Happily I slip them off and carry them in my hand. Once we reach the elevator, I knock the guard unconscious with a swift thump on the head while Kud punches a code into the elevator keypad. The doors slide open, but before Kud can step inside, a guard rushes over to us, his eyes scanning the area. He bends over and checks his partner as the elevator doors shut, blocking us from him.

"Human contraptions. Such annoyances," Kud mutters as the elevator glides downward.

When the doors open, I'm shocked to find a room that looks like a giant vault. It's a metal chamber about two stories high, stockpiled with what appear to be ancient artifacts. I step out onto the Plexiglas bridge, my jaw gaping open.

"This place is amazing," I whisper.

Paintings, armor, and weapons line the walkways. Below, cases are stuffed with hundreds of glittering precious jewels, stones, and relics. Glass cabinets cover the back wall, and lights flash on panels beside them. I am afraid to breathe. Everything is so quiet and still.

"*Sinbunjeung,*" a voice says from a tall pedestal at the stairwell entrance. A green light blinks on a console on top of the pedestal, waiting for us to enter a code.

"I'm afraid the computer won't accept my identification." Kud shrugs and pulls out the miniature turtle that I found. He holds it before me in his palm and nods to the floor below. "Look familiar?"

I follow his line of sight to spy a massive bronze-coated turtle resting on the floor below us. It's about eight feet long and five feet high. The jaws of the turtle are wide open as if it's about to take a giant bite out of someone. The claws of the turtle's feet are sharp knives.

"You think the orb is somewhere near that statue?" I ask.

"Let us hope," Kud says. "Because we have about twenty seconds to find it before something happens."

Sure enough, a timer has been triggered. Big red numbers are counting down on the console.

"Crap." I assess the area, not sure where to begin to find the orb. I've never trained for anything like this.

"Fifteen, fourteen," Kud begins counting down, lounging against the railing. He crosses his arms. I shoot him a wide-eyed, exasperated look. "You're just going to stand there? Someone has to take care of the guards when they arrive in"—he glances at the timer—"eight seconds."

"Ugh!" I take off down the stairs. Alarms blare and red lights erupt the moment my feet touch the main floor. I scramble to the turtle, pulling out the White Tiger orb on the chain that Samshin, the goddess of life, gave me. Light from the orb can shine through the clasp of the necklace, and the chain keeps the orb safe. I whisper to its milky white surface, asking for the location of the Black Turtle orb, but the White Tiger orb remains unchanged.

"It's not here," I yell up at Kud.

"Impossible." But his stance stiffens and his composure shifts.

I grin. "What's it like to be wrong?"

"If I'm wrong, I hold you responsible for leading me to this mistake."

"Fabulous," I mutter. I comb every freaking inch of the statue, but I come up with nothing. There are no secret compartments or hidden buttons. The only thing out of the ordinary is a plaque on the front with ancient Chinese characters. I cock my head. There's something about the words that tugs at the edge of my mind. Maybe it's just that it reminds me of the sign on Haemosu's sick little hangout: "All who enter will surely die."

Above, the doors of the elevator open. Guards pour out wearing full protective armor and helmets. They hold their guns at the ready, scanning the room with them. One of the guards calls something over his radio.

A part of me wishes they could take out Kud and arrest me. It would be so nice to get arrested and have an excuse not to be responsible for saving my country. But no, thanks to Kud's cloaking spell, they can't see either of us. Kud merely steps before each guard, one by one, and presses something onto each of their suits that causes the guards to collapse to the ground.

He picks up one guard's headset and rattles off in Korean that the area is clear and it's a technical malfunction.

"You better not have killed them," I say in a growl.

"Did you find the orb?" He tosses the headset to the floor.

I narrow my eyes. "It's not here."

"Try harder."

I grind my teeth and close my eyes. It's hard to focus with alarms blaring and red lights flashing and armed men who may possibly be dead lying on the ground. I rub my palms over my eyes. *I can't do this.*

Then I take a deep breath. I pull the image of the turtle into the forefront of my mind and hold the White Tiger orb with my right hand. As a seeker orb, it has the power to lead its wielder to his or her heart's desire. The tricky thing is that the orb doesn't always think like a human does.

The orb warms in my palm. Shocked, I open my eyes to find that the lights are back to normal and the sound has shut off. A beam of white light shines from the orb, not on the statue, but on the case beside it. Using my knife, I pick the lock on the case and pull out an ancient coin illuminated by the orb's glow. The coin is cold against my sweating palms.

One side of the coin holds an image of a robed man surrounded by a winding wall, and the other side shows rows of armored men. The robed man looks familiar. From the image of the wall, I guess that he's the emperor who built the Great Wall of China. I silently thank my IB Chinese teacher.

"Got something." I run back up to Kud but stop at the top of the stairs, the pile of guards turning my stomach sour. It's one thing to see them falling to the floor from a distance and quite another to stand over them.

"Don't worry." Kud grabs my waist and lifts me over the bodies. "I just put them to sleep. They'll wake up from a horrid nightmare with a headache, nothing more. What did you find?"

When I show him the coin, he sneers. "What? No orb?" He curses. "Just rubbish from China."

He takes it from my palm and smashes it to the floor, grinding his shoe's heel into it. Even though the coin is metal, it breaks apart into small chunks, as if it too is unable to withstand Kud's wrath. I know the feeling.

Normally I would find joy in seeing him so distraught, but my only chance to escape Kud's control is to find that other orb and give it to Palk. We are running in mindless circles. The Guardians who first hid these orbs are playing games with us even though they've been dead for over a thousand years.

Maybe my plan to return the orb to Palk is the most ridiculous one on the planet. Maybe I should be content to live in misery for all of eternity.

But I can't just give up. As Kud steps into the elevator, I snatch up the pieces of the coin. The White Tiger orb showed the coin to me. There must be a reason for it. I have to believe that, or I'll have nothing left to believe in, nothing left to hope for. And without hope, I will have nothing. I swallow my fears as we ride back up on the elevator. I just want to get this whole night over with.

"You're really attached to that coin, aren't you?" Kud eyes my clenched hand.

"It's our best lead yet."

I slip on my high heels as I follow Kud back into the ballroom. I expect the place to be in evacuation mode or high alert after what just happened, but everyone appears to be exactly as we left them. Gossiping, drinking, eating, and having a perfect night of bliss. Those days are forever lost to me.

Kud hooks my arm into his and smiles down at me. "That wasn't so bad, was it? Perhaps your little coin will tell us something after all."

I stare in surprise at Kud's sudden change in demeanor. How can he transform from raging mad to civilized and rational in a mere five seconds?

"I suppose." Something feels off. Kud is far too pleased with himself, but maybe I'm just struggling with his humanity. "What changed your mind?"

"Do you know the waltz?" Kud kisses my hand and draws me toward the dance floor, where a few others are dancing.

My "no" falls on unhearing ears as Kud practically drags me forward. My mind swirls as the contract in my arm yanks me after him. I resist its pull, but as I do, my arm burns hotter until tears prick my eyes from the pain. And that's when I realize I can't say no to him, not even to dancing a stupid dance. The contract won't let me resist him. I try to process this as I stumble along behind him.

Some of the guests glance our way and whisper, but no one bothers to intervene. Maybe they don't see what is happening for what it is, or maybe they just don't want to get involved.

At the dance floor, Kud takes one of my hands and slides his other hand behind my back. He's pretty good at the waltz, unlike me. I'm so bad I actually make him look like a lousy dancer. I wish I made him look bad at everything.

"Shouldn't we leave before someone finds those guards?" I ask. "Or notices a missing coin?"

Kud leans in close and whispers in my ear, lingering for too long. "We must be discreet. Leaving now will be too obvious. We must wait for the right moment."

His lips nearly brush my forehead, and I frown, confused. Ever since we left the elevator, he's been back to acting like the perfect gentleman. I don't understand—and then I see why. My heart sinks to my toes. My knees buckle, and I'm sure I would've landed in a puddle on the floor if Kud hadn't been holding me. His grip tightens, and he dips me backward and then pulls me up.

But I can't focus on the dance or the people around me or how we've snuck into the President of Korea's secret vault and should be escaping while we still have a chance. I've lost all ability to breathe or think.

Because there, in the corner, is Marc. He's wearing a black jacket and a white shirt, the top two buttons carelessly left undone, and his hair is as disheveled as ever. He's talking to that same girl I saw the other night on the roof, laughing and popping an hors d'oeuvre in his mouth. Until he spots me. His face freezes as his eyes lock on to mine. His smile transforms into a lined grimace, and those beautiful eyes harden. His chin lifts a notch and his eyebrows rise, partly in shock and partly in challenge. The red scar along Marc's jaw, a reminder of our battle with Kud, stands out.

Kud whispers in my ear again, drawing me closer. My muscles are jelly, and I can't seem to shove him away or think of anything but Marc.

How he's there. And I'm here.

In Kud's arms.

Finally I'm able to gather my wits, push myself away from Kud, and stalk out of the ballroom into the main entrance. I'm not sure why Kud has finally released his vise grip on me, but I don't care. I just want to get out of here and leave before I fall apart. I can't let Kud find out I'm still in love with Marc, and I can't have Marc see how I behave around Kud because Marc might not understand that I'm manipulating the god of darkness.

I glance over my shoulder despite all the warning bells in my mind urging me to keep walking. Marc is speaking into something on his wrist. That can't be good. He must be alerting the rest of the Guardians.

Once I reach the hallway, away from the crowds, Kud grabs my hand. I whirl around and dig my heels into the plush carpet.

"You did that purposely. You wanted him to see the two of us together."

Kud's mouth curves. "I needed to know if you still cared for him."

"Why? I'm in your service now. What does it matter?" I'm yelling, but I don't care because Kud now knows the truth. That

I've been lying to him about not caring about Marc. There's no doubt that he will use Marc against me.

Three of the Guardians of Shinshi stroll up: the girl, Jung, and Marc. My heart beats wildly as they line up before Kud, and I grip the coin pieces more tightly in my hand. "What are you doing here?" Jung asks.

"I should ask the same of you," Kud says.

"Someone tipped us off," the girl says, pursing her plump lips. I try not to focus on how beautiful she is, with her short black hair cut into a cute bob and her blue silk dress hugging her body. "But somehow I suspect that was you. You wanted us to be here. Why?"

"You are on Palk's sacred ground." Jung moves closer. "You were not invited."

"I thought I would stop by for a hello." Kud smooths back his hair and adjusts the cuffs of his shirt. "But I see he isn't here now, is he? Tell him to send someone of importance to speak with me next time, not the dregs of society."

Jung's jaw tightens, and then his gaze falls on me. "Jae." When he says my name it comes out strangled. "I have to know. Whose side are you on, ours or Kud's?"

How can he ask me that in front of Kud? I close my eyes, groaning. Jung can't know, none of them can know the position I'm in. How much I've had to sacrifice so that they can stay safe. But the sacrifices must continue, I know. There will be no end to my separation.

"I am a slave of Kud," I manage to say, and I show the three of them the contract swirling on my arm. "I must follow his orders, as it is written on my arm."

"It's just a tattoo," the girl says. "You still have free will."

"It's more than a tattoo." Marc lets out a long breath and rubs his eyes, as if what I've said is too much for him. "You probably can't see how it's burning and moving as we speak. It controls her."

"So now you understand that she is truly mine," Kud says with a victorious smile. "I suggest you leave her alone."

"I can't believe it." Jung's face is full of loathing, and his mouth twists as if he's tasted something sour. I look away, crossing my arms. I hate myself on so many levels. "That you would turn your back on us so quickly."

"It's not that simple." My voice is a whisper. I will my eyes to explain everything to Marc, but there's so much pain in his face that I know he can't see what I'm trying to tell him. If only I could get away from Kud's all-seeing eyes and explain everything to Marc.

"You don't belong here and are not welcome," Jung tells Kud, and points to the door. "Leave now or there will be consequences. Haechi will escort you out."

Haechi stands by the door, his giant body swallowing half the entranceway. A growl emits from his mouth, and he lowers his head so that the lights glint off his horn like fiery waves. I swallow my fear and my sadness that I'm on the side of his enemy. I've seen him fight with Haemosu and stand against Kud's most horrifying creatures, only to strut away victorious. This is Haechi's territory.

I wonder if Kud would be able to fight Haechi here and win. And then the next thought sickens me because I realize that's why Kud has me here. To fight for him. Just in case.

As if reading my thoughts, Kud sets his hand on the small of my back. "We should go, don't you agree, my princess?"

"Jae Hwa." Marc grabs my arm. His voice chokes, and he presses his lips together.

"Leave her be." Jung snatches Marc's hand from my arm. "She has picked her side. She's dead to us now."

I gape at Jung. How could he say that? But then I realize he's right, or at least close. If I'm not dead, I'm most certainly dying with every passing second in Kud's hands. Each day I live in his land, slivers of my soul are cut away.

I glance between Kud and Marc. I know what I must do. I hate myself so much for it, but it's the only way to keep Marc alive and the rest of the Guardians safe.

"Jung is right." I hook my arm through Kud's. "I am dead to you, and you mean nothing to me. Sure, there once was a time when we had something." I try to shrug nonchalantly. "But those feelings for you died the moment I signed my contract with Kud."

Marc jerks back as if I've hit him, and then his body shudders. He opens his mouth to say something, but nothing comes out. Jung moves in front of Marc and crosses his thick arms, glaring daggers at me. Tears itch in the corners of my eyes, but I push them away. Far, far away.

"Come on, man." Jung drags Marc back, protecting him from me. Me, the monster. "Let her go."

"Well." Kud cocks his head toward me. "Shall we?"

Kud and I stroll pass Haechi, whose eyes never leave mine. He studies me as if searching my soul only to find it lacking. I despise every step I take. If I could, I would run. The contract burns across my skin and into my veins, demanding obedience.

I must play the part. Everything depends on that. So I lift my head high, even though I'm shattering into a million pieces inside. Even though I'm nothing but a broken vessel.

CHAPTER 5

This time, Kud sucks us into his world through one of his TV-screen look-alikes. I stumble behind Kud, my dress tangled around my ankles, my contract arm burning from being dragged along, and my stomach twisting from the quick jolt into the Spirit World dimension. Usually I travel through the starry skies, where I can ease between worlds, rather than through Kud's screens, which are jarringly fast.

The moment our feet enter Kud's realm, he transforms back to his black-cloaked horrible self. Now he paces around the rotunda while I lean against the pedestal, waiting for the room to stop spinning and my breathing to return to normal. Every screen in the room has the coin pieces magnified. Kud is muttering and cursing and spouting all kinds of thoughts, but I can't hear his words. Or even care to.

All I can see is Marc's face. The devastation. The hurt. I've ruined him. More than anything right now, I want to slip away and hide.

But there is nowhere I can go without Kud knowing what I'm doing. I need a place to rage without him seeing my hurt and suffering. My best friend is dead, my father can't know I'm alive, and now I've lost Marc, too. And even worse, now that the Guardians know I'm alive, they've most likely told Grandfather. I wonder if he despises me for what I've done.

I had always had that hope, that secret place in my heart of hearts that I could escape to and remember Marc's and my last meeting on top of Seoraksan. There had still been love in his eyes then. Tonight I crushed that love just like Kud crushed the coin under his heel.

Then a new thought begins swimming through my mind. The White Tiger orb had been trying to tell me something. Sometimes its answers are not cut-and-dried. Maybe this coin is another clue to the location of the Black Turtle orb. If only I could talk to Grandfather. He'd know what to do.

Kud whips out his scepter. It's made from three silvery snakes twisted together to form an oval peak at the top, where the three heads merge into one, with six eyes always watching and three tongues flicking out, ready to strike. Kud begins smashing the screens, one by one, his cloak whirling around him as he screams obscenities.

An image on one of the screens catches my attention. It's a traditional-style home sitting on a bluff overlooking the sea. Grandfather's house. Anger burns within me at Kud for watching Grandfather. I suppose I've known he was doing it all along, but there's a difference between knowing it and seeing it.

"Wait!" I scream, and I rush to stand in front of Kud's scepter seconds before he smashes the screen that displays

Grandfather's house. "I have an idea. One that could help us figure this problem out."

"I had such high hopes for you, but now I see how wrong I was," Kud snarls. The warmth he had when we danced has vanished. "You may have fooled Marc and the Guardians, but I saw that look in your eyes. You still love him. You would turn your back on me and fight for their idiotic cause if I didn't have you bound to me. I waited a millennium for you, all in the hope that you would join me in reaching insurmountable power. But you are worthless."

I stumble back in surprise. Kud is jealous of Marc.

Kud's lips curve, and he jabs his scepter into my stomach. I scream as lightning bolts streak from the snakes' tongues into my core, and I drop to the ground in agony. Every inch of my body is on fire. I can barely process what is happening as I twist and jerk haphazardly. Not long ago Kud was twirling me around on the dance floor, and now he is unleashing his rage on me.

I scream for the pain to stop, wishing I could just die and be out of my misery. Finally, Kud lifts the scepter away from my body and stares down at me. He's waiting for the Spirit World to heal me so he can do it all over again. This has been his habit since I entered his domain.

"My grandfather," I manage to say between gasps. "He would know what the coin means. I could ask him."

"You know, you got your conniving genes from your grandfather," Kud says. "A trickster, that one. Who knows what devilry he's plotting against me this very moment?"

"I could make him think I snuck away from you." I grimace as I roll to a sitting position. "He'd never know he was betraying the Guardians."

"I have trouble deciding whom I hate more, Palk or your grandfather. The grief your grandfather has caused me—"

Then Kud does a very strange thing. He pulls back his hood and tilts his neck to reveal a jagged cut. Yellow pus bubbles out and oozes down his shoulder. "Your grandfather did this to me. Cut me with a blade forged from Palk's pure light. He may not have destroyed me, but it is my constant reminder that he must suffer."

I gape at the wound, and as I do, courage rushes through me. Grandfather may not have realized that his actions long ago would have an impact on me today, but for the first time I see that Kud has weaknesses, too. I rise on wobbly bare feet, my shoes having fallen off somewhere.

"Still," Kud continues. "The idea of him betraying his own pleases me very much. It's a tempting proposition."

"You could watch me." I slouch against one of the broken viewing screens, trying not to look eager. "He'd never know."

Kud flips his hood back into place, shrouding his features, and slams the end of his scepter into the stone floor. I stumble as my arm yanks me over to the screen where Grandfather's house is pictured. In the moonlight, I see the ocean slipping in and out on the beach and a light breeze bending the trees to its will.

"You will have fifteen minutes," Kud says.

"I'll need more time." I clench the coin pieces harder as if they will bring me good fortune.

"That's a matter of opinion." And with those words, the contract on my arm drags me into the screen, pain searing up and down my veins.

. . .

I land on the sandy path before Grandfather's house. Though time and Kud's patience are short, I close my eyes, drink in the briny air, and savor the grains of sand beneath my bare feet. The first time I visited Grandfather's home was for Lunar New Year this past winter. I arrived thinking Grandfather was a loon and left with a sense of purpose. I push aside the fact that my dress is torn down the side, probably from when I fell while Kud was electrifying me, and how I'm sure my hair looks like I stuck a finger in a socket. I try the front door. It's unlocked, so I slip inside.

The wooden floor is cool as I pad down the hallway, passing by the winged-horse sculpture and the manikin of General Yu-Shin Kim. Memories haunt me: coming here with Dad, eating rice cakes, drinking tea, and discovering the mural of Princess Yuhwa riding Oryonggeo, the five-dragon chariot.

Discovering the truth of my past and my future.

I enter the back room. The geometric-shaped screens covering the windows reveal the ocean glimmering under moonbeams, the waves sloughing across the shore. And there, sitting on a silk cushion at a square table and reading an ancient book, is Grandfather. He lifts his head, and when his eyes find mine, they open wide.

"Jae Hwa," he whispers, almost as if he's not sure if I'm real.

Dark circles ring his eyes and his cheeks are sunken, as if he's spent too many hours training and studying instead of sleeping and eating.

"Haraboji." I step closer, and suddenly he has me wrapped in his arms. We cling to each other. I wish I could freeze this moment and never let it go, but the contract on my arm begins to burn. Kud's reminder of the purpose of this visit.

"I heard you were alive," Grandfather says in his deep voice. "The Guardians alerted the Council after they faced you at the intelligence service. I suppose I never stopped believing that you weren't dead after you left us that day at Marc's house. Marc refused to speak to me about what happened, and we all guessed there was a reason for it."

"Those were the terms," I explained. "I exchanged my service to Kud for Marc's life. And I was to let everyone I love believe I was dead, or Kud would kill them."

Grandfather nods, his brow wrinkled with worry. "Are you able to speak freely?"

"I have fifteen minutes," I say, avoiding that question. "Or less. Is Dad okay? I've been so worried about him."

"He's alive," Grandfather says vaguely.

I don't like that answer, but there isn't time to ponder the meaning of his words. I hold out my hand, showing him the broken coin pieces.

"Do you know what this coin means? I asked the White Tiger orb to lead me to the location of the Black Turtle orb, and it led me to this coin."

Grandfather picks up the coin shards, piecing them together like a puzzle. He mutters something under his breath. "Shall we go for a walk? There's something I wish to show you."

"Walk? I suppose. But it needs to be quick."

I follow Grandfather down another hall, where he opens a door. It leads to an empty room. I'm about to ask him why we are here when he shuts the door behind him.

The room vanishes.

We float in an endless midnight sky, stars glistening around us and singing songs of light. Grandfather nods once to me, finally acknowledging a secret he's been withholding from me, from all of us.

"I am sorry I have kept this from you, but this is something I'm not allowed to divulge, even to the Council," he says. "I am the link, the human who communicates with the Tiger of Shinshi. When I began my quest to stop Haemosu, I was summoned by the Tiger of Shinshi to help with communication between immortals and humans. The only other person whom he has spoken to in this generation is you. Because I am the link, I'm able to know things humans wouldn't normally know, and this knowledge is why the Council puts up with me."

My mouth is dry as I take it all in. "What about Kud? Can he see us?"

"Not here. This region belongs to the Tiger of Shinshi, and Kud's power is limited, as is ours. But our time is short. It won't be long before Kud's hold finds you."

A slice of gold sparkles in the distance, growing closer by the second until I realize it's the Golden Thread. A massive tiger materializes before us, his orange fur radiating the cord's glow.

The Tiger of Shinshi.

"Great One." I bow, and as I do, the burning sensation of my contract grows on my arm. My time is almost up. "Warden of Three Thousand Li, Defender of the Chosen, and Guardian of the Golden Thread."

"Jae Hwa, daughter of Korea," he says, and the air shudders around us. "The Golden Thread is weakening. The land of Korea is broken, and it is only a matter of time before the thread snaps in half and all is lost."

"Why are you telling me this?" I ask, worry curling through me. "I can't save Korea by myself."

"You speak the truth." The tiger's ginger eyes assess me. "But you are the wielder of the White Tiger orb, which has shown you the location of the Black Turtle orb through the pieces in your hand. I do not know of another who has the ability to undergo the tasks required to reclaim this lost artifact."

"I want to help," I say. "Nothing in the world would give me greater pleasure than destroying Kud, but his power over me scares me."

"Yes, it is troubling," the Tiger of Shinshi says.

"Kud also wants this artifact." I bite my lip as the pain from my contract digs deep into me. I'm not sure how much longer I can resist the pull. "I'm trying to make him think I am getting it for him. But I don't think I can do it alone."

"Have the Guardians assist her," the Tiger of Shinshi tells Grandfather. "We cannot afford to lose this orb."

"I will try," Grandfather says. "But they believe that no matter how true of heart she may be, she doesn't have control over herself, and Kud will end up controlling the orb in the end."

"This is true, which is why she will need their and your help." Then the tiger turns back to me. "The artifact you seek was taken to China by one of the Guardians a thousand human years ago. It is my hope that it is still accessible. But beware! Once there, you will be alone, for the immortals of Korea cannot assist you outside our boundaries. You bear Kud's mark, so the immortals of China will believe you to be an enemy and will do everything in their power to kill you. So will their human Guardians."

"What if I fail?"

"You must not. For the sake of our beloved Korea."

The pain in my arm is unbearable. I hunch over, pressing my forearm to my chest. "Haraboji!" I cry out in pain. "I'm being pulled back."

"Jae Hwa!" Grandfather's face contorts and he grabs my shoulders, trying to hold me in place. "If anything should happen to me, remember this place. If you escape, take my place as the next link between humans and the Spirit World."

But my arm whips out, dragging me away from them. I stretch out my free arm toward Grandfather, but I cannot reach him. I memorize his face as I sail away, knowing this could be the last time I speak with him.

• • •

"I know where the Black Turtle orb is," I tell Kud as I lift my head off the stone floor. The combination of all the traveling through dimensions has taken its toll on me. I crawl to the corner and throw up. Sweat pours down my face, and my hands shake.

"Where did your grandfather take you?" Kud roars.

"He showed me where to go to find the orb." I wipe my mouth with the back of my hand. My emotions are out of control. I can't even think properly. The only thing clear in my mind is that this monster is destroying everything in my life, and it's time to play hardball.

He thinks I'm tough. He thinks I'm special. A once-a-millennium-kind-of-girl. It's hardly true, but I have to make it be so if I'm to do the impossible. I'm going to send him to the darkest, deepest hell. Nothing is going to stop me.

I shove aside my pain, the lingering image of Grandfather's face, and the sad eyes of the Tiger of Shinshi. And I smile up at Kud. My expression causes Kud to stop his pacing.

"I also discovered that only *I* am able to get this final orb."

"Who told you this?"

"An old book of Grandfather's," I lie. "So you need me. Let me free for one hour in Seoul and I will tell you the location."

Kud cocks his head to the side. I can't see any part of his face other than the two glowing silver eyes beneath his hood. "Where is it?" His voice chills my bones.

"One hour. I need to make sure you've been keeping your end of our bargain."

He nods slowly. "You will have your hour."

"Alone."

"How will I know you will return?"

"Seriously?" I lift up my arm, and the swirling bronze liquid on my forearm glows in the dark light.

"Fine. You may have one hour. But you will be restricted to speaking to the living."

I nod, my mind racing as I formulate my plan. Tonight I'm going to dance on the edge of Kud's contract. It's risky, but I don't know if I'll have another chance, and I need to do two things before I go to China and most likely die.

CHAPTER 6

The walls of the apartment buildings loom over me on either side as I make my way to the back parking lot that all of the apartment balconies look over. I move to a dark corner and blend into the shadows, glad I changed into my black jumpsuit. Gingerly, I set down my backpack.

"Stay there," I say to it. "I'll only be a moment."

I stand back, assessing the silent cars to make sure the backpack will stay safe. I can't risk taking it up with me. This area is so familiar, it causes a pang of sadness to wash over me. There isn't time for sentimental thoughts, though; I only have one hour. I pull out my crossbow and clip on the grappling hook. The hook flies into the air and lands on the railing of the balcony next to mine. Close enough.

I clip in to the ascender, pull myself up to the balcony, and then slide over the partition between my old apartment and the neighbor's. But when I stand at the balcony door and press my fingers against the glass, I find my muscles unable to move. The furniture is still in the same location. A sliver of light cuts across the floor from my room, but the rest of the apartment slumbers in darkness. Dad must be sleeping.

I should turn back around and leave, but I can't. I need to make sure Kud has kept his side of the bargain about leaving Dad alone, and Grandfather's vague words worry me. It doesn't take me long to find the key I placed under the potted plant long ago. I slip inside, clinging to the shadows.

I creep through the living room, and that's when I spy Dad. The glow from his computer illuminates his face; otherwise I wouldn't have seen him. He's sleeping on the couch, still wearing his suit, his tie tossed to the ground.

Dirty dishes, discarded takeout containers, beer bottles, and piles of clothes surround the couch. The room smells like rotting food. It's a far cry from the immaculate place we kept while we both lived here. There was a time when Dad went off the deep end drinking after Mom died, but he quit when we moved to Seoul. He had promised we were going to make a fresh start in Korea. It wasn't easy, I know, especially with the pressure to drink with his boss and coworkers after work, but he had always stayed true to his word.

Until now.

Every fiber within me wants to hold his hand, to tell him I'm okay, to tell him not to worry. But in the end, perhaps Kud is right. It's better for him to think I'm dead than to know the truth about what I've become. I shuffle to my room. My light is on, and I wonder why—or if Dad ever turns it off.

I step inside. Clothes litter the floor and drawers hang open. It's exactly like I left it. An origami creation rests on my dresser:

a blue dragon. I pick it up and notice writing inside. I unfold it and read Dad's words.

> *Jae Hwa,*
>
> *My heart aches from missing you, and nothing will numb it. Haraboji says you are dead, taken by some creature, but I refuse to believe him. Perhaps this is how he felt when Sun disappeared. Haraboji never stopped looking for her, and now it's my turn. So this dragon is my wish for good luck and holy power.*
>
> *I pray for your return every day.*
>
> *Appa*

"*Appa*," I repeat.

I haven't called Dad that since I was little. I press the dragon to my chest and tuck it into my pocket, even though I know I shouldn't. The contract on my arm forbids any form of communication, and I wait for my arm to burn in punishment for my actions. But it doesn't, so somehow I've tricked Kud.

A sound like thunder rolling in the distance fills the apartment. I freeze, every nerve tense. A snake-like shadow slithers across the wall. I spin around, only to be greeted by the wide-open mouth of an *imoogi*, fangs and teeth bared. Its hood juts out as it gears up to attack. The red eyes home in on me. The last time I faced an *imoogi* was in North Korea, where three of them were feeding off the souls of innocent tuberculosis patients at a clinic. Knowing there is one here, feeding off my dad, sends rage through me. This creature will die.

I don't even have a second to breathe before it blasts out a stream of fire. I cartwheel to the right, but the fire doesn't hit where I stood. Instead, the stream follows me as if it's a serpent itself. I run and push off the wall, flipping over the fire and landing on the other side of the *imoogi*.

My mind frantically searches for a way to kill this beast. I have no weapons other than the White Tiger orb. It heightens my abilities and powers, but could it repel fire? I whip out the orb, clutching it in one hand and holding my other hand out as if to hold back the flames. White light engulfs me in a shimmering explosion.

The fire halts at the barrier, and the *imoogi* roars as it whips its head around. It snaps its massive jaws at me. Power surges through me from my fingers, racing through my bloodstream. I stand taller, my hair and dress whipping around me. But how much longer can I hold off the fire and the *imoogi* before the power of the orb overwhelms me, as it has done so often in the past? I'm still human—my constant curse and blessing.

I turn and race to the kitchen, slamming my bedroom door behind me. I flip over the kitchen island and throw open the utensil drawer. We hardly ever cooked in our kitchen, but I'm pretty sure we have knives somewhere. My hand closes around the hilt of a carving knife, and I block out the memory of Mom cutting the turkey with this knife when we once cooked meals together as a family, when she was alive and we were normal.

The *imoogi* smashes through the door, creating a giant splintered hole. I risk a glance over at Dad on the couch. He still sleeps. The *imoogi* must have enough power still to keep our fight's sound within its own realm; otherwise everyone in this entire apartment building would have already called the police and fire departments.

I leap onto the island and dive through the air, knife raised, ready to plunge it into the *imoogi*'s forehead. Fire circles me, hungry to consume my skin. The orb's power holds the flames at bay, but my skin still chars.

Then my knife and the *imoogi* meet. I sink the silver blade into one eye, focusing the power of the orb into the blow. The *imoogi* screams and sweeps its muzzle to the side, tossing me across the room. I land against the wall by the front entrance. The old pain in my back from fighting the *imoogi* in North Korea flares up, and I sink to the floor, screaming in pain.

Furious, the *imoogi* whips its head back and forth. It snarls and lunges for me. My anger at this creature forces me back to my feet, and with another cry, I plunge the knife into the creature's other eye.

The *imoogi* screams in protest, plummeting to the ground. It flops across the floor.

"Leave this home and never return, you wretched creature," I say.

I lift the knife once again, but the *imoogi* vanishes. I stare at the spot where it stood and then crumple to the ground, releasing my hold on the orb. Using the orb's power has drained my strength, and it takes every ounce of my energy just to lift my head and assess the room.

The knife clatters to the floor as I realize the *imoogi* is finally gone. Maybe it's my imagination, but the air feels lighter, less oppressive. The door is still smashed, but that isn't my fault. Kud should never have allowed one of his creatures to enter.

What will Dad think of this when he awakens? Will he call Grandfather? Will Grandfather tell Dad the truth?

I try to write a note to Dad explaining everything, but not one pen or pencil will work for me thanks to Kud's power. On the coffee table I find Dad's phone. I scroll through his contacts until I find Grandfather's number. I press Call and rest the phone in Dad's palm.

I pray Dad will be able to piece together tonight's events. Time is running short, so I lean down and kiss him on the forehead. Even then he doesn't wake, and I curse Kud for it.

My feet whisper across the floor as I slip out to the balcony. I glance back, memorizing Dad's face illuminated in the computer screen's light, and promise myself I'm working to right all the wrongs.

CHAPTER 7

As I hurry down the main street in Yonhi-Dong, the air smells exactly as I remember: a blend of cooking *bulgogi* meat, a hint of coming rain, and fumes from the buses. The air vibrates as if it's alive and breathing, and I soak it all up. The sky still holds its blanket of night, and I guess that there's a few hours left before morning arrives. Ever since I've been in Kud's realm, morning and night haven't had much meaning; the sky there is always murky gray or pitch black.

The neon signs glow, illuminating the darkness and dispelling some of the gloom that even now has crept into my heart. A light drizzle begins as I pass by the ginseng store, turn right, and begin to hike up the hill. This is my first summer in Seoul. My friends have said that it'll be dreary because of the rainy season, but as water streams down my face and soaks my shirt and jeans, I take it all in. It's cold and wet and real. I revel in this moment.

Bushes line this road up the mountain, and as I hike higher, the scents of flowers and evergreens sweeten the air. When I reach the guard shack and the Korean gate halfway up the hill, I stop and stare at the sign. Seoul Foreign School. I breathe in deeply and consider turning around and forgetting about my past.

But I can't. My school was a huge part of my life. It's where I first met Michelle, Marc, and all of my friends. I take a step closer. And then another. I hug the shadows of the bushes to avoid being noticed by the security cameras as I scurry under the gate and up the final leg of the hill.

I come to the first building and tail one of the security guards making the rounds inside. He doesn't bother checking to see if anyone is following him. I don't blame him. Who would want to come here in the middle of the night? I slip inside as the glass door shuts behind him, and I duck into the shadows.

The guard's boots clip down the hall, retreating from where I huddle under the stairwell. I dig in my backpack and pull out the jar, holding it up between my hands. The celadon is cold in my wet palms.

"Remember when you threatened to set me up on a date with Marc?" I say to the jar. I smile at the memory. "I was so ticked at you. But you were right. He was the perfect guy for me."

I stare at the celadon, memorizing how the green pattern swirls in endless circles, never beginning, never ending. If only everything good in life were like that. Endless and forever.

"Your mom found your journal and photos from the North Korea trip. Don't be mad. I think she wanted to make your trip into a living memory, so she published them in the *Korea Times* under your name. Kud came and confronted me about it. He was so mad that it showed the truth about North Korea." I giggle as I remember when Kud jammed the paper in my face. "You would've liked the article."

I stand, suddenly overwhelmed by the flood of memories. I hug the jar to my chest. Michelle feels closer this way. If only I had kept her closer when she was alive, she might still be living, laughing, and bossing me around.

"I miss you," I whisper to the jar. "It's so hard to be alone. Marc despises me. Dad thinks I'm dead. And Grandfather—" I shake my head, shoving back tears. "I may have saved my family, but I've brought them shame by doing so."

I take off down the hall. Lockers line the walls on either side. I tuck the jar against my hip with one hand, and I reach out and let my other hand brush along the lockers as I walk. School is out for the summer, and since this is an international school, most of the students have migrated back to the far corners of the earth for their holiday. The air has a musty and unused scent to it. But as I walk, the memories bombard me.

Then I pass by the art room. The place I first laid eyes on Marc. It was the only class we shared. He was painting on his canvas, choosing bright colors of red, purple, and yellow. His strokes were wild and bold, but that wasn't what caught my attention. It was that intense look in his eyes as his brush swept over the canvas, filling up the white. His hair hung over his eyelashes, and a streak of red paint ran across his cheek.

At the end of class, when we were washing up, he strolled over to where I stood at the sink.

"You're new here, aren't you?" he said.

I nodded, trying not to get lost in those green eyes of his.

"This place is nothing like your school back home, I'm guessing?" And he smiled. I ducked my head to focus on the black paint pouring out of my brush, swirling down the drain. "It's not so bad. Soon you'll make friends from all over the world. You'll have a place to crash on every continent."

"Even Antarctica?" I lifted my eyebrows at him.

He laughed and pointed at me. "I like you already." Then he backed up, saying, "See, you're already getting the hang of it. Just give it time."

Time.

I leave behind that memory as I shuffle the rest of the way down the hall and out into the courtyard. I expect one of the guards to notice me, but no, I'm left to my wanderings. Perhaps no one expects a skinny, lonely, half-dead girl to be wandering around in the rain.

I pass the fountain and the gardens until I reach the back wall, which runs between Yonsei University and Seoul Foreign School. There's no way I'm going to risk alerting all the guards by using the back gate to leave the school's premises, so I scramble up the hill, where the wall is lower and easier to climb.

The rain has made the concrete wall slick, so it takes me a few tries to scale it, but once I do, I easily drop down onto the path on the other side. I run a short distance until I find the cemetery. The rain pours on me, flattening my hair against my cheeks and drenching my clothes.

The last time I was here was when Marc and I were trying to sneak into the Guardians of Shinshi's headquarters. The place isn't far, just down the hill in the first building on the Yonsei

University campus. But the headquarters is the last place I want to be.

I set my backpack onto the muddy grass and unzip it. The spade I've brought ends up being the perfect equipment choice, and I dig out a small hole in the ground. I kneel in the mud, placing the jar before me, and then I pull out Michelle's two butterfly clips. The gems on the wings glisten in the rain. I'm not sure how long I sit there, but soon the rain stops and I'm left alone with the mist curling around my body and Michelle's jar. Time is running away from me. Soon my hour will be up, and I'll be summoned back to Kud's land. Even still, I can't force myself to open the lid.

"Do you think I made the right choice?" I ask the jar. "I didn't know what else to do. He killed you, and Marc was next. It was all happening so fast, and I had to act."

I stare at the jar as if I expect Michelle to say something back.

"What are you doing?" a girl's voice says behind me.

I jump up and spin around in attack form. For a moment I believe it's Michelle, but then I realize with disappointment that it's not. It's a girl who looks like she belongs at a traditional Korean funeral, wearing a snowy-white *hanbok* that is dry and unsoiled despite the rain. Her black hair is coiled into an intricate braid that cascades over her shoulders. But the moment my eyes fall on the spear strapped to her back and I take in her shimmering appearance, I remember her perfectly. Princess Bari, the guider of the dead.

She lifts her eyebrows meaningfully at my raised fists. Slowly I lower my hands.

"Still human, I see," she says. "And most definitely still delusional. I confess I had to come see you for myself. Kud has never captured a human girl for his assassin. Either you are very special or very stupid."

I grimace. "Probably very stupid."

"That was my guess." Bari nods at the jar on the ground. "Why are you talking to a pot?"

"My friend." I swallow, unable to explain what happened because, looking at this situation from her point of view, I must appear delusional. "I've come to bury her."

"You do know you are talking to a pot."

"But these are her ashes. Kud only sprinkled a few of them in the car wreck to trick her parents."

"This is ridiculous," Bari says. "She's not in there."

"What?" I grab hold of Bari. "You know where she is? But I saw her die right before my eyes."

"You poor soul." Bari sighs and looks at me with pity. "She has passed on from this world into the heavens."

I step away, shaking. I knew this already. But hearing Bari actually say it makes it all real. I had come back to the human world because I wanted to be alive, to feel. Now I'm not so sure. Maybe it's better not to love, better to lose my humanity in Kud's world.

Numbly I turn and pick up the jar. I slide off the lid, easily now, and pour the ashes into the hole. Then I scoop up the mound of dirt and cover the remains. I press one butterfly clip into the top of the mound and slide the other into my hair. I stare at the mound as Bari comes to stand beside me.

Dawn is creeping along the horizon, and the burn of the contract is fierce, tearing at me, screaming for me to return.

But not yet. I must say my final words.

"Go and find peace, my dearest and most faithful of friends. But I promise in this moment, on this day, that I will not rest. I will find no peace until your death is avenged. So let it be."

Bari eyes me in the muted light, and a smile creeps across her face as if what I've just said brings her joy. "As your witness, so let it be."

CHAPTER 8

"The Black Turtle orb you seek is in China," I say, once again back in Kud's stinking, rotting land.

"China?" Kud's voice sounds startled and slightly panicked. I can't resist a laugh. "How is a treasure of Korea in *China*? This is impossible. The orbs were created and bound to Korea."

"Are you sure they are bound to Korea?" I place the pieces of the coin onto the pedestal in the center of the room and point to the picture of the Chinese emperor. "This was hidden in the secret vault of the president's house. It's a vault that isn't supposed to exist. And without the knowledge that the orbs exist, no one would be able to understand the message on this coin."

"Where in China?" Kud barks at me. His tentacles wrap around my chest, squeezing me. The contract on my skin burns.

I choke. "Is this the way you treat a princess? I'm not telling you anything until you let go of your death grip."

Kud loosens his hold.

"Long ago, the Guardians of Shinshi sent one of their own to China to hide one of the orbs as a safeguard in case one immortal gathered too many of the orbs and tried to usurp all of the power." I glower at Kud. He waves his hand for me to continue. "The emperor on the coin is Qin Shi Huang. It's my guess that the orb is located in one of the places he built. The Great Wall is pictured there, but so are the terra-cotta warriors. I'll need to do a little more research, but we're close."

"We must put a plan into place to find this final orb before the Guardians do. There is just one problem. I am bound to Korean soil."

Yes. I smile. *So the Tiger of Shinshi said.*

"Which is why you need me to make this happen for you." I move closer to Kud. "You've been searching for this clue for practically eternity, and in less than a month, I've found it for you. Let me go to China and get this orb."

Kud stares at me, his silvery eyes boring into mine until I want to shrivel into a ball and forget I even said anything. Yet I stand my ground, holding his gaze.

"I won't fail." And I mean that with all my heart.

"I think it will be better to keep you close by my side," Kud says, and then he turns to the two creepy things he recently created. "But you two—my creations—I command you to complete this next step of the task. Go to China. Bring this orb back to me."

They bow. I frown. My plan is slipping away. I can't allow his creatures to get the orb or to be anywhere near me when I do. I have to go on the mission myself if there's going to be any chance to get the orb to Palk.

Kud waves his hand dismissively at the three of us. "Leave me."

I grasp for some way to change Kud's mind. Somehow I need time to convince him that I should go on this mission, not those two stiffs.

"What?" I ask, hoping this crazy idea of mine will work. "No celebration?"

"You wish to celebrate?" Kud laughs. "The task is not finished."

"A dinner celebration would be perfect," I say. Before he can say no, I add, "And wear something other than those old rags you've got on."

I look pointedly at the writhing material snaking around me. Then I spin around and stalk to the door, cringing at my audacity and expecting him to fly into a rage. But he doesn't. For once, I'm grateful his plotting and scheming is keeping him preoccupied.

. . .

Back in my room, I begin rummaging through my dresser for jewelry and makeup. There's a magic about these drawers; every time I open one there's something different inside. Some people might find it cool to have mystery drawers. I find it unsettling to never know what I'll find within them.

Still, I always wonder if one day I'll open a drawer and find a key out of this place—or something else that could help me escape. The only things these drawers have given me so far are random trinkets to help me pass the long, endless days in Kud's land.

After I slam the drawers open and shut, the chest finally produces two silver rings, dangle earrings, and a tube of lipstick. Tonight I will be prepared. Next, I flip open the wooden chest against the wall. Stacked inside are multiple *hanboks*, all black. I pull them out of the chest and throw them over my shoulder until the floor is littered with dresses.

"None of these will do." Then I notice a long, sequined black dress, shimmering like a sea of black pearls, with two slits that run from thigh to floor. This will give me mobility if the need arises.

I strip out of my black jumpsuit and slide the dress over my head, allowing it to slink down my body to the floor. I adjust the spaghetti straps. It hugs my figure, making my chest look bigger than it really is and giving me hips I didn't know I had. If I had my bow and arrows, I'd feel better, but this will have to do.

I take my silver brush and run it through my long hair until the black strands practically shine in the lantern light. After I put on my lipstick, I stare at myself in the shattered mirror.

"Perfect," I say as I plan Kud's demise.

. . .

"You should've picked me," I tell Kud from across the dinner table. "Not those stiffs who haven't lived in the real world since the Mongol invasion."

I shift uncomfortably on my silver cushion. It's hard to sit on a cushion in a floor-length sequined dress and come across as confident, capable, and at ease.

Kud has set our little celebration dinner on the balcony of his palace. The view is staggering and altogether depressing. The palace was built on top of a mountain peak, and on either side of the peak, the rocks rise up in a swoop to form the image of a dragon: one side as the head and the other as the tail.

Fingers of mist curl from marshy bogs and barren trees. The sterile, rocky landscape below us is accented by bone sculptures placed sporadically along a winding trail. The statues are one of Kud's hobbies. They are oddly lifelike and take on the images of humans. I wish I knew why he'd chosen those particular people to sculpt from bones.

"To your success." Kud lifts his wineglass in the air, completely ignoring my comment.

I eye him through the fire drops that rain down between us from upside-down candles. The drops splatter into the basin at the center of the table. Kud's in rare form tonight. Not only is he dressed in human clothes, but he's taken on the image of Kang-dae again.

Honestly, I wish he had worn his rags, his creepy eyes, and his bodiless form. It's much easier to manipulate a corpse than a real human being. My goal tonight is to become like Min, one of the girls I absolutely despised back at school. She had the hots for Marc and loved to flaunt all her everything in his face to get his attention.

It must be working, because when I strolled out onto the balcony where Kud had set up our dinner, he did a double take. It was exactly the reaction I was aiming for.

Channel Min, I tell myself. *Channel Min.*

"I am the perfect candidate to find this orb, and you know it," I continue, fiddling with my chopsticks. "I don't know why you can't see that."

"Actually I don't like the thought of you leaving my presence." Kud leans back in his chair and takes a sip of his wine. "Especially to a land where I have no control. I'd rather have you here with me. Aren't you enjoying your life of eternity?"

"Blissful as it may be, I think you're making a mistake."

The sigh escapes my mouth before I can stop it. I take a bite of meat. It tastes like chewy rubber. The last time I ate *kalbi* was with Marc and Michelle. Now she's dead, and I'll never be with Marc again. I need to stop thinking about both of them, or I'll drive myself mad.

"Have you tested your creations?" I ask Kud. "Are they able to handle the task you're giving them?"

"But of course."

"I seriously doubt it. Do they even have names? Do they know how to travel through customs?"

"Kwan and Sang Min?" Kud shrugs and looks out at the view spread before us. "They will not fail me."

"Oh, they will." I stab my meat with the end of my chopstick in anger. "And when they do, I'll be laughing, and I'll never let you forget their inadequacies for all eternity."

Kud laughs then, throwing his head back. The contract along my arm lights up. The brazen letters sparkle across my skin like fireworks. "I look forward to it, princess."

"Bring them to me," I tell Kud. "I wish to test them."

He lifts his eyebrows, and then his mouth quirks. "As you wish."

With a snap of his fingers, the two assassins enter. Now, in the murky light, I can see them better. Kud introduces them with a wave of his hand before continuing with his drinking. He has yet to touch his food.

Kwan, the one I'd thought was bald, actually has a long rope of hair that falls down his back. He's wearing pantaloons, and his muscular chest is bare except for a cloak that's wrapped from one shoulder to his belt, which is filled with an assortment of weapons. He grips a spear, the tip pointed to the sky.

The other one, Sang Min, has the same pants and belt, but he wears a vest and his long hair flows down his back. Tonight he's wearing a mask that hides his shriveled face. A jagged sword, which looks larger than me, is strapped to his back.

They both stare at me with empty black eyes.

"If they go to the airport looking like that, they'll be arrested for *sure*," I tell Kud, waving my hand dismissively.

"Don't be ridiculous," Kud says. "I'll have them disguised in something more contemporary. They will be fine."

"And when they get to China, what will they do?" I stand, pressing my palms on the table and leaning over my plate, a smile on my face. "They'll wander about and get their butts kicked into the sea by the Chinese Guardians. That's what will happen."

"You underestimate us," Kwan says in a toneless voice.

"Oh!" I lift my hands into the air. "The thing speaks. Well, this is an improvement, Kud."

Kud leans back in his chair, clearly amused. "I'm glad you think so."

He thinks this is some kind of joke. Fire races through my veins. He has no idea how much I want to snap his head off his neck.

In one fluid motion, I swing myself onto the table and grab my plate and goblet. I fling the two objects, one at each assassin. Then I snatch up my chopsticks and somersault off the table onto the ground before the assassins even realize that I'm attacking them.

When I land, Kwan moves to block my blow with the side of his spear while Sang Min tries to stab me. I side-kick Sang Min and jab Kwan in the arm with one chopstick. They both grunt, but before they can move, I slide between the two of them so I'm behind them. I grab Sang Min's long hair and yank him backward. He resists, but I kick him hard in the stomach. He whips around and swings his sword. I lean back just in time, and the sword slices the empty air above me.

These two aren't bad fighters, but I'm accustomed to fighting and pulling from the power within the Spirit World. I roll across the ground, but this ends up being my mistake because my dress tangles between my legs.

Sang Min thrusts his sword at me, missing my ear by inches, while Kwan hurls his spear across the balcony. I whip out the White Tiger orb and use it to push out a force field. The spear clatters off the barrier and falls to the ground. I've been testing the orb's abilities each day, and I discovered this new power when I was thinking about the assassin that Kud sent to kill me at Kukkiwon, the Tae Kwon Do arena. That assassin had used a similar force field created from the Spirit World. The force fields require huge amounts of power, and creating them exhausts me, so I rarely do. Still, they're useful for emergencies.

I expect these two dead things to pause in confusion, but they just keep attacking me as if they're mindless robots. They probably are. So I flip back through the air, landing behind Sang Min. I grab hold of his belt, and with the help of the orb's power, I toss him off the balcony. He screams, his voice echoing across the land. He'll be screaming for a long time because I'm sure we're about a thousand feet above the ground.

"Too bad you don't have a railing," I tell Kud, who is now standing, his arms crossed. I don't have time to decide if he's happy or upset because Kwan is spinning his spear through the air. He flings it at me again. I leap back, sidestep, and then spin into a roundhouse-kick, smacking him hard in the face and sending him sprawling to the ground.

Black blood drips from his mouth. I sprint toward him, and as he staggers to standing, I split-kick him. He collapses to the ground.

I'm barely out of breath. This is what happens whenever I'm in the Spirit World. I have power. Maybe not as much as Kud or Palk, but enough that I can hold my own against other mytho-logical creatures. These two may have been great warriors in the human world, but they have no connection to the Spirit World.

I stroll to where Kud stands by the table, one hand on my hip. "Poor things. I don't think they even had a chance. And imagine how clumsy they will be in the human world. Still." I shrug, grab his glass, and toss it over my shoulder. It hits the ground, shattering. "I haven't had that much fun in a while."

With my other hand, I grab the White Tiger orb and run it along the chain. Kud's eyes follow it greedily.

Then I lean in close and whisper into his ear. "Let me go to China. You know I'll be perfect."

"Oh, I don't doubt that." He trails his cold fingers along my shoulder and up my neck and tucks a strand of hair behind my ear. "You have proved your point. You may go, but never forget that if you disappoint me"—his lips are a breath from mine—"Marc, your father, and your grandfather will be tortured until my wrath is appeased."

CHAPTER 9

The rain pours around me, as it does in June in Seoul. I stare up at Severance Hospital, the memories of all the times I visited Komo rushing through me. But today I can't focus on what I can't have; instead, I must focus on what I must have. I'm supposed to leave for China tomorrow, but in order for my trip to be successful, I need to get Marc and the Guardians of Shinshi on my side. I can't do this mission alone.

"Do you wish to enter, princess?" Kwan asks.

"You can't call me that in public," I snap. "In fact, it's best if you don't talk at all. And put those sunglasses on, for heaven's sake. With those eyes, you'll give every elderly person a heart attack."

While Sang Min and Kwan put on their glasses, I adjust the traditional black *hanbok* I've chosen to wear, and I pull the mesh veil over my face. I'm sure I'll stick out, but with my cane and the *hanbok*, I'm hoping everyone will think I'm an old woman. Snapping my umbrella up, I hobble across the parking lot into Severance Hospital and make my way toward the wing where all the funerals are held. It's really unfortunate Kud insisted I bring along Sang Min and Kwan. I need to talk to Marc in private. Convincing Kud to let me attend my own funeral was tough enough, but now I've got to figure out a way to talk to Marc without Kud or his goons realizing it. It won't be easy.

Once I enter the funeral corridor of the hospital, my whole body freezes up. At the end of the hall, I spot Dad. He's wearing the traditionally acceptable black suit with a hemp cloth tied on his arm. He's shaking hands with a lady I don't even know.

I lean against the wall, my heart beating a million times a second. I can't pass by him. He'll recognize me right away. Or maybe he won't, but I'm not sure if I have the strength to get that close to him without breaking. Then everything I've done so far will be for nothing. I can't let that happen. For once I'm relieved Sang Min and Kwan don't say anything, standing silent as death by my side. The three of us are hardly friends, but at least they seem to understand the seriousness of this situation.

A group of students from my school rush out of the elevator and hurry down the hall. My funeral was supposed to start at four o'clock. A glance at the hall clock tells me they're late.

"Do you know what happened to her?" one girl asks.

"No clue," the guy next to her says. "But I heard it was suicide."

They continue down the hall, chattering on about me like I'm something off the menu rather than a real person. Suddenly it's hard to breathe. My classmates are going on with their lives, unscathed. Meanwhile here I stand, living in hell, attending my own funeral, unable to be with the ones I love. Fighting for my mere existence.

But the reality is that they are right not to show sympathy for me. I chose this path. I agreed to the quest to find the White Tiger orb. I entered Kud's land of my own free will and signed my life away to Kud in exchange for Marc's and my family's lives. So this is my living hell. I can stand here and wallow in misery or do something about it.

Standing straight, I take off down the hall. My dad has already entered the room, so I assume the ceremony has started. At the door, I pause. The room is packed and smells of lilies. Should I feel happy that people evidently miss me? Or maybe they're just curious, like my classmates who came at the last minute. There's a book by the door where people have signed in. It's supposed to be a memory thing for my family, I guess. But Dad won't look at it. I know that. He'll probably drown himself in his work like he did when Mom died.

I slide my finger down the names until I find Marc's.

Marc Grayson.

I'd recognize that handwriting anywhere. It flows like clouds on a summer day. He has this thing about not typing anything unless he has to. Something about holding on to traditions. Just seeing his name there fills me with hope. He hasn't abandoned me completely. I duck into the room, hobbling with my cane, and scan the crowd for his face.

There are a few rows of chairs facing the front of the small space, but almost everyone has already lined up to pay their respects at the casket, which is surrounded by vases of lilies. I wonder if they know the casket is empty. A part of me thinks it's wrong to be deceiving them like this, but it was part of the contract with Kud. I severed all my ties to the human world to be with him.

Two women stand in the front, wailing and moaning and making all kinds of ruckus. The sound is dreadful, and I just want to scream at them to shut up. I don't even know who these crazy ladies are, but I'd bet a small fortune that Dad paid for them. It's not uncommon to pay for mourners at a funeral, and most of the women in our family are dead. Thank you very much, Haemosu and Kud.

Standing next to the casket is Dad, shaking hands with the line of people. He's got bags under his eyes, and his cheeks are hollowed out as if he hasn't eaten in days. His black suit hangs on him, and there's a blankness about his face that makes me wonder if he even knows whom he's speaking with or what he's doing.

Next to him is Grandfather. Of course he's wearing a traditional white *hanbok*. Only he would do something like that, to make a statement about not forgetting the old ways. He stands stoically next to Dad, his arms crossed and his jaw set. He refuses to shake any of the hands of the people who walk by him, and he stares at the plaque on the far wall.

Man, he's ticked, I realize.

Then I spot Marc against the wall, hands in his pockets. He's wearing a suit. A suit! I can't even believe it. His hair is wild, sticking out all over the place as if he's run his hands through it so many times that it's forgotten which way it's supposed to go. Tucked beneath his arm is a bouquet of daisies, my favorite flower. Their bright canary color sticks out amid the black of the room. I cover my mouth, holding back a cry. He remembered.

Then his eyes land on me, and his eyebrows rise ever so slightly. He knows it's me. I jerk my head to indicate for him to go out into the hallway, and then I duck back out of the noise-and-crowd-infested room. Kud's two babysitters follow. Not good. What I need to say to Marc is something they definitely can't hear.

My mind races, trying to find an excuse to get rid of them.

"I think I spotted a *gwishin* at the far end of the corridor," I tell Kwan, trying to let my voice quiver with fear. "They gave us problems before and nearly killed the master. Go check the situation out. Hurry!"

They nod and take off down the hall. I let out a relieved breath just as Marc exits the room.

"Marc!" I say. And then I'm speechless, and my brain and tongue seem to have forgotten how to work.

"You gave it to him, didn't you?" Marc says, his face full of rage. "The Guardians' object from the intelligence service."

I don't know what I was expecting, but it definitely wasn't this.

"How could you?" he says. "What happened to you? You said you did this for us. I was a fool to think you could escape his power." He points to my arm where the contract is hidden beneath my jacket.

"I had to." I scramble to find the right words, knowing all the while that Kud is listening to our every word and watching us through his viewing screens. "It was the only way. You have to believe me. I did it for us."

"No, you didn't. You did it for you and your fear." Marc points his finger at my chest. "You gave in to his demands because you were too afraid of the consequences. And now look at you. I don't even know who you are! Do you know how many people died for that artifact? A sculpture that we were trying to get at that very moment so it wouldn't fall into the wrong hands."

I clench my fists, the memories taunting me.

"You're not the girl I fell in love with." His eyes are hard as emeralds. "I loved the girl who stood up to the warriors and the monsters. Not the one who bows to their every whim."

I hang my head. He's right and yet so wrong. He doesn't understand. If I could just explain everything to him—but I can't. Because Kud is waiting for me to break my part of the contract so he can rip Marc to shreds.

"Today I mourn with the rest of them because the girl I love is dead. She gave her heart to the devil, and I'll never forget that."

Marc smashes the flowers into the trash can and spins around, nearly knocking into Kwan and Sang Min. He stops for a moment, stares at them, and then shakes his head before marching off down the hall.

"Wait!" I yell and run after him, pushing past Kud's stiffs. "That's not fair and you know it. Nothing has ever been that simple."

He punches his fist into the wall, the plaster cracking under his power, and he keeps walking. I sag to the floor below the hole he created, watching his back and listening to the wails from my funeral.

CHAPTER 10

"That didn't go so well." It's Princess Bari.

"Being of both worlds bites harsher than death," she says. The corner of her mouth quirks up in what's almost a smile, but it doesn't reach her rich brown eyes. "He will never love you the same. You should forget him."

"Never." I leap up before her. There's a fierceness to my voice that scares even me. Or maybe it's the fact that I know she's right, and I can't live with that truth. "Every person is different. We all make our own choices."

She lifts her eyebrows and points meaningfully with her eyes to my wrist. I grab my arm and tuck it close to me.

"I have business to attend to," she says. "Death calls."

"Bari." I grab her arm. The material of her dress feels softer than silk. "You have to help me. You understand this transition from human to spirit better than I do. There must be a way to escape."

"Not even death can help you," she says, and she strides through the wall, her skirts flowing behind her like trails of snow.

I start pacing the hallway, clenching my fists.

"There was no sign of a *gwishin*," Kwan says. Kud's two creations stand before me, stoic and completely creepy. They literally look dead with their gray skin and stench.

"Do you still feel?" I ask them abruptly. "Does death save you the pain of feeling? Or are you still haunted by your previous life?"

A flicker of emotion flashes across Kwan's features, but it's gone so quickly that I wonder if I just concocted the notion to make myself feel better. Something nags at the corner of my brain. I'm close to solving something. I just don't know what it is.

"Be right back," I tell the Stiffs. I slip inside the room that Bari just entered, except I use the door.

The room hangs in darkness, the stillness only interrupted by the wailing next door. My fingers fumble along the wall until I find the light switch. The lights flicker on, and the room comes into view. It mirrors my funeral room exactly, except it doesn't have all the complications of mine. Just a coffin and silence.

Of course my babysitters follow me. I grimace. Somehow I need to lose them.

A flash of white flickers around the coffin. I edge closer. Bari may seem innocent, maintaining her teenage appearance, but anyone who carries a jagged spear around isn't someone to startle. Something shifts in the room, almost as if the presence that was once here has vanished. I jog down the rows of chairs to the coffin. The spirit of the human has left, and I'm too late.

Then I remember the orb dangling from my neck. I slip it out and cup it in my palms. In a whisper, I say, "Take me to Bari."

The orb's warmth drenches my palms. Its power seeps through my pores into my bloodstream. A beam of white light shoots out from the orb, pointing to the wall behind the coffin. I drop the orb, letting it dangle from my neck and guide me. There's a door at the far end of the room.

"Princess," Kwan says, startling me in the silence. "We are deviating from the master's plan."

"Shut up." I yank on the door handle.

It's locked, so I lift my skirts and withdraw the knife I've strapped to my thigh. I convinced Kud to give me a weapon after he took my Blue Dragon bow. Unfortunately, since this knife was crafted in his world, it won't harm him or any of his creatures, unlike the Blue Dragon's weapon.

I touch the knife's tip to the door, and it slides open. A dark corridor stretches before me, and at the far end I spy a flutter of white that reminds me of snowflakes. I duck inside and slam the door behind me, blocking off my babysitters. I start jogging down the hall, and as I do, the lights flash on; they must be sensor activated. Another door opens at the far end, and even though I push my muscles into a full-on sprint, the door slams in my face.

Once again I dig my blade into the lock, glancing around to make sure no doctors see me with a knife. I'm entering a stairwell now, and I see Bari gliding down the steps, her dress floating around her. A basket is tucked in her elbow.

"Wait!" I grasp the railing and lean over the edge. "I need to talk to you."

Bari glances over her shoulder and smiles, her face ghostly white. Then she takes off, even faster.

I thought we were in the lower levels of the basement before, but I must have been wrong. I don't know how deep this hospital runs. I feel dizzy as I race after her. Down, down, down. My breath comes out heavily, and I clutch the orb for strength. Energy flows into me through my fingers. Renewed, I take off faster, desperately tearing down the stairs, leaping down them three or more at a time.

Soon the lights dim, and the stairs change from concrete to stone. Tiny glowing pebbles fill the walls. The air changes, too, from the moist summer of Seoul to a dryness that leaves my throat parched and chalky.

Finally the stairs end, leaving behind a dark dirt floor. As I begin to walk, I realize it isn't a floor but a dirt path. Naked trees line the path, their branches lifting straight toward the sky as if desperate to escape. Bari strolls on ahead, silver against the darkness, her *hanbok* swirling around her, iridescent against the night.

My feet falter as I look about me. Tall walls stretch before us, and traditional lanterns let out a pale, mournful glow from above. A double-door gate looms ahead that reminds me of the wooden one at Gyeonbokgung Palace in the heart of Seoul, except three times wider and taller. A ghostly white stream of light coils around the edges of the doors as if it's ready to snap out and strangle any unwanteds that come too close. White carvings of doves and winged creatures that look like bats glow within the wood.

In the center of it all rests a yin yang made from two massive jewels, one black and one white, their insides swirling like volcanoes about to erupt. Yet this symbol isn't connected. The two edges, which should touch, are separated by a wide, starry gap.

A lump forms in my stomach as I glance behind me. An open stairwell spirals into the sky, and from this perspective, I'm surprised I didn't tumble over its edge and plummet to my death.

Bari spins around, her skirts billowing up around her in a fan, and points her sharp-toothed spear at me. Weasels leap out from unseen holes in the ground and circle me, snarling and gnashing their teeth. I know these creatures all too well. But the last time I fought them, it was with three others and in the human world. Above, giant birds soar, circling us. I step back, holding up my arms as a sign of peace.

"Why do you follow me, servant of Kud?" Bari asks.

I eye the point of her spear and the creatures around us. I had thought we had bonded the other night at Michelle's graveside, but evidently she's already forgotten that. "I'm more of a slave than a servant. I don't wish to fight. I just wanted to talk to you in private. Is this the land of King Daebyeol, ruler of the Underworld?"

She nods warily.

"And Kud can't overhear our conversation, correct?"

"True." She cocks her head to her side and narrows her eyes. "But my lord can."

"Good." Despite the dry air, my hands are sweaty. I wipe them on my *hanbok*, eyeing the weasels warily. One bite means death. "I need you to talk to Marc for me. Tell him I want to meet with him here. That way Kud won't hear what I have to tell him."

"Dearest sister of the Spirit World, there are rules about humans being brought to the Underworld."

"Forget rules! Kud wants to get all the orbs so he can rule not only his realm but every other realm in the world. This isn't about some stupid love skirmish. This is bigger than me or you or all of Korea combined."

She stands there, unmoving. The air remains stale, not even a hint of a breeze, but her dress continues to blow. In fact, the air is so stifling, I'm finding it hard to breathe. I have to focus on taking long, even breaths.

Bari considers me through calm eyes, and then she turns to face the gate, as if that will speak to my demands.

"The Spirit World is being ripped in half," she finally says, her voice full of aching sadness. "It has been happening so slowly, at first no one noticed."

I move to stand beside her. It's weird, but she doesn't have to say much. I remember when Palk showed me the separation of the Spirit World through the great rift and the feelings of anger, frustration, and loss that I felt.

"There is a way to fix it," she says.

"What?" I nearly yell the word, and the weasels snap at my ankles, snarling. "Why is this the first I've heard about it? Why didn't Palk tell me?"

"Because the humans have forgotten the purpose of who they are, and therefore so have the immortals. It all began when Kud found the Red Phoenix orb. The Tiger of Shinshi ordered the Guardians to hide the remaining orbs in the far corners of the land, hoping that would stop the rift. It slowed down the separation, but it wasn't enough. No one knows how to unite the two sides, but I believe that if we could remember our purpose, then we could unite Korea once more."

"That sounds impossible."

"Yes." Bari bows her head. "It does. I will need to think your proposition over and get back to you."

"But don't you see? You immortals have been sitting around and mulling this over for centuries, and now it's nearly too late. I'm leaving for China soon, as in *tomorrow* soon. I don't know if I can stop this madness, but you can bet I'm going to do everything I can while I'm still breathing. I *need* to talk to Marc. He's the only one who can help me convince the Guardians to stop Kud."

I grab Bari's hand. It's cold to the touch, but I *can* touch her. Which is another reminder that my time as a human is fleeting. Bari stares at our touching hands and then up at my face, her eyebrows raised. She knows this, too.

"Please." I'm begging, but I don't care.

"Meet me at the Cheonggyecheon Stream tonight."

"We can't meet there," I say. "Kud will be able to monitor my every move."

"Trust me, my impatient sister, and I will bring the boy you love. And if I don't, know that I did what I could. Now close your eyes and return to where you belong."

CHAPTER 11

I pace the sidewalk of Sejongno under King Sejong's statue, checking my watch. Seven o'clock. I only have another thirty minutes—with Kwan and Sang Min as my babysitters, per Kud's orders. I'm supposed to be using this time to book a hotel room and flights.

I imagine twenty different scenarios for how things could work out between Bari and Marc. Maybe Bari will never find him, or maybe he will refuse to even come. The Saturday night crowds are already gathering and heading down to the Cheonggyecheon Stream to see the lit falls and flowing streams. Couples are holding hands and laughing while I try not to focus on how I'm standing here alone.

"You're upset."

I turn toward the voice. It's Kud, disguised as Kang-dae.

"No," I say quickly, wiping away any traces of my panicked expression. Knowing my luck, Bari will show up right now with Marc, and everything will be ruined. "I'm formulating a plan for the trip before I go make my bookings at the Internet café. I want to make sure everything runs smoothly. The fresh air helps me think better."

"You look beautiful tonight." He traces the line of my jaw and pulls me to him. He smells like spice. A part of me cringes, knowing he's so close, while the other part yearns for acceptance and attention. But I don't want it from him. Never from him.

"I have a few moments," he continues. "And I thought I'd steal the time with you before you leave. Do you know how hard it is for me to let you out of my sight? I've waited too long for you to lose you so quickly."

"Yes, um." I search my mind for ways to get rid of him. I come up with nothing. "You shouldn't feel obligated. You're so busy."

He chuckles and brushes his lips across my forehead. "You are far too tame tonight, my brazen princess. I can't help but suspect you are up to devious things."

My heart tumbles about as I realize my whole plan will unravel before it has even unfolded. I grab his black button-down shirt with both hands and pull him even closer. Having him this close terrifies me, but I will do nearly anything to keep him from suspecting.

"I'm starting to see things differently lately," I say, twisting his button between two fingers.

Then he hooks his arm through mine. "A night stroll might be just what we need."

A night stroll? I can't just promenade around with him. There isn't time. What will Marc think of me? I glance around, searching for Marc and Bari, but they are nowhere in sight.

We take the stone stairs down to the canal level. A wave of dizziness floods me, and I have to lean on him for support. He wraps his arm around my waist, and for once I'm too weak to resist. I want to shove him far away from me, but I don't have the strength.

The sound of rushing water fills the air, and as we walk along the stream, he points out his favorite artwork hanging along the walls on the sides. The last rays of sun fade along the horizon, allowing the colorful lights to illuminate the stream. Laser beams cut across the waters, creating beautiful designs to the beat of the music lilting over the speakers. Time flashes past me, yet everything seems to remain still. Kud tells me stories from a thousand years ago that make me laugh. But when we reach the end of the canal, I can't remember a thing he's said.

He takes both of my hands. "Jae Hwa," he says, and he kisses my hand. "I must go."

I start in confusion, taking in the crowds jostling around me. My watch says it's eleven o'clock, but it doesn't seem possible that we've been walking around downtown for hours. Bari and Marc must have seen us. I rack my brain, trying to figure out what exactly happened all evening, but attempting to remember causes my temples to throb. I press my fingers against the sides of my head to stop the pounding.

"This is only the beginning of our future of eternity. I must attend to business, but I will make every effort to be there in the morning to send you off at the airport. And don't worry," he says. "I will be watching you carefully, my pet. I always keep a close eye on what is mine."

He stares at me with those dark eyes, and my heart starts beating wildly, afraid he can read the intentions of my soul and the desire in my heart to destroy him. I try to smile and keep my hands from trembling. I doubt I fool him for a millisecond.

His lips turn up in a crooked smile, which would make any other girl's heart flutter, but not mine. There's something desperate about his expression, needy even, and I pull away. My pulse throbs against my temples. His grip strengthens. He won't let me go. The contract on my skin burns, and my muscles weaken.

That's when I realize he planned this whole night. Maybe he suspected what my plans were, and instead of just keeping me locked up in his land, he decided it would torture me more to know how close and yet how far away I'd been from talking to Marc.

He leans down, and I realize he's going to kiss me. I try to pull away, to scream, to punch, but my body won't obey. His lips press against mine.

The noise of the crowd fades. The people jostling against me disappear. The lights from the city spin around us, and I fall down into a swirling funnel of darkness. My feet touch emptiness until that emptiness fills my core. A scream claws at my throat, but I'm so cold, even my voice is frozen.

"Never forget," his voice whispers in my ear. "You are mine. *Forever.*"

Those words whoosh around me like a wailing wind, curling through my mind and every inch of my body.

Forever, forever, forever.

CHAPTER 12

"Hold this." A voice pounds against the void. "Jae Hwa! Do it."

But I can't budge. I twitch my fingers, and that movement alone pains me. It would be so much easier to shrivel into myself and forget everything. Then a hand slaps me across the cheek, and my head whips to the side. My cheek stings.

"Don't you dare give up." The voice sounds just like Bari's, except it's a whole lot less calm and composed.

I allow her to guide my hands until they tingle. A fire rushes through me, warming up every inch of my body. I draw in a long breath and blink my eyes open. Sure enough, it's Bari standing in front of me, her usual serene expression replaced with worry lines.

"I have been waiting for you for hours," she says.

"Hours?" I shake my head as if that will clear the fog that fills my mind. "What time is it?"

"Time for us to have tea." She grabs my hand and drags me after her. Each step feels like I'm walking on pins. I cry out in pain. "This night is turning out to be such a bore. Remember how you promised me a modern girl's night out?"

"No. I don't."

"You are so difficult."

"You wouldn't be the first to say that," I mutter. Then the events of the evening flood my mind, and I remember what happened. I was supposed to meet her and convince Marc to go to China and help me get the orb. I open my mouth to ask where Marc is, but then she stops, presses her finger to her lips, and looks meaningfully to our right.

Sang Min stands on top of the bridge, snarling as he watches me. To our right is Kwan, spying on us through empty eyes. Kud has no trust in me. Not that I blame him.

After considering the facts—my life completely sucks, nothing has gone my way in forever, and I seem cursed to keep messing everything up—I decide to follow Bari's lead.

We scurry through the crowds. A glance behind us tells me that Kud's two assassins are following us. Bari picks up her pace. She's as fluid as water, slipping through people as if they do not exist. I, on the other hand, have to actually skirt around them.

At the sidewalk she spins to head to the waterfront. We rush down the stairs and into the canal area, which is packed with people.

"What's the rush?" I ask.

Then I see them. Standing on the sidewalk above us are more than twenty of Kud's creepy walking dead guys. They all wear black long-sleeved tunics, pantaloons, and sunglasses. It's a peculiar combination. Despite their strange appearance, only a few people give them a second glance. One girl lifts her camera and snaps a picture of them.

"Your master really has taken a liking to you," Bari says.

"No kidding."

We come to the waterfall section, where there's a small boat for decoration. Bari jumps into it.

"I can't get on that," I say. "It's for decoration. I'll probably sink it, or we'll get arrested or something."

"You say this? One who has no care for rules or danger?"

"You've got a point."

I step in next to her. She grabs my hand. "Close your eyes," she says as she pulls her spear out from behind her back.

But I hesitate, lifting my eyes to the men in sunglasses striding toward us and then to those leaning over the sidewalk railings above. The sound of the waterfall rushes through my ears, mixed in with the calm zither and flute playing through the speakers along the canal.

Bari plunges her spear into the bottom of the boat. White light sparks from its tip, blinding me. People on the side of the canal start pointing at us, taking pictures and clapping. They think it's a show, I realize. *Un-freaking-believable.* The light converges into a solid line and begins to whirl around our feet. My eyes widen. Bari's spear is burning a hole in the bottom of the boat.

"What are you doing?" I yell, still clutching Bari's hand.

"A shortcut." Bari eyes the Stiffs who are pushing their way toward us, and she frowns. We have a few seconds at most before one of their hands will be able to grab me.

Finally the wood beneath us shifts, and the bottom of the boat falls out with a jerk. A hand grabs my arm, but the force of the fall yanks me out of the Stiff's grip. Bari and I plunge into darkness.

My heart slams into my throat, and I scream, clutching Bari's hand so tightly I'm surprised it doesn't snap off. Apparently I am ill trained for hanging out with Bari. I haven't ridden a free-fall ride in a long time, but this is far worse than any I can remember.

Stars funnel around us, swirling in a chaos of sparkles. We plummet into a void broken only by a glimmer of light twinkling below.

As we move closer, a glowing land is revealed, filled with flowers and gardens. Our bodies slow down, and we land gently in a field of lilies, their fragrance filling the air. They radiate light like hundreds of lanterns. I brush my hand over one flower, letting its smooth surface tickle my skin.

"This is my home," Bari says.

"It's perfect."

"*Kamsahamnida.*" Bari almost smiles.

She leads me across the field to a pagoda, and there, leaning against the red-pillared entrance, is Marc. He's wearing a pair of jeans and a blue-sleeved T-shirt. My heart melts into a puddle, and I wish I could take back all of the horrible things I've said and done to him. It takes every ounce of my strength not to just go running into his arms.

"You found her," he says to Bari. His voice sounds bitter. "I didn't know if you could get her out of Kud's sight."

"It was harder than I thought it would be," Bari says. "Kud spent nearly the entire night with her."

Marc's eyebrows rise. "Do you spend most of your nights with him?"

Cringing at his tone, I climb the stairs of the pagoda to stand before him. He stares at me warily, unmoving. It's as if there's an invisible wall between us. I shift my feet before finally sitting on the bench.

"No," I say. "He must have suspected something. I doubt I could've escaped if he hadn't been called away on business."

"He had about twenty of his dead warriors watching her," Bari says. "I had to take the shortcut here."

"More like the heart-attack-cut," I say.

"He sounds quite taken with you," Marc says dryly.

"I have never seen him so obsessed with a mortal." Bari snaps her fingers, and a table with a tea set appears in the center of the pagoda. "Why did he kiss you?"

I glare at her, wishing she'd stop repeating all of this to Marc. Telling him Kud is obsessed with me and kissing me is definitely not helping this conversation.

"He didn't kiss me," I say, but then a thread of doubt drags at the dark corner of my mind. I touch my lips, and I suddenly remember the horrifying image and feeling of his lips touching mine. And then endless darkness. "Did he?"

"You *kissed* him?" Marc stands upright, and his face turns red. Then he spins away from me and stalks to the other side of the pagoda. "I don't even know why we're here. Why are we here, Jae?"

"He kissed her, not she him," Bari says as she pours the tea. "He likes to play games, doesn't he? Because after he left, you couldn't move. It took all my power and that orb hanging on your neck to wake you up."

I nod slowly. "Yes, I remember you yelling at me. And slapping me."

"What is going on, Jae?" Marc strides back to stand before me. His face is contorted, and I see how tortured he is.

"I have to stop him, Marc. But I need you to help me."

"You know that's not going to happen. I can't work with you. Not after what you did back at the intelligence service and the Blue House. Your ways are not how I do things."

That was a slap in the face. "I deserved that comment," I say. "I didn't handle that situation well. If I could have figured out how to get in contact with you earlier, I would've. But I didn't even think of asking Bari to intervene for us until I saw her at my funeral."

"Your dad isn't coping with your death very well," Marc says. "And your grandfather isn't either. Do you know how torn up he is over all of this? Knowing you're working with the monster who helped Haemosu torture your family for generations? And that silvery sheen is stronger than ever before. How much longer before you're not human anymore?"

I duck my head and press my palms over my face. Finally I look back up and stare Marc in the eyes. "I can't go back to the way it was. I've made a disaster of things, but honestly I don't know if I would do anything differently. Nothing is simple. There is no black and white here. And telling me how much I've messed up—" My throat constricts, and I choke up.

"I'm sorry," Marc says, his voice quieter now. "That was cruel of me. I shouldn't have said all that."

I take a few deep breaths before continuing. "I'm going to China to get the final orb. Grandfather told me to go there, but the Tiger of Shinshi says I can't do it on my own. He said I need the help of the Guardians. If I'm going to get my humanity back and stop Kud, I need your help."

"That sounds like the worst idea yet," Marc says, his jaw muscles working.

"Just listen to me." I stand and grab his arms. He flinches, and I let go. "If I can get the final orb and return it to the Heavenly Chest, Palk could use the orbs to defeat Kud because Palk would have the advantage."

"Wherever this final orb is, it should stay there. It's been safe in its current location for centuries. There is no reason for that to change."

"But there is. Kud has resurrected these warriors from the past and sent them on missions around Korea trying to find the final orb. If I hadn't gotten to the clue first, one of those creatures he's created would have. They are bound to him and would have handed the clue over to him anyway. This way, I'm in control, and I have a better chance to stop him."

"Don't forget," Bari says, handing me a teacup. "You're bound to him, too. Don't tell me you were able to stop him from controlling you tonight."

I sigh and plop down on the bench in defeat. "Maybe you're right. But I have to try and stop him. I can't keep living like this. Kud was planning on sending his two top assassins to do the job. The only way I convinced him was to kick their butts so Kud could see I was the better choice."

"I don't get why you need me," Marc says. "Just telling me means I need to stop you. Don't you see that we aren't on the same side anymore?"

"But we *are* on the same side. We both want to destroy Kud. Nothing has changed."

He shrugs, unconvinced, but he says, "I'm listening."

"I can't determine the exact location of the orb. The clue was a coin that had Emperor Qin Shi Huang on it. I think the hiding place has something to do with him, but I'm not sure. The terracotta warriors are pictured on the coin's other side, and since they are outside of Xi'an, that's where I'll start."

"Did you bring the coin with you?" he asks.

"There's no way Kud would let me take that thing out of his realm again. It's hard enough coming up with excuses to leave his presence. Tonight I was only allowed to come to Seoul to make flight plans and book hotel rooms for the trip to China. We leave tomorrow."

"We?" Marc's eyebrows rise. "You and Kud?"

"He can't leave Korea," Bari says. "None of us from the Spirit World can. We are bound to Korean soil."

"He's sending me with his two assassins."

"To keep an eye on you," Marc says.

"Of course." I shrug and then look at him pleadingly. "I need you to go to China, too, and help me find this orb. Help me take it back to Palk, because I don't trust myself completely. Please. If there is any love left from who we were, I'm begging you to help."

"The Council will never agree to this," he says, yet I sense a crack in his barrier. "Xi'an, huh? China is a big country. I'm guessing there's no way I can stop you from going." He stares at me and then groans, running his hands through his hair. Beside me Bari mutters something about the evil of all this, and Marc begins pacing the pagoda.

Finally he stops and nods to me. "I'll go." I practically squeal, and I grab his hands. "But only to keep a close eye on you. I will do everything I can to make sure one of the Guardians or I get the orb first. The Triads are the Guardians of China. I will work with them and do everything in my power to stop you."

I drop my hands and step back, nodding. "I'd rather us work together than have you trying to stop me, but I can live with that. I will be staying at the Shangri-La Hotel in Xi'an, and I should arrive around midmorning. Contact me when you arrive."

The invisible barrier between Marc and me tugs at my chest. The loss of everything I once had weighs down on me, and I sag back onto the bench. Desperation fills me until it feels as if it's seeping out of my pores. I need to hold him, to feel his lips on mine, and to hear his voice whispering in my ear that he loves me.

But now I know the truth. All that we had is lost forever.

CHAPTER 13

The trip through Incheon International Airport pulls my nerves as tight as a bowstring. Thing One and Thing Two flank me as we walk across the shiny polished floors. I focus on keeping my head down, hoping my wig will stay in place. It would be weird to have someone recognize me, because I'm supposed to be dead.

I have no clue how we got through security without a full-on interrogation. They didn't bat an eye at the false passport that Kud arranged for me or my pink hair, neon-green skirt, and combat boots. I made sure to wear an outfit that my family and friends would never imagine me wearing so they wouldn't recognize me if they happened to see me. Kud wouldn't think twice about killing them if he thought they were going to get in the way.

When we arrive at gate 27 to wait for our plane, I sink into one of the seats, relief flooding me. Considering how weird the Stiffs look, it's a miracle we weren't held for questioning. The two of them don't bother to sit beside me; instead they move to the wall and stand there, staring out through their sunglasses. I try to resist rolling my eyes, but it's too hard. They just look ridiculous.

A flight attendant calls out our flight number. "Boarding begins in five minutes," she says.

Seeing as I have a few minutes, I hurry to the concession store to grab water and something to read. I browse through the magazines, but my eyes keep getting drawn to the newspaper racks with headlines of "War Imminent in the Koreas" and "Nothing Will Stop North Korea" and "A Madman or Power Hungry?"

One magazine cover sticks out from the rest, titled "Korea: A Struggle for Unity." It features the yin yang on the cover with a jagged line cutting the two sides apart. I skim through it, and one line resonates with me: "What was before will be no more." It's so true. If war breaks out, South Korea will no longer be what it was. Just like my life. I bite my lip as I trace the dividing line with my finger, wishing for the strength and knowledge to stop this madness.

These headlines mirror the power struggle in the Spirit World. Again I realize that what I'm about to do will impact not only me but the entire country.

A man wearing a baseball cap, jeans, and a Korea Legend soccer shirt bumps against me. I scoot away, annoyed, and grab a teen magazine, suddenly wanting to forget the madness and just be a normal teen. Maybe I can live vicariously through these teenagers.

"This magazine would suit you better," the soccer fan tells me.

The man has a beard and long bushy hair that practically covers his eyes. He's older, old enough to be my dad's dad, but there's something about the cadence of his voice that's familiar.

"Here." Korea Legend guy pushes the magazine into my hands.

It's an archaeology magazine. It's more like something Marc would read. The front cover shows a desert and a bunch of rocks around pillars. Pretty dull reading.

"Page thirty-two might be of interest to you," he says.

Then he moves to leave, but I grab his arm and turn him to face me, my heart stuttering. As he looks up, I recognize his eyes.

"Haraboji," I whisper.

He presses one finger to his lips. "Shh."

I spin back to face the magazines, my heart racing, the pictures before me blurring. I want nothing more than to throw myself into his arms and explain everything, but there's so much to say that my words stay choked in my mouth.

"Marc told me everything," Grandfather says. "I have intervened too much already on your behalf. The Council is against you, afraid you do not have free will, but Marc—he might be persuaded to join your endeavor."

I nod. "Maybe. He said he would go to China with the Guardians to get the orb before I do. Do you think we have a chance to succeed?"

"Do not worry about success, for it is fleeting," he says from behind me. "Focus instead on courage and belief to reach your final goal."

Nodding again, I grip the magazine against my chest. I turn to ask another question, but he has already disappeared.

I wonder if he was a figment of my imagination.

· · ·

"Put that away," I snap at Sang Min and rip what looks like a hairbrush out of his hands. It's actually his weapon. When he pushes the bristles of the brush together, it ejects a long silver sword. He growls and frowns at me as I stash the hairbrush back in his bag under his seat.

I glance around the plane to make sure no one is watching us. Sang Min's growls alone could attract unwanted attention and suspicion. "Don't snarl at me like a barbarian. If security finds out you're carrying weapons into the country, they'll flip. Or maybe I should let them. Then I wouldn't have to babysit you."

I think about my own weapons stashed inside my backpack. First I have a cable and my ascender, which have come in handy more often lately. Then there's my Blue Dragon bow, which I convinced Kud to give me for the trip. I used the "don't you want me to return to you?" card. I was shocked when he agreed. When it isn't strung, the bow looks like it's just a piece of bent wood. It passed security in Seoul because most security officers have never seen an unstrung horn bow—and because I didn't bring any arrows. The bigger issue will be whether I can find a place to buy arrows in Xi'an.

On my other side, I detect a slight smile from Kwan. With his bald head and long braid, he looks anything but normal.

Still, I wonder if we would've gotten along if I knew him as a human.

"So how did you get mixed up with Kud?" I ask Kwan.

"I made a deal I couldn't keep," he says.

Interesting. The thing can think for itself. "Man, do I ever know about that. Do you mind me asking what the deal was?"

"I was a warrior stationed at Kusong during the Koguryo Kingdom." Kwan rubs his temple and blinks rapidly. I'm not sure if he's trying to remember or if the memory is too painful. "The Mongol devils had been rampaging across our country and finally attacked the city. I called upon the god of darkness for help. I told him if he saved our city, I would give him my firstborn son."

"He gave Kusong the victory?" Kwan doesn't answer, so I take that for a yes. I press him further. "You gave him your firstborn?"

"I never gave myself a chance to have a firstborn," Kwan says.

I'm opening my mouth to ask more questions when the pilot announces we're landing at Xi'an. I lean back in my seat and adjust my seat belt one more time, thinking about Kwan's words and his sacrifice. I'm willing to make sacrifices for my country, but I don't think I could go to that length.

Then my mind shifts to Grandfather. After he disappeared, I searched the whole gate area, but I never spotted him again. I keep replaying those few seconds in my mind, wishing I had said something else, told him how much he meant to me.

Finally I open the magazine to page thirty-two.

It's an article on Emperor Qin Shi Huang's tomb. I read it hungrily, searching for clues. There's a diagram of what archaeologists believe to be the layout of the tomb, but no one knows for sure. Due to the poisonous gases from the mercury rivers that weave through the tomb—and the fact that members of every crew the government has sent to investigate have gone missing or mysteriously died—no one has reentered the tomb in a decade. I can't help but think there's a connection between the orb and this place. I read through the article, memorizing the details.

A normal, sane person would read this article and think these were just odd events. But to me, this article screams mythological creatures. Something must be guarding the tomb. If I had written the article, I would've named it "Dangerous Mythological Creatures Guard This Tomb" rather than "The Abandoned Excavation."

I study the face of the emperor in the magazine. He's heavyset, with a mustache and a full black beard that reaches just below his chin. I notice how, even in the ancient paintings, his eyes are narrowed and his thick eyebrows point up, giving him an angry expression. He is one of the most powerful and feared men in all of Chinese history. His legacy still lives on today through his terra-cotta warriors and the Great Wall.

Still, the coin didn't picture the tomb on it, and Marc is right. China is a massive country. The possibilities for where a tiny orb could be hidden are endless.

I think back to my sparring matches with Komo. She'd stand before me, hands prepped and feet bouncing back and forth. But her sharp eyes told me she knew how the fight would play out even before I did.

My aunt was all about visualizing. I close my eyes and allow her voice to play in my head as if she were still here, guiding my steps. A plan begins to form in my mind, but it crumbles before it can manifest itself. Because no matter how much I try to focus on Komo, a nagging voice tugs at my thoughts, reminding me that I'm about to enter a whole new land, a place where I don't belong.

CHAPTER 14

As Thing One and Thing Two go through their customs line, I wait by one of the massive pillars, tapping lightly on the straps of my backpack. Maybe Kud put a cloaking spell on his creatures, because no one notices how creepy their eyes are when they take off those sunglasses.

My hand trails unconsciously to the White Tiger orb dangling from its chain. Kud had warned me to use it sparingly.

Each time you unleash the orb's power, he had said, *every nearby creature of the Spirit World will be drawn to it. Only use it when you must.*

If I had a clearer idea of where to go and what to do, then I wouldn't have to rely on the orb. As I watch Kud's cronies strut stiffly over to me, I get the feeling I will most definitely be using the orb before all of this is over.

We brought only backpacks, so after the three of us converge, we thread past the luggage conveyor belts toward the glass-walled exit. Everything in this section of the airport sparkles, from the white marble floor to the bleached walls to the silvery ceiling, pinpricked with tiny white lights.

As we step outside, I'm assaulted by the acrid smell of pollution. The concrete ceiling presses in on me, and an urge to run free from the crowds makes my heart speed up. Even though it's nearly ten o'clock, the air holds a brownish hue, giving the world an ominous tint. I shiver despite the heat.

We weave through the crowds chatting and rolling their suitcases, and head straight for the taxi queue. Yet as we enter the line, a nagging feeling burns between my shoulder blades, as if eyes were boring holes into my back. I freeze, then glance around casually, like a curious tourist might. I don't see anything out of the ordinary, but I'm sure we're being watched. Having Marc around would be helpful right now. Unlike other humans, he can see mythological creatures—even when they don't want him to see them. I'm much better attuned than I used to be, but right now I only feel exposed and useless.

As I slide into the cab after Kwan, I fidget with the straps of my backpack, never once letting my eyes leave the windows.

"Take us to the Shangri-La Hotel," I tell the driver.

He says something to us in Chinese. I don't like the thought of being jammed, defenseless, inside the back of a taxi. We've just become the perfect target.

"Do you speak English?" I ask.

"No English." He taps the steering wheel to the beat of his music. Some annoying pop song. I eye the stereo's Off button and resist the temptation to touch it. Instead, I scribble the name of our hotel in Korean and Mandarin on a piece of paper. My written Mandarin is much better than my spoken version, thanks to my IB Chinese class. Now I wish I had worked on my verbal skills. The driver eyes my writing and tries to ask me more questions.

"Just go," I say in Mandarin and wave my hand, trying to convey forward motion.

But the driver smiles and opens his door. He says something else and holds up one finger. "Find English."

I bury my face in my hands, wishing I had taken my Chinese classes more seriously. Kwan rolls down the window and nudges me. I follow the line of his finger to where he is pointing.

Across the pavement, the air shimmers. My breath leaves me as a red-bodied beast materializes out of the wavering light. It shakes a head that looks like a mix of a dragon and a snake. Its body has five legs with talons the color of steel. The creature shrieks, the sound so loud and piercing that all three of us clamp our hands over our ears.

Our driver slides back into his seat, humming to the music, oblivious to the screeching monster. I lean over and grab his shirt.

"Drive!" I scream, shaking him. "Drive!"

The creature bounds into a full sprint, straight toward us. Giving me an annoyed glance, the driver starts the car, muttering under his breath. The grind of the ignition hitting the starter makes me cringe. The driver creeps the taxi onto the main road. We're moving too slow. I want to leap out and push us.

"The creature is too fast," Kwan says.

I dive headfirst into the front seat. "Move over," I tell the driver.

His eyes widen, and he shakes his head at me as if I'm crazy. He slows to a stop at the side of the road.

He has no idea how crazy I am. I grab his shoulders and push him over to the passenger seat as I slide into his place in the driver's seat. The taxi driver starts screaming at me and grabbing my arm, but I ignore him and slam my foot on the gas. The car jerks forward, and the taxi shoots down the road.

The driver shoves his palm into my face. I grab his wrist and push on a pressure point. He yelps. If he could see what is chasing us, he wouldn't be fighting me. It'd be so much easier if I tossed him out of the taxi, but I don't know where to go, so I'll have to put up with his screaming. And now I'm glad I don't speak Mandarin fluently. I'm sure he's calling me every horrible name in existence.

The beast lands on the back of the car, and its claws dig into the metal, making a horrible screeching sound. The roof shudders and sinks inward from its weight. I jerk the car across two lanes of traffic, horns blaring, and careen onto a side road. The creature smashes its tail into the car's back window, shattering the glass. Kwan and Sang Min pull out their weapons as the tail lashes across the backseat like an iron whip.

Sang Min grunts, holding up his sword against the tail pressing down on him. Kwan tries to stab the tail.

"The skin is too thick," Kwan says, far too calmly for this situation. But then what should I expect from a walking corpse? "I cannot break through it."

I yank the car onto an open stretch of road and gun the gas. The beast sinks its claws into the roof of the car, trying to hold on. It shrieks again as if it's angry, shattering my eardrums. I jerk the taxi left and then right. Thankfully the taxi driver is now too preoccupied with screaming at the beast that's ripping his car apart to get upset about my driving. The creature must be too busy fighting us to worry about keeping its body cloaked.

I jerk the car to a skidding stop, almost sending us all flying through the windshield. The beast slides onto the hood of the car. Its unblinking eyes find mine. I can see the anger in them.

You bear his mark, it says in my mind. *You are not welcome.*

It knows. The Tiger of Shinshi was right. I glance down at my arm where the contract is hidden beneath my sleeve. Then I gun the gas and spin the car to the right. The creature tumbles off and its claws rip through the hood, unable to manage the shift in direction. As we spin away, the creature flicks out its tongue, slicing off the bumper of the car. We fly down the road, wind whipping through the open slashes in the roof and the shattered back window.

The taxi driver starts yelling at me, probably calling me a spoiled-stupid-idiotic foreigner. At this point, I'm happy to agree with everything he has to scream at me. I keep my foot on the gas pedal and try to keep us from wrecking. This probably isn't the time to tell the driver I'm too young to get my license. I watch the rearview mirror as the beast's form slowly fades from view.

"You did well," Kwan says from the backseat, motionless as the dead.

"No thanks to you two corpses," I say, finally letting go of the gas and parking on the side of the road. I slide to the passenger side and push the half-hysterical driver back behind the steering wheel. "If we were left to your devices, we'd all be dead right now."

They stare at me blankly.

"Oh! That's right. You're already dead. Fantastic. Just perfect." I rummage through my backpack for my Mandarin translation guide. Finally I find the phrase I need. "Take us to the hotel."

The driver gapes at me with wide eyes. He finally seems at a loss for words. I shut the music off and push my hair out of my face.

"Drive," I say in English, and I point behind us.

Somehow he gets what I'm saying, and he starts driving again.

"That creature must have been guarding the airport," Kwan says. "We did well to escape."

"No." I'm still shaking. "Either it failed and it's sending reinforcements, or it let us go, which makes me even more nervous."

CHAPTER 15

When we drive into Xi'an, we are met with a city full of life and bustle. Buses, motorbikes, and cars clog the streets, while in the bike lane thousands of people wearing business suits, dresses, and jeans pedal their way to work.

I drink in every detail. China is so different from Korea. The buildings are an eclectic mix of modern concrete blocks and old-fashioned structures with flared roofs. Small, traditional-style tiled houses are crammed in next to towering skyscrapers, and bright red lanterns hang along the street as if in preparation for a celebration. Billboards display officers saluting the Chinese flag beside reminders to follow the rules. Directly next to those are signs for Western companies such as KFC.

As we enter the oldest section of the city, we pass by the ancient walls, which are about four stories high and open for anyone to walk on. We join the throngs of cars circling the famous Bell Tower of Xi'an. The tower is a massive three-tiered pagoda on top of a stone platform. The platform itself is huge, and the arch in its center is big enough for a car to drive through it. The pagoda's eaves are made of dark-green tiles, and gold plating shines on the point of the roof. Red pillars placed every few feet set off the intricate designs painted on the walls. Flowers fill in the area around its base, and people sit and chat on the nearby concrete steps.

Despite the everyday normalcy for the people here, there's something about that tower that sends goose bumps up my arms. I wish Marc were here. He'd know if I was losing my mind or if there really were dangerous mythological creatures standing watch.

The car idles at the light, and I hate just sitting here exposed. My nerves sizzle as if they are on fire. A quick glance at the rearview mirror tells me nothing is following us, so I tell myself that maybe I'm feeling these emotions because I've been stuck in Kud's land, away from people, for so long. Then I see a swarm of police officers running down the pagoda's steps and out onto the sidewalk. They're pointing at our taxi. I suppose a taxi with a missing bumper, a smashed back window, and claw marks streaking down from the roof does look rather unusual.

The taxi driver spots them and opens the door with shaking hands, begging for help as he stumbles toward them.

"Crap." I fumble with my door. "The police are heading our way," I tell the Stiffs in the backseat.

I slide out of the car, and Kud's goons follow me. I don't bother shutting my door, just shrug on my backpack and take off in a sprint. Pumping my arms, I weave between the cars. One truck slams on its horn as it swerves to miss me. I don't move fast enough, and the fender swipes my shoulder, knocking me onto the hood of a car. The momentum of the hit sends me rolling across the hood, and I fall flat on my back, the hot pavement burning through my clothes. I lie there a moment, expecting something in my body to start screaming in pain, but it doesn't seem like I've broken anything. I'm guessing I'll have some major bruises tomorrow.

Groaning, I move to stand, but freeze when the end of a gun bumps into my forehead. Police surround me, guns pointed at my chest.

I inch my palms into the air, kneeling. "I surrender," I say, hoping someone speaks English.

One of the officers rushes over to me and slaps on a set of cuffs. He pats down my body roughly, checking for weapons, and tosses my backpack onto the ground. I try to remain calm and resist glancing down at it. Tucked inside is my Blue Dragon bow. I can't lose that weapon.

Unfortunately that's the first thing the officer points out when he opens my bag. He says something to one of the other officers, zips it back up, and tosses the pack to one of his buddies.

With a shove, I'm led forward. Pedestrians have stopped in their tracks, snapping pictures on their phones. My only consolation is that even if the photos show up in the news, my dad will never think to look for a girl with pink hair. The police try speaking to me. I offer a stony glare.

Finally I say, "I don't speak Chinese."

"American," one says, and then he calls a report into his radio, which I'm sure isn't good. "You ran from a police officer."

I shrug. Knowing my luck, this will seem like a minor crime by the time I'm finished with this country.

Then my taxi driver comes barreling through the crowd. The two top buttons on his blue uniform have popped off, probably from when I grabbed him. He points at me, his eyes wild and his hair sticking up as if he's touched a light socket, and he screams something.

"This man says you tried to take over his taxi and physically harm him," the English-speaking officer says with a furrowed frown.

This guy has no idea. I saved his life. He was nearly ripped to shreds by a giant beast. But I don't say any of this. Instead, I give the officer my most confused, blank expression, and stick out my bottom lip.

"I have no idea who this man is," I say. "I'm taking a break from classes and backpacking around China. College can be so stressful, you know?"

Inside, I'm cringing, waiting for him to tell me I don't look old enough to have graduated from high school—which is true—or show a picture of me driving the taxi. Before he has a chance, another group of officers pushes through the pack of bikers who have paused in their travels to gape at me and the scene I'm creating.

The tallest one marches up and flashes a badge in my interrogating officer's face. "We'll take it from here."

This new officer wears a slightly different uniform, so blue it could be construed as black. His hair is cut close to his scalp, and his features are harder, more angular. He peers into my backpack, and his eyebrows rise. He looks me over, and there's something in his rich dark-brown eyes that tells me he *knows* all about me. But that doesn't make any sense. He can't possibly know about me or my mission.

He flicks his wrist, and two of his officers grab my arms and haul me forward. I'm practically airborne, my boots skimming across the pavement. I jerk backward, but their grip is tighter than a noose.

"It is fruitless to resist," one of them whispers into my ear. "This is our land, and here we are more powerful than you."

This freezes me. They do know. And in that moment, everything tumbles into place. These police officers aren't officers at all. They belong to the guardians of China, the Triads, who are the equivalent of the Guardians of Shinshi in Korea.

"How did you know about me?" I ask.

But that question is pointless; they don't respond other than a sliver of a smirk from their leader. As I'm being dragged along, I realize they're taking me to the bell tower. At the base of the stairwell I see Kwan and Sang Min. They have managed to get handcuffed as well. Their faces, as always, are unreadable. This is a definite bonus of being a corpse. You have no emotion to betray you.

At the stairwell, the tall officer pulls out a key and touches it to a place in the wall. A door slides open, revealing a staircase. This is so not good. I'm going to die before I have a chance to even try to succeed.

"Please," I say, pulling against my captors' hold. "Let me go, and I promise to leave peacefully and not hurt anyone."

This gets the leader's attention. He spins on his heels and cocks his head to the side. "You won't hurt anyone?" He laughs, and the others around him snicker. "You have no idea what you are up against, little girl. You waltz into our land as if you own it. You defile our sacred ground."

"That is so not true!" Okay, so I may have destroyed a taxi and angered one of their mythological beasts, but none of that was my fault. "I have broken no rules other than speeding. Where are you taking me?"

A flicker of hesitation crosses the leader's face, as if he wonders if he's made a mistake. I seize that moment and twist my body, kicking the guard on my left hard across the face. Then, as his body reels backward, I throw myself down so the other guard's fist hits air instead of my face. Lying on the ground, I roll onto my back and swipe my feet across his legs. He tumbles to the ground with a grunt.

I leap to my feet, screaming, "Hairbrush!"

Sang Min jerks his arms, and his handcuffs snap at the chain like a plastic toy. Then he rips open his backpack and whips out his hairbrush. It shivers as he stretches it toward me, transforming into his jagged sword. I hold out my cuffs, and he slices through each side. The handcuffs clatter to the ground. I try to take a step, but my knees crumple beneath me. I'm out of breath, and everything around me feels off-kilter. I wipe the sweat from my forehead, unsure of what's wrong with me. Could this be happening because I've been outside of the Spirit World for too long? If I don't get my act together quickly, I'll be dead.

"Please!" I tell the officers. "We don't want to hurt anyone. Just let us go."

"You bear the dark lord's mark," one of them says, and he draws a sword from within his coat. "You must die."

The Tiger of Shinshi hadn't been joking when he warned me. I do the only thing I can think of. I press my hand against the orb hidden beneath my shirt, using it for strength. Instantly power surges through me, but with it comes a twinge of guilt and worry. I know I'm playing with fire every time I use the orb, but I tell myself this is a life-and-death situation.

Meanwhile Kwan has broken free of his cuffs, too. He slams his backpack into the man pointing a sword at my throat, shoving him to the ground, and side-kicks another's stomach. Then he tears open his pack and pulls out an empty water bottle, tossing it into the air as he punches the oncoming officers. The bottle shimmers and spins until it lands in Kwan's hands as a giant spear.

But the soldiers are prepared, too. The leader and his men charge at Kwan and Sang Min. Despite the modern clothing I've dressed Kud's cronies in, they stand like warriors from ages past. Sang Min growls and charges at the Triads while Kwan waits, crouched with his sleeves rolled up. As they attack, Kwan's spear arcs through the air, smashing against two Triad Guardian swords.

Sparks fly.

Meanwhile, one of the officers races toward me, his knife lifted and aimed at my heart. Feeling revived from the orb's power, I spring onto my toes and throw myself into a three-sixty spin, knocking the knife to the ground. As the officer staggers backward, I front-jab him in the face; blood sprays through the air from his broken nose.

Once the man falls to the ground, crying in agony, I whirl to find Kwan about to thrust his spear into a man's chest.

"Don't kill them," I yell at Kwan, and then I back-flip through the air and slam a front-kick into the final guard. He smashes against the wall and slides down, unconscious. I turn and face the leader, yanking off my pink wig and tossing it to the ground, pretenses over.

"You're right," I say into his ear so only he can hear me. "I'm not who I appear to be. I am Jae Hwa Lee, descendant of Princess Yuhwa of Korea. And I am here to save my people from the hand of darkness that wishes to destroy our world as we know it. All who stand in my way will face my wrath."

The leader's face turns ashen. He steps backward, taking in the scene around him. "I—I knew it was you. I—I just didn't— The mark."

"Give me my backpack."

His hands shake as he tosses it at my feet. I pick it up and loop it over my shoulder.

"Tell your leaders my words," I say. "I hope I never lay eyes on any of you again."

Then I nod at the Stiffs and take off down the street, the two assassins following at my heels. Cars continue circling the tower, horns beeping, bikers pedaling, pedestrians walking. It's as if the fight we just experienced never happened.

"There must have been a cloaking spell on the tower," Kwan says from behind me, as if reading my thoughts.

"Yeah," I say. "There is great power here. It won't take long for the Triads to gather their greatest warriors, find us, and kill us. We need to complete our mission. And fast."

CHAPTER 16

The Shangri-La Hotel lobby is pure elegance, with a blend of ancient and modern architecture. I scan the area while I casually saunter up to the receptionist, once again flanked by the Stiffs. I try not to think about how my tights are torn from being thrown to the ground, or how strange Thing One and Thing Two must look wearing sunglasses indoors and ripped shirts.

In any other circumstance I would find myself starting to relax in an atmosphere like this. Rich mahogany-colored walls and sand-textured pillars fill up the space. The middle of the room is covered by a floral carpet and cream-toned chairs and couches. Massive palm trees splay over the sitting area.

But it's hard to focus on these things. All I can see are the four Guardians of Shinshi lounging in those chairs. Jung sits in the chair closest to the elevators, reading from his tablet, and beside him is that girl who's always with them. Her hair is pulled back in a ponytail, and she wears tight black pants and a white sleeveless mock turtleneck.

My steps slow as I think about Jung, who is obviously their leader. There wasn't any kindness in his eyes when he last faced me. How far will he go to stop what I'm trying to do? I wouldn't be surprised if he tried to kill me. How would I react if he did? I clench my fists as I think about the situation I'm in.

From the corner of my eye I spot Kumar, typing furiously on his laptop. His dark head doesn't even pop up at our appearance, but I would recognize this Indian boy anywhere. He was recruited by the Guardians of Shinshi not long ago, and he's Marc's best friend. He used to be one of my close friends, too, I think with a pang. The four of us—Marc, Kumar, Lily, and I— would go on double dates together at the *no-rae-bongs* or the movies. My heart tears a little more at that thought. It's amazing how, just when I think I can't feel the pain of the separation anymore, it rears its ugly head and nearly cripples me.

But as I pass by the chair where Marc is lounging, reading *Reference Daily*, I stumble and it's suddenly hard to breathe. Just seeing him. He came like he said he would. He may not love me, but maybe we can still be allies.

We had agreed to meet here, but I hadn't thought he'd bring the other Guardians into our plan. I should have known better. Hadn't he warned me that he was going to do everything he could to stop me? How could he have done anything other than bring the Guardians here?

Still, it could work. If I could convince them to join me— although that is highly unlikely since even Grandfather couldn't. The only way to pull this off is to make sure the Stiffs don't know anything about Marc or the Guardians. I can't let Kud's goons even realize the Guardians are here in our hotel. I just hope they don't recognize Marc from the hospital. I square my shoulders and clutch the straps of my backpack more tightly.

"Checking in for three," I tell the receptionist. "We have a suite reserved."

"Of course." The receptionist's eyes widen as she scans my clothes. My request and my dress don't exactly match, but she pastes on a smile anyway. "The Presidential Suite."

"It should be paid in full." I hope she won't try to start any investigating. I booked the most expensive room at the hotel. If I have to live in the dark god's lair for all of eternity, I deserve some perks.

"And send up a full meal spread while you're at it." I tap Kud's credit card on the counter. "Cost does not concern me."

Once I have our room keys in hand, the three of us head to the elevator. I step inside, turning to face the closing doors. Just before they seal shut, my eyes find Marc's. He holds up two fingers.

Two o'clock.

• • •

The Presidential Suite is everything I'd thought it could be and more, with chandeliers hanging from tray ceilings, plush furniture, and mahogany-paneled walls. It's a bit over-the-top. I let my backpack fall to the floor, skirt the couches and a tall vase of flowers, and plop down on a cream-colored chair. A sigh escapes my lips as I sink into the thick cushions. My muscles ache, and my lungs burn from running through the polluted city. I've nearly forgotten what it's like to be a human. This has been the longest time that I've been in the real world since I signed the contract with Kud.

Kwan and Sang Min glide across the room, their bodies so silent that it makes my skin crawl. Sure, it's a hotel suite, but still. Sleeping within twenty feet of these two will be weird. And creepy.

"You should call him," Kwan says as he pulls aside the curtain of the window and looks out at the city.

Sang Min pulls out the phone Kud gave us to keep in communication and sets it on the mother-of-pearl table beside me.

"After I take a shower." I scowl at Kwan's back. "Speaking of which, go and cover every mirror in the suite."

Kwan and Sang Min stare at me, unmoving.

I widen my eyes. "Like now."

After bad experiences with a *gwishin* and with Kud emerging from mirrors, I'm wary of them. At least in Kud's land no *gwishin* would dare enter, but here, who knows what types of creatures might emerge? I tap my fingers on the armrest as the two scurry into action. If I talk to Kud, his voice will linger in my thoughts, and he's the last person in any dimension I want to talk to. All I want to think about is Marc. I want to hear his voice. See that dimple pop up in his cheek. Listen to his laugh and drink in the sight of him as his eyes sparkle. That's what I want to think about.

There's a knock on the door. I shoot out of my chair while both Stiffs magically appear on either side of the door, weapons drawn.

I hold up my palms as I cross the plush Persian carpets. "Let me open it. If it's a human, you'll give them a heart attack. And put those sunglasses back on while you're at it. You look deader than dead otherwise."

My whole body tenses as I peer through the peephole in the door. A server with a cart of food is standing in the hallway. The door creaks as I crack it open. The guy smiles when he sees me.

"Your dinner, Madame."

I crack the door wider, grab the cart, and shove it into the room, scanning the hallway all the while. The floor is silent. The attendant looks at the retreating cart, his face scrunching in worry.

"But—"

"*Xie xie.*" I say thanks in Chinese, sign the bill, and then give him an exorbitant tip. Knowing I'm throwing Kud's money away makes me feel better until I realize Kud couldn't care less. I'm practically snarling when I slam the door in the guy's face.

The cart proves to be full of all kinds of amazing foods. I recognize many of the Chinese dishes, including sweet-and-sour pork, *baozi*, noodle soup, and dumplings. There is also a weird mix of international foods, including pepperoni pizza, hamburger sliders, and sushi rolls. I grab a *baozi* and a sushi roll, wishing it was *kimbap*, when I notice a slip of paper tucked beneath one of the sushi rolls. I peek to see if Kud's cronies are watching me. Sure enough, they both haven't moved from their post at the door and they're staring at me. At least I think they are. It's hard to tell with the sunglasses.

"Hungry?" I ask. They don't move. "There's plenty of food here. You do eat, right?"

Kwan slowly shakes his head no. The sushi in my mouth suddenly tastes bland. I eye the slip of paper again, my heart skipping as I grab the plate of sushi.

"Guard the room," I say with a mouthful of food. "I'm going to get some rest. And I don't want to be disturbed by any Guardian or mythological creature. Got it?"

"I am sure he is waiting for your call," Kwan says, arms behind his back, feet spread apart.

Will Kwan not give it a rest? Can't he figure out that I don't want to talk to Kud? I pop the rest of the sushi roll into my mouth and face Sang Min. "Do you talk? It's weird that you don't say, like, anything."

He takes off his sunglasses and stares at me with those endless black pools for eyes. I get the feeling he's debating whether to stab me in the heart or slice off my head. I groan, grab my backpack, and head to the bathroom.

Once the door is shut and I've turned the lock, I slide to the floor. With my back against the door, I unfold the piece of paper.

256

I frown. 256? That's it? Nothing else fills up the white space on either side of the paper. I balance the sushi plate on my knees as I consider all of the possibilities of these numbers. This note has to be from Marc. He's the only one who knows how much I like *kimbap*. Since sushi was the closest thing on that cart to *kimbap*, he would guess that I'd choose to eat that first.

Marc raised two fingers down in the lobby. My guess is he meant for us to meet at two o'clock. And now the note of 256. Could that be the location? It has to be.

I check the clock by my bedside. It's 1:30 p.m. I smile. In just thirty minutes, I'll be talking to Marc again. And Kud will never know. Or he won't as long as I can keep the Stiffs away. I hold back the sigh that wants to escape again and take a deep breath instead, closing my eyes and visualizing today's events. Then I whisper a prayer to God, who I imagine doesn't want anything to do with me. Still, I cling to a ridiculous hope that he still cares.

I march back out into the main living room, head held high. Thing One and Thing Two still haven't moved. The phone also hasn't moved from where Sang Min left it on the table. I stare at it, knowing Kwan is right. If I don't call Kud, he will suspect something is wrong and send in more of his goons to finish the job for me. I clench my fists and then sweep it up, punching speed-dial.

"You have delayed in calling me, darling." Kud's voice is smooth as honey over the phone.

"We had complications," I say and drop back into the chair. "A beast attacked us at the airport, and then Triads showed up and arrested us from our taxi."

"Fascinating."

"Quite." I close my eyes and resist grinding my teeth. "Anyway, all is back on track. I need to do some investigating tonight on some leads I have. We're close."

"Excellent."

"I knew you'd be pleased." I frown, hating the thought of him being happy. "But you will be so much happier when I return. Just don't forget how invaluable I am to you."

"Princess, you know I forget nothing."

"Yes, there is that." I am planning on this. I want him to remember for eternity the pain and suffering he will feel once I use the orbs to dethrone him and send him to the pits of the Underworld forever. I smile, suddenly feeling so much better.

"*Annyeong kyeseyo,*" he says.

I hang up and throw the phone across the room. It hits a vase, which tumbles over and shatters across the floor. Kwan ignores the vase but picks up the phone. After examining it, he places it on the coffee table, unharmed. *Figures.*

"I need some time alone to relax," I tell them, trying to regain my composure. "A shower sounds perfect. Why don't you both head out and find me some arrows for my bow. That would be helpful."

Kwan's eyebrows rise, but other than that, I get no response. So I stand up and slam the door to my room, causing the wall to shake, and then I lock it.

I'm not sure how long I'll have before the Stiffs start suspecting that my intentions aren't totally true to Kud. My watch says I've got five minutes before two o'clock, when I'm supposed to meet Marc. I turn on the water to the freestanding bathtub, letting it run, and then strap on my equipment belt with my ascender, clamps, and knife, just in case things turn sour.

Then I turn on the bedside lamp and the music on the alarm clock. Chinese opera fills the room as I open the door to the balcony and slip outside. Another reason why I picked this room—the balcony.

This high up, the breeze is intense, tearing at my long hair and tugging on my clothes. The distance to the ground makes my stomach slightly queasy, but I shove that feeling aside. I've done this before, maybe not this high up or during the day, but it's all pretty much the same, right?

Mind over matter, I chant to myself. I give myself a little pep talk about how powerful the brain is and how, with the right mentality, I can climb down twenty floors.

The red fire-escape box holding a rope ladder is tucked just beside the balcony door. After I unravel the rope, I tie my own cable to the ladder's end, because from the look of the ladder, it will only take me halfway down. Then I toss it over the edge of the balcony. But before I can swing over the edge, I notice the curtains in the living room twitching. Kwan's gnarled fingers tug aside the drapes. I dive back inside the bedroom, sliding across the wooden floor. I wait, holding my breath, staring at the door.

A million scenarios flash through my mind. Sure, the Stiffs will do pretty much anything I tell them as long as it doesn't contradict their glorious maker. But there's no doubt that Kud has given the Stiffs orders to kill me if I deviate from the plan.

After waiting for a precious minute, I crawl back onto the balcony, peering around the edge at the window. It's free from decomposing fingers, crooked noses, or empty eyes. If I don't hurry, Marc will think I've stood him up.

I suck in a deep breath, rush to the balcony railing, and begin climbing down the ladder. The wind swings the rope ladder back and forth. I clutch the edges as I'm tossed from side to side. My feet won't cooperate, and keep slipping off the rope. The problem with hanging the rope off the edge of the balcony is that I'm slightly away from the wall of the building and am left to swing freely in midair.

Soon the ladder reaches its end, and I climb the rest of the way down on my cord.

Every few seconds I scan the area, making sure no one has spotted me yet. When my feet finally hit solid ground, my arms burn from holding my weight. I've landed in the gardens in the back of the hotel, just down the path from the pool. I stare at the ladder hanging out in the open air. If anyone notices it, they'll investigate which room it comes from.

I swing the end of the cord into a line of bushes to keep it somewhat hidden—as long as no one looks up. It will have to do.

A quick glance at my watch shows that it's 2:10 p.m. I'm late.

I sprint down the garden path, ducking past pagodas and ornate benches. The air smells of blossoms and dampness from the lily pad–filled streams that weave throughout the courtyard. I slip through the side door and step into the lobby of the hotel. Air-conditioning washes over my face. A *guzheng* performance is being held in the lobby, but even its lilting strums can't calm my nerves.

I decide to start with room numbers. I dart up the stairs to the second floor, rereading the number 256 in my mind, over and over. There are so many things that could go wrong: Chinese mythological creatures attacking me, the Stiffs realizing I've left and prowling the halls, or the rest of the Guardians figuring out that I've been chatting with Marc and trying to interfere and stop me.

Suddenly I find myself staring at a door with those numbers: 256. I can't seem to lift my hand to knock. Deep breaths. I lick my lips and somehow manage to raise my fist and knock once.

The door swings open.

Jung.

CHAPTER 17

He grabs me by the front of my shirt, yanks me inside, and slams me against the wall so hard I'm surprised I don't crash through it. I grunt, the wind knocked out of me. Stars swirl through my vision. I had expected Marc, not the rest of the Guardians, and anguish washes over me at Marc's betrayal.

Before I can recover, the girl I keep seeing with them thrusts a pitchfork-like weapon at me. I scream as its two prongs sink into the wall on either side of my neck, missing my face by millimeters. It's a bident, I realize, similar to a trident but with two prongs rather than three. Grandfather had owned one of those. Its metal burns my skin, alerting me instantly that this weapon was forged in the Spirit World. This bident has powers beyond its steel and sharp edges.

My eyes widen as I realize I can't move my neck. If I shift even a fraction of an inch, pain sears my nerves. "A little close, don't you think?"

"Not close enough is what *I* think," the girl says, blowing her bangs out of her eyes. She grabs my wrists and slaps on handcuffs. Then she checks my equipment belt, taking out Kud's knife and pocketing it. "She's got an ascender, a tether, a knife, and a room key in her leather pouch. Planning on climbing something?"

"I like to be prepared," I say.

Jung's eyes are hard as onyx as he kicks the door shut and draws his long sword, grim-faced. He's got the Tiger of Shinshi tattooed on his shoulder. With his massively broad shoulders and tall physique, he's not someone to mess with.

Jung and I never really connected. Maybe because I always blamed him for taking Marc from me for training all those weeks after Marc became a full-fledged Guardian. Or because I felt as if Marc and Jung had this connection from their training that I never had with Marc. And then there's the fact that I have never gotten over how Jung tried to stop me from rescuing Marc.

He had his reasons. I had mine.

And even now as he draws closer, his jaw tightening, I can tell we still don't see eye-to-eye.

"How could you have joined Kud's side?" Jung asks. "Of all people, I never would have expected you to turn."

"I didn't have a choice."

"We always have a choice." Jung holds the point of his sword at my throat. "Just as I do now."

This is exactly the scenario I had worried over—and should have expected from Grandfather's and Marc's warnings. But I'd hoped I could sway the Guardians. I've been a fool.

"Don't touch her." It's Marc, standing by the windows. His arms are crossed and his mouth is set in anger. Seeing him just standing there, letting them do this to me, hurts more than I wish to let them see. "Hana, let her go."

"You don't think she'll kill us all?" the girl, who must be Hana, says.

"Your weapons are meaningless." I try to bring confidence to my voice. "Or have you forgotten I hold the White Tiger orb?"

"Is that a threat?" Jung's eyes bore into mine.

"Maybe," I snap back. "Listen. I don't have much time, and I don't wish to waste it arguing about who trusts whom. My goal is to get the Black Turtle orb, and I need your help to do it. I met the Tiger of Shinshi and he gave me his blessing, but he said I couldn't do it without you. Kud's going to find the orb through one of his creatures; it's just a matter of time. So we can either beat them to it or let him have it without a fight. But if we can't come to an agreement, I'm out of here."

Slowly the girl pulls the bident out of the wall and back to her side. The steel burns my cheeks as she pulls it back. I press my hands to my face.

"It burned her," Hana says, inspecting my neck. "She's not completely human."

My pulse picks up speed at her words. It's a truth I've been in denial about ever since Bari and Marc told me I was taking on a silvern sheen. There have been moments when I've felt my humanity slowly slipping away. I've tried to forget that and focus on how my footholds in the human world and the Spirit World have been useful.

But it's only a matter of time before I will have lost my humanity forever.

I look to Marc, waiting for him to say something, but he only rubs his hands over his face and turns his back to me, leaning against the wall.

When Jung doesn't move, it's Hana who jerks her head, indicating for me to enter the main room. Her face remains calm; she's more in control of herself than Marc and Jung are. Of course, she and I have never met, so we don't have emotions getting in the way.

Now that I'm not about to be killed, I have time to study this girl who has entered Marc's life. She's tall and willowy, her long black hair pulled back in a slick ponytail, and she's still wearing the sleek black pants and sleeveless white mock turtleneck she sported in the lobby. The shirt shows off her sculpted, muscular arms. She's got sharp features that tell me nothing gets by her. From the hard line of her jaw and her easy hold on her weapon, I can tell she's been around the block a few times as a fighter. I don't want to think about what Marc sees in her, so I look around the room instead.

Their suite isn't as lavish as the Presidential Suite, but it has a living room, a dining room, a kitchen, and multiple bedrooms. In the corner, I spy Kumar ducked behind his screen, typing away. But as I step beside Marc, Kumar finally looks up. He clears his throat and adjusts the collar on his white button-down shirt. As usual, he's dressed as if he were heading to a photo shoot for J. Crew, a hint of stubble on his chin and his long hair neatly combed back.

I want to grab him and pull him into a big hug. To tell him to go back to Lily and forget about this whole mess. That it isn't worth it. The only thing that matters is to be with the ones we love and to love them with every breath within ourselves.

"Kumar," I whisper. My throat is too tight to say anything else.

"Jae." Kumar rubs the sides of his computer. "Hey. We've missed you. I went to your funeral. That was—" He clears his throat again. "Glad to see you're not, um, dead."

"I can't say the same." Jung perches himself on the armrest of a chair. "I want to believe you. Let's pretend you're telling the truth, that you want to get the Black Turtle orb to save Korea from Kud and all of that. But the truth is that contract on your arm forbids you from doing exactly that. You're strong. I've heard you're a kick-ass fighter, but Kud's a god. An immortal with an incredible amount of power. There's no way you could stand up to him or resist his commands. So, if that's the case, why should we trust you?"

"Kud has no power in these lands," I tell the group, rubbing the contract on my arm, glad to be free of its burn. "None of the immortals of Korea do. That's why Kud needs me. He thinks I'll get him what he wants here, especially because he has threatened to kill all those I care about if I don't obey him. But this is so much bigger than me or the people in my life. Kud is planning a massive war. The war between the North and South may have begun, but it won't end in the Koreas. He means to take over the world.

"If I fail this mission, Kud won't care because he has been creating creatures to replace me. Basically, he's taken dead corpses and breathed life back into them. They are still human, so they can travel outside of Korea. And since they owe their allegiance to Kud and are soulless, they will do his bidding without thought or care."

"Walking dead." Jung nods. "We've heard about them."

"So you can either stop me or help me." I dare a glance at Marc. His eyes remain hard and wary. "The Stiffs won't negotiate, and the two with me are here to help me get the orb. If I fail, then they will still continue with the mission. And who knows? Maybe Kud has sent more of these corpses to other locations or even here. I don't know."

"How can you guarantee that you're not tricking us?" Hana asks. "For all we know, every word you just uttered could be sprinkled with pretty little lies."

"I can't. You will have to trust me." I suppress a wince. Even to me, those words sound hollow and empty. How can I prove the intentions of my heart?

"I don't know what to believe," Marc says. "You said one thing at the Blue House, and here you say the complete opposite."

I don't blame them for doubting me, but I can't stop an edge of annoyance from pricking my temper. Marc set me up. He knew I'd come if I thought I was just meeting him and not the whole group. I need to stop depending on others to help me. I need to start realizing I'm on my own.

Kumar's eyes shift back and forth between the other Guardians and me. "I hope we can work things out," Kumar says, and then after receiving a scathing look from Jung and Hana, he adds, "It's not the same without you."

"How about this," Jung says. "You tell us where the orb is, and we won't kill you."

"I don't know where it is," I say.

"Yet you found the turtle statue and the coin." Jung taps his sword on his knee. "Marc said it gave you a clue. And now you're here."

"I'm probably chasing shadows, but my grandfather gave me an article about the terra-cotta warriors and Emperor Qin Shi Huang's tomb. He thinks it may be in one of those places. I was hoping you all might know something."

"Let's pretend you aren't lying," Hana says. "We help you get this orb, and then you arrive back in Korea. The moment you land on Korean soil, Kud will have control over you again, and you won't be able to resist him."

I stare at my contract, remembering all the times where I couldn't fight against the pain. Maybe the Guardians are right, and this is a pointless endeavor. I shake my head. "No, you're wrong. He does have power over me, but he won't have power over the orb if I claim it as the owner. I can stand against him. I know I can. If you help me, I know I can do this."

"Tell her," Jung says to Hana. "Tell her what you are."

Hana eyes me closely. "I'm from Jeju Island, trained by Master Rim. After the events between Kang-dae, Marc, and you, the Council requested that I come out of hiding and join the Guardians. I'm a seer. And the truth is, you will betray us with this orb. I've seen you stand against us in my vision. I'm not sure if it's intentionally or unintentionally, but because of this, we can't in good conscience allow you to find this orb."

"What?" I practically yell the word. "I don't know who you are, but I refuse to believe you or your supposed future. How do I know that *you're* not lying?"

"Listen." Jung clears his throat. "For the sake of your grand-father and for finding the third orb, we're going to let you go free. My suggestion is to run away. At least you are free from Kud's power here. Whatever you do, don't go after the orb."

I'm flabbergasted; I'm at a loss for words.

"Let's talk," Marc says to me, and he opens the door to an adjoining room. "In private."

"She's poison, man," Jung yells after Marc. "Don't trust her for a second."

I glare at Jung before following Marc into the bedroom. Once we're alone, I lean against the door. He stands before me, dark circles ringing his eyes and hair hanging in his face. He's beautiful, and my insides cry at the hurt I've caused him. If only I could erase every painful memory.

He jams his hands into his pockets and takes a deep breath. I remain still, almost not daring to breathe, not wanting to ruin the magic. Because right now, this second, it's just the two of us. No Guardians or Stiffs or Kud hovering over us. It takes every bit of my willpower not to throw myself into his arms.

"I can't believe our relationship has come to this," I say, tears streaming down my face. "You know me better than anyone. I'd never do what Hana says I will do."

Marc pulls out a piece of paper. It reads:

Room is bugged. Meet me by the pool in 10 min.

"We can't help you complete Kud's orders," Marc says, obvi-ously for the Guardians to hear in the other room. "It's against the code of our Order, and we've been commanded by Mr. Han, the head of the Council, to do everything in our power to stop you. Go back to your room, think this over, and when you're ready, tell us where the orb is and let us retrieve it."

I should be devastated by his words, but all I can focus on are his lips and the way his hair has fallen across his eyes. Then he reaches out and brushes his fingers across my cheek. I shiver at his touch. He steps closer; his lips brush against my ear.

"I've missed you," he whispers. "More than I ever thought possible."

He misses me? I search his face for proof that he's teasing. Or lying. But all I find is warmth, and it's seeping into every inch of my skin. He presses his body against mine, and his hand rests on the door just above my head. The room spins, and I have to grab on to him to keep from collapsing.

"If you are wise"—his voice is louder now, even though his face is centimeters from mine—"you and your two men will leave the country this instant."

I can't speak. It's too much having him this close, seeing that look in his eyes. It was so much easier to see the distant look he once had.

But this.

This I can't handle. I know I'm starved for human contact, but now I see I've been dead without Marc. A walking corpse wandering aimlessly, just like the Stiffs.

And now that I know he cares, my heart starts pounding a mile a minute. I must leave. I can't breathe. The knob slips through my sweaty palms as I fumble to open the door. My face burns, and the room spins slightly as I stumble out.

"I can't—" I head for the door, unable to form a complete sentence or thought.

Marc still cares for me. No, it is more than that. I saw it in his eyes. *Love.* He loves me. Still. After everything.

Jung is speaking again, but the room spins and rings and my heart soars.

"If you go after this orb, I will kill you for your betrayal," Jung tells me as I'm stepping into the hallway. His tone pulls me back to reality.

"You've chosen your side." Hana grips her bident, her chin lifted high. "And so have we."

My eyes take in the three of them. How has it come to this? We should be working together, not against one another.

I march out of the room, slamming the door behind me. Once more I've started down a path without a clue whether it's the right one. Father loved to quote Robert Frost and his poem "The Road Less Traveled." Am I making the right choice by turning my back on the Guardians? Will taking this path make all the difference?

My steps quicken as I stride down the hall. It's easy to know the right choice in hindsight or when I'm standing outside looking in. But here in the middle of the storm, I'm lost. Still, if Marc is keeping secrets from them, there must be a reason.

As I head back toward the lobby, away from Marc's scent and presence, I'm able to think more clearly. My thoughts fly to the ladder and my babysitters—and whether they have discovered what I've done. Ten minutes suddenly becomes a lifetime.

The hall presses in on me with its close quarters, and I break into a jog toward the garden, needing to breathe. There is something about knowing that these hours may be my last that pumps my legs faster. But as I run, my breathing becomes labored. My legs shake under me. It's like I've been running for miles, but it's been only a few minutes. I don't want to admit why I'm feeling this way, but deep down I know it's because I've lost too much of my humanity to be out of the Spirit World for so long. I pause to catch my breath before continuing.

I find the cord to the ladder tucked within the bushes, safe and untouched. A soft breeze rushes through the gardens, and the place is nearly deserted, with only a few couples strolling the paths. Other than the kids shouting and splashing in the pool at the other end, only the cicadas and crickets make any noise.

Up on the twentieth floor, both of the living room curtains are still shut. Since neither of the Stiffs has found the ladder or attacked me, I'm hoping my running shower and music have fooled them. I allow myself to relax, and I slip into the shadows to wait for Marc.

I don't wait long. He comes strolling out in quick, long strides, and although it's obvious he's trying to be inconspicuous, his head whips back and forth as if he's searching for something. He's about to take a different path when his eyes land on the shadows where I'm hiding. He stops in his tracks and then turns onto the path toward me.

"How did you see me?" I ask once he's closer.

"The orb." He slips through the bushes to join me. "It's like a blinking radar."

I look down at my shirt where the White Tiger orb is concealed. Even I can't see it. "Even though it's hidden?"

"It's not hidden from me. Sometimes my sight is infuriatingly frustrating, but in this instance, it helped me find you."

"So I take it the Guardians didn't approve of you helping me."

"Definitely not. I broke the news to them not long before you came. As you saw, Jung and Hana don't trust you because of her vision. Your grandfather hoped that once we were here, away from the Council's influence, I'd be able to sway them, but that wasn't the case. Kumar was pretty cool about it, but he insisted on bugging the room because he was worried you'd try to kill me. Hence the note."

"I wish things weren't this way. Nothing is ever simple anymore."

"It never was." He lets out a long breath. "And probably never will be."

We stare at each other, and his face softens.

"How is it that every time I see you, you are more beautiful than the last time?"

My heart flutters. "I thought you hated me. Despised me."

"No." He pulls back, his forehead wrinkled. "No, never. I was mad and hurt after what you said at the Blue House, that's true. And at first I believed you. But on the flight over here I started thinking about everything you said, and it made sense. You were trying to protect me, and pushing me away was your way of showing you loved me."

"If I had told you the truth at the Blue House, Kud would've killed you and the other Guardians there. Without hesitation."

"It's agony, Jae. You've no idea how it kills me to see you as his captive. It's literally like someone is stabbing me over and over every time I lay eyes on you. It should've been *me* that he took. It wasn't supposed to turn out this way."

I lightly touch his arm. He doesn't cringe. "I made the choice. There wasn't a good choice. Just a choice. You can't blame yourself for any of this, but we can change things. We don't have to live like this. If I can get that other orb and get it to Palk, we have a chance of defeating Kud. And then we can be together again."

"There's no way he'll let you out of his grip once you land on Korean soil again. You need to run as far from Korea as you can. Go somewhere else and live there."

I bite my lip. "I think the Spirit World's grip on me is too strong. Ever since I left Korea, I've slowly been getting weaker. I keep using the orb to gain strength. You know how the immortals don't have limitless power in the human world? I think I'm slowly becoming like that."

There's panic in his eyes, but he says nothing. Instead he swallows, and his jaw works as if he's restraining everything inside him that wants to come out.

"I don't have much time." I look pointedly at the ladder. "I'm going to search for the orb tomorrow. Will you help me?"

"The Grand Council is gathering."

His words bring my thoughts to a stumbling halt. Not long ago I learned that the Guardians of Shinshi weren't the only Guardians. Every country has their own protectors, designated to defend and keep the treasures of their lands safe. The Grand Council consists of one or two Guardians from every country. They only convene for great emergencies or when things get out of hand.

"I didn't know the Grand Council still met," I say. "Why did they call a meeting?"

"The Triads called it when the skirmishes started up between North and South Korea—they realized the fighting was tied to Kud's growth in power. It's a big deal. The Grand Council hasn't been called since Stonehenge was made into a tourist attraction."

"Wow." I stare up at the sun, peering through the clouds. "This is big."

"Yeah. They're trying to figure out a way to get that orb before you do."

"They are meeting because of *me*?"

"You always did like to stir up trouble, Fighter Girl."

My chest tightens at his nickname. I can't remember the last time he called me that.

"Jung has been asked by the Guardians of Shinshi to represent the order," Marc says. "He's requested that I go with him. So tomorrow we'll go and listen to what they have to say."

"Where's the meeting being held?"

He presses his lips together, and I see the boundary between us has surfaced once again, severing our connection. We still are on separate sides, a chasm apart, and I wonder why the love we once had isn't enough. He runs his hands through his hair.

"You have to tell me, Marc." I grab his forearms, but being this close and not pulling him closer is too much. I let him go and whirl around, my arms crossed. "I wish I'd been able to convince the Guardians to help me. I don't know if I have the strength or the ability to find this orb. What if it's heavily guarded like the White Tiger orb was? And I'm not sure if I'm strong enough here. Every time I run I become exhausted. Plus, once Kud's babysitters find out what I'm doing, they'll do everything in their power to kill me."

"Maybe Jung and Hana are right. Have you thought about that? After hearing what Kud did to you last night at the canal, I've been wondering if it's too risky for you to get this orb. Maybe this is one of those times you shouldn't get involved."

I close my eyes, hating how he had to bring up last night. The memory of Kud's kiss and the missing hours makes my skin grow cold. The words of the Tiger of Shinshi vibrate through me: *You must not. For the sake of our beloved Korea.*

Hadn't he said we all needed to work together? But perhaps he hadn't foreseen that the Grand Council would be involved. I turn back to face Marc.

"Maybe you're all right. Maybe I'm worthless now, but you don't understand. I can't let this go. The Tiger of Shinshi said he believed I was the only one who could gain access to this orb. I feel responsible for what's happening, and I can't sit by and watch the Guardians mess things up and allow Kud to destroy the world. Whatever happens, Marc, I love you. And I'll never stop."

I push past him, seize the cord, and start climbing toward the ladder.

"Don't go." Marc grabs my arm.

"Kud's creatures will be suspicious soon, if they aren't already. Do what you have to do. I know you and the Guardians mean well. I wish we could work together. But all I ask is that you don't try to stop me from doing what I know needs to be done."

He releases me, and I've never felt so alone. The wind picks up the higher I climb, but I'm glad for it. It wipes away my tears so quickly that I imagine they never existed.

As I scale the hotel, my strength wanes. I just don't have the energy I once did, and that scares me to the core. There has to be a link between this and my growing connection to the Spirit World. I'm losing my humanity. With this realization, my resolve to win this battle dissipates. When I reach the top of the ladder, I collapse onto the balcony floor, wondering if there's any hope for me at all.

CHAPTER 18

With the break of dawn comes a sense of panic. I jerk up in my massive king-size bed, my heart beating wildly. Something is wrong. Or is it? I clutch the sheets, taking in the streams of sunlight trickling through the cracks in the curtains. The geometric lights give off a soft glow, still lit because I never turned them off.

Everything feels different. It's as if there has been a shift in the world and things are stirring. I pull my bow out from under my pillow and tuck it to my chest, rubbing its smooth wood.

It's been a long time since I've slept so well. I didn't wake up screaming, and I don't even remember dreaming.

I toss off my covers and squeeze into black pants and a shirt. A wave of dizziness washes over me, and I have to lean against the wall for support before I'm able to slip on my boots. I tell myself it's nothing. I just need some food and I'll feel better. I throw open the door, only to be greeted by the Stiffs, standing exactly where they were when I left them last night.

So weird.

I frown. Kwan almost smiles. Sang Min definitely snarls.

"I must have overslept." I open the minifridge. Nothing looks appealing. "Any problems?"

"Two *taotie* attacked," Kwan says with a shrug. "It was nothing."

"A *taotie*?" My muscles stiffen. "What is that?"

"A monster that eats everything that moves. It's known to be obsessed with consuming everything it encounters."

"You should've woken me." I abandon my search for food to peer into the closets and check the locks on the windows. "I could have helped."

Sang Min grunts and fiddles with the hilt of his sword. Kwan shakes his head. "The *taotie* kills through fear. Through emotion. It was powerless against us. But you, it could consume in moments."

"So you're saying you're a bunch of brain-deads and I'm a complete basket case."

Kwan frowns. "I do not understand."

"Forget it." I wave my hand and pick up the phone, punching number eight for room service. "Yeah, I'd like a full-course breakfast sent to the Presidential Suite. And make sure you've got chocolate croissants."

"We are wasting time," Kwan says, and he sets a dozen arrows on the table before me. "We must find the orb. Now."

"You need to chill. The White Tiger orb will lead us to the location, and I need breakfast first. But these." I pick up the arrows, inspect them, and nod. "Well done."

As I stow the arrows in my pack, I decide not to mention how I feel sick to my stomach and dizzy, or that the Guardians are off making plans and having meetings without me. Because I'm dangerous, volatile, and according to Hana, a traitor.

Instead I plop down onto the soft sofa and stare up at the gold-framed painting across from me. Rows and rows of terra-cotta warriors fill the painting, lined up beneath a huge dome. Something about that picture bugs me. I'm not sure what it is. I nibble at the nail of my pinky and then stop. *Unbelievable.* I'm now a freaking nail-biter.

I jump back to my feet and start pacing the room. A new idea sprouts in my mind. Marc may not be able to tell me where the Grand Council is meeting, but I'm sure the White Tiger orb can. I know Kud said I should use it only in emergency situations, but something tells me that if I don't hurry and find this orb, I'll be too weak to even attempt the mission.

If I could make a surprise visit to the Grand Council, maybe I could convince them of my true intentions and they could help me stop Kud. Still, I highly doubt I could just walk the streets of Xi'an in broad daylight bearing the orb. I don't have Haechi or Palk watching my back here. I've got nobody. Freaking nobody.

Breakfast arrives, and I take two giant bites of the croissant before diving into the stack of pancakes, drenching them with butter and syrup. Then I attack my rice porridge. It's creamy and steaming hot. I almost moan in delight. Every once in a while I glance up to see Kwan and Sang Min watching me. The creepiest part is that I'm starting to not find them all that creepy anymore.

I'm washing it all down with a cup of coffee, hoping for a caffeine jolt to give me more energy, when I notice a post-card tucked next to the rose on the tray. It's an aerial photo-graph of the terra-cotta warriors. I pause, my heart kicking into overdrive. Casually I flip the card over to see a cursive *M* scrawled on the bottom.

Marc.

He's left me a clue. Maybe my words last night got through to him, or maybe there's something within him that still believes in me. I set down the coffee mug and sit up straighter, a plot crystalizing in my mind. If the meeting is held at the terra-cotta warriors' pavilion, then all I need is a taxi. Everything is falling into place until the mirror in the far corner of the room catches my attention.

The blanket once thrown over it has slipped off onto the floor, and I take in my reflection: a pale-faced girl with long, wild hair, who is too thin and too tiny to be thinking of standing in front of the most powerful council in the world and telling them how they should run things. One look at me and this council will laugh me out of the room.

"How old do I look to you?" I ask Kwan, taking another sip of coffee.

"Kud should have kept you at home."

At this I set down my coffee mug and lift my chin. "Are you questioning the master?"

Sang Min grunts and Kwan whips out his spear. He touches the head, and it sinks into the shaft so that the spear looks like a walking stick.

"We're going shopping," I tell my babysitters, pocketing the postcard.

As expected, they frown—well, Kwan frowns and Sang Min snarls.

"We do not have time for shopping," Kwan says.

"Fine. You two trot off and get the orb while I go shopping."
I snatch up my backpack, determined to not let my bow leave
my side, and march to the door. As I turn the handle, I glance
over my shoulder. "Good luck with that."

I suppose I must hold some value, since they decide not to
kill me at that moment. The three of us step into the elevator.

"I knew you'd see things my way." I smile as I push the elevator button. Somehow I'll need to lose them in the market and
slip away in a taxi. "I've always wondered what it would be like
to have personal escorts."

The main lobby is packed full of people. I study the room
briefly, examining each person. My back stiffens, and my nerves
go on high alert. There's something odd about the couple we
pass. Maybe it's their bright eyes or their long necks, as if their
bodies have been stretched too far. As we stroll to the boutique
adjacent to the lobby, a man reading the paper raises his eyes
to study me and slowly licks his lips. A chill washes over me.
Maybe I'm hallucinating and these feelings are side effects of
being away from Korea and the Spirit World for so long. Or
maybe there's something seriously wrong with this place.

We're just about to cross the threshold and head outside
when something cold and scaly slithers across my neck and
down my arm. I spin around but stumble, my legs tangled in a
rope. The Stiffs also turn, and as they do, everything shifts into
slow motion.

"*Zhulong*," Kwan mutters under his breath. The spearhead
erupts from his walking stick, and Sang Min unsheathes his
weapon. I follow their gaze back into the lobby. The bodies of
the people we passed shimmer and contort, revealing their true

selves. Human eyes slant into snake eyes, and long tongues flick out of human mouths. Half-human, half-snake, the creatures tumble to the floor and slither across the marble, over the carpet, toward us.

Eyes intent on me.

There isn't a single human in the entire room. I scoot backward, sliding on my butt, but I realize that what I had thought was a rope is actually a snake wrapping its body around my legs.

"Yessss," the female *zhulong* hisses. "Wes gots yous. Tricksty little girl."

Then it begins to speak in Mandarin, and my brain doesn't translate well due to sheer panic. Not that I have time to care. The other creatures converge on us. The Stiffs spin their weapons in an arc, slicing down centimeters from my legs, and sever the snake's body. The creatures all hiss and shudder as if Kud's cronies had cut them instead.

"Dies!" they cry out as one. "All girls must dies."

I leap up, free of the snake's grip. "Did you hear that?" I ask the Stiffs as I fumble with the zipper to my backpack. "They just called you girls."

Sang Min grunts beside me. Kwan spins his jagged spear through the air over his head, and then the two of them open their black mouths wide and scream. The room shudders. I clamp my palms over my ears and crouch down against the guttural, inhuman sound. Terror and dread jab through my skin like knives.

I stare up at the Stiffs, their heads leaned back as if they are howling to the moon. I can't believe I slept sound as a baby in the hotel suite with them there. Being with them for so long has made me forget how truly horrifying they can be as an enemy.

The moment their roar dies, the snakes shake their human heads and hiss back, launching their bodies in a frontal attack. Kwan and Sang Min retaliate, slashing their weapons with wild fury. The zipper of my backpack slips between my fingers, but I finally wrench out my bow and notch an arrow.

A massive woman-snake slithers past Sang Min and rears her head back, preparing to strike. Her long black hair swings around her, and her shiny dangle earrings distract me. Blinking against the glare, I pull back on the string and let my arrow fly. It sinks directly between her eyes. With a cry, she topples to the ground, eyes glazed. There isn't time to be thrilled, because the onslaught of snake-like creatures is merciless.

I scramble to my feet and notch another arrow. I sink this one into a man-snake. The glasses he's wearing fly off and tumble to the ground. My fingers freeze, and for a moment I'm fooled into believing I've shot a human.

But these creatures are not innocent humans. I can't think of them in that way.

These snakes are trying to kill you, I tell myself. Don't hesitate. I try to focus on the creatures' bodies rather than their human-seeming faces.

One after another, I let the arrows fly until my goong dae is empty.

Then I run to each of my victims, ripping out the arrows to be used in my next onslaught. The snakes' bright blue blood drips off the arrowheads as I scamper over the mounds of bodies. The stench of their open wounds makes my stomach churn, and I bend over to throw up. But before I can do anything, a lady-snake drops from the ceiling and wraps her body around my neck.

"Sweets for me?" she asks.

I push against her thick body, my arm muscles protesting sharply. She's got spiked hair, and her face is caked with cherry red lipstick, streaks of blush, and yellow eye shadow. Her long tongue flicks out, licking my cheek. I bite back a scream and punch her face instead. The last thing I need is for her to sink her fangs into my neck.

Then the rest of her body slides around my torso, while she squeezes my throat like a steel cord. The room spins and I wheeze, gasping for air. Desperate, I try to move my hand to stab an arrow into her, but my arms are crushed against my sides. My feet are still free, so I backpedal until I'm able to slam my back against a wall, throwing all my weight so that her body is crushed. She grunts from the impact, but her grip never loosens.

In my peripheral vision, I spot Kwan and Sang Min in action, swooping across the snake-humans. They are death in physical form, and once again I'm torn between being disgusted with myself for being on the same side as them and being thrilled that I have such powerful allies.

The orb burns against my skin, hidden beneath my shirt, as if it's aching to be used. I hesitate, Kud's words of wariness echoing through me. If I use it, all nearby Spirit World creatures will feel its presence. Memories of the beast that charged after us at the airport flash through my mind. Still, I'm going to have to use it at some point in order to find the Grand Council and then the location of the Black Turtle orb.

My muscles scream in pain, and I relax for a moment. The snake-woman's grip tightens on my throat in response, and she shifts more of her body to wrap around my neck. Black spots fill my vision. Kwan and Sang Min are too busy fighting for their lives to worry about me. I realize I can move my arms again. My hands shake, and my fingers grow numb as I grope under my shirt to find the orb. My hand clutches around the orb's sphere, but it's too late. My knees buckle and everything darkens around me.

And then I'm falling.

The ground is soft as air, and I'm floating. The sweet scent of cherry blossoms replaces the reek of the snakes' rotting bodies. I hear birds chirping rather than hisses and screaming. But heat pulses in my hand as if it's holding a burning coal. I want to run and find an icy stream to cool my scorched fingers.

My eyelids pop open, and the room revolves in a rush before righting itself. I sit and reach for my throat, which is raw and burning. In my other hand I'm holding the orb. Its pulsing white light radiates through the room, pure and unblemished. I drop the orb and try to stand, but I slip on scaly skin and tumble to the ground. I had been lying on a pile of snakes. All around me the snake-humans lie still. Kwan and Sang Min also lie in a heap on the floor, unmoving.

In fact, the room is oddly silent. My pulse pounds against my temples. I'm not exactly sure what I did, but it will only be a matter of moments before others come to hunt me down. I take off, but it's nearly impossible to walk. I'm slipping and falling over snakes. Oozing blue blood sticks to my boots and clings to my pants.

I scan the area for my bow. I know precious time is ticking away, but there's no way I'm leaving that behind. As if reading my thoughts, a ray of light from the orb shines on one of the corpses. I slip and slide over to a body that is wider than me. My palms are slick with blue blood, and as I plant them on the snake's body, I can't help but cringe. I grunt and groan until the body rolls over. The Blue Dragon bow lies unharmed beneath it.

It takes me a moment to gather up my arrows and stagger back to where I'd left my backpack leaning against the wall. I pull out the postcard Marc gave me and trace my finger over the letter *M*. I eye the front door of the lobby, but this hotel has obviously been taken over by *zhulong*. Who knows what lurks outside the front entrance. I don't wait to see if anyone notices as I slip out the back door.

CHAPTER 19

I pump my legs as I run down the cobblestone alley. The tile-roofed houses are a mix of concrete and bricks, and normally I would consider them quaint. But today they press against me, leaving no easy escape route if an attacker should appear. I duck beneath a line of clothes hung out to dry and skirt around a stack of woven baskets. Trash blows past my feet, and I splash through a puddle.

A light drizzle of rain patters against my cheeks. Every crack, every corner, every open window is a possible entry point where an enemy could leap out and stop me. And just as that thought settles into my brain, I hear the pounding of feet drawing nearer behind me, *thud, thud, thud.*

I try not to think about what could be chasing me, and instead I set my jaw and focus on the path before me. The alley abruptly shifts, turning into an even smaller passage. I push aside a red balloon-shaped lantern dangling in front of my path, vault over two clay pots, and keep sprinting. A roar fills the alley, rolling like a hurricane and rattling the hexagonal-paned windows. Sweat trickles down my forehead. I gasp for air, and my legs wobble, ready to collapse.

My fingers itch to grab the orb and suck in its power, but I know better than that. Too much of the orb always overwhelms me—hence the passing out back at the hotel lobby.

The alley opens up into a street, and at the end I see my hope. A taxi. I'm barreling down the alley, eyes intent on the little blue car, when something yanks my backpack strap, drawing me back. My back arches against the pull, and my boots slide out from under me. I fall on my butt, mud sloshing in my wake.

I swivel and raise up the orb between myself and my attacker. When I look up, I nearly drop the orb in shock. The beast before me looks so much like Haechi that I can't focus. Images of when I first met Haechi flash through my mind: how he was trying to help me, and how I'd been so very wrong about him.

But then I notice the differences between Haechi and this creature. It has a goat-like body that glows a brilliant blue color, and its single horn juts out like a unicorn's. Its fangs snarl, spit raining across my face. Then its hoof-like feet rear up to crush me.

I shove the orb higher, aiming at the creature. It roars even louder, as if angered by the power of the orb, and then it falls back, shaking and rolling its horned head. I have no idea how to handle this situation, and once again I miss Marc and his knowledge about all these sorts of things.

Remembering how painful it was to kick Haechi, I decide not to engage this guy. So I scramble to my feet and practically dive into the taxi.

"Drive!" I scream at the driver. Then realize screaming at him in English won't help, so I hold out the postcard, saying, "*Xie xie*, drive to the terra-cotta warrior exhibit."

The car takes off down the street. I grip the side of the door, peering over my shoulder and waiting for the creature to come galloping out after us. But it never does. I lean against my seat and let out a long breath. A hint of a smile reaches my lips. In the insanity of everything, I've somehow managed to escape Kud's cronies.

I slide the orb back beneath my shirt and allow my muscles to relax. The music playing over the radio and the sweet blossom scent in the taxi soothes me. Rain patters on the windows, and I allow my eyes to close. I'm not used to being physically challenged. Was running always so difficult before I became a slave to Kud, or is this because I'm attached to the Spirit World? It's all so confusing, and moments like these make me want to give up and leave all the saving to someone else. I mean, really, there's a whole council gathering together to stop Kud. They can take care of it. Do I really need to get involved?

But then I remember Dad, Grandfather, and Marc. I can't abandon them. I can't risk their lives just because I'm tired. I sit up, shoving back the sleep that tugs at me. My eyes connect to the rearview mirror, and my heart dives into my stomach. The man staring back at me is the officer from the bell tower. The Triad Guardian guy.

"You!" I fumble at the door handle, but of course the doors are locked.

"Don't even think about escaping from me this time." He points a gun back at me and cocks the hammer. I freeze. "I assume you are still human enough that this device will kill you if I shoot a bullet through your brain."

I decide to go for what he's least expecting. The truth.

"Yes, it will kill me. And if you kill me you'll definitely throw a wrench into Kud's plan. But you won't stop him. He'll just send more of his dead things to do the job. I'm the best chance you have of stopping him."

"You?" The guy laughs. I grip the handle of the door and nearly rip it off. "My dear, you think too highly of yourself. What you need is a dose of humble tea."

"Whatever." I look out the window, trying to take in the situation. My bow and arrows are tucked away inside my backpack. Without looking down, I slowly unzip it. If I can just slip out one of my arrows before he realizes it, I can stab him before he gets the chance to shoot me with his gun. "Where are you taking me? Why not just shoot me and get this over with? Or are you too scared to kill a little girl?"

"I don't have time for your mind games. You will find out the answer soon enough. Why don't you just relax?"

Outside, I try to focus on the buildings and street signs, but everything blurs. I'm just pulling out an arrow when I see him slip on a gas mask and touch a button on the dashboard. I grip my arrow and try to thrust it into the guy's brain. But my arm fails me and falls to my side. He's drugged me, I realize. Then I fall against the back of my seat, and the darkness swoops in and consumes me.

. . .

I wake as I'm thrown to the ground, my cheek scraping across a concrete floor. The impact sends pain reeling through my skull, and I can't stop the groan from escaping my lips. A trickle of liquid trails down the side of my face. Blood, most likely. I blink against the yellowish light. The concrete walls swirl up and down in my vision. I try to stand, but my legs are too numb. Whatever drug they filled the car with has some serious side effects.

Male voices speak around me. I can't understand a lick of what they are saying, so I assume they must be the Triad Guardians. My mouth opens and closes, but I'm unable to speak, and my tongue feels thick and dry. I run my hands over my throat, which still aches from that darn snake-thing trying to choke me.

A hand grabs my chin and lifts my face upward. "Who would have ever guessed that a stick like you could cause such trouble," he says.

"You guys don't get it," I finally croak out. "We're on the same side. We both want the same thing."

"And a comedian!" The man chuckles. The two others join in. Or I think it's two. It's hard to tell with my double vision. "But don't worry, we will tie you up all nice and snug. Will that make you happy?"

"Yep. I'll be just thrilled," I say.

A girl leans down next to me, her long hair falling over my cheek and smelling of roses. She's probably a nice girl. I almost feel bad for what I'm about to do. In one swift movement, I twist and jam my elbow into the girl's face, hitting her nose hard. She falls back and holds her face. There's blood everywhere. I roll across the ground just as the other guy swoops down to grab me.

I snap up my legs and kick, throwing him against the wall. I leap to my feet, and my knees nearly buckle from their numbness.

The head guy whips out a chain at me. The shackles on its end wrap around my wrists and connect with a snap. I'm now handcuffed to a chain ringed with spikes. They sink into my skin, ripping across my wrist. I cry out. The pain is like having a swarm of bees stinging me. But I can't focus on the pain or it will cripple me. I grit my teeth, knowing I still have a few more seconds of surprise on my side. I have to take advantage of every one.

I take a deep breath and backflip—without touching the ground this time because my hands are bound. The moment I land, I spin into a roundhouse and nail him with a hard kick in the neck. The girl and the other guy are behind me, and I back-kick and side-kick them in succession. My energy is draining, and with every kick I can feel my strength leaving me.

The taxi guy yanks on my chain, and I scream as the spikes dig into me. I race at him and shove my wrists at his body, allowing the spikes to sink into his skin. He crumples to the floor while I stagger to the other side of the small room to give myself space to assess the situation.

But I don't have to worry. My three captors are lying on the ground, moaning. Blood drips across my face and wrists as I stumble back over to the guy who was my taxi driver. After digging through his pockets, I find a ring of keys.

"You seem like decent people." I gasp in agony as I twist my wrists to unlock the chain. "But you sure know how to make enemies."

My hand trembles as I slide the key into the shackle lock. After it unlatches, I slowly pull the iron thorns from my wrist. Tears well up in my eyes, and I grit my teeth to keep from screaming too loud. The last thing I need is more of these guys showing up and beating the crap out of me.

Then I drop the handcuffs on the head guy's chest and hit him hard across the head with the chain so he passes out.

"That should keep you busy," I mutter. "Sweet dreams."

Thankfully, the door is unlocked. I stagger out into a long corridor, which looks more like the tunnel of a dungeon with its flickering yellow bulbs lining the corridor's ceiling like a ghost trail. I lean against one of the clammy concrete walls, trying to muster my strength. Every fiber in my body aches to touch the orb, but I know I need to wait to use it until I absolutely have to. It's almost as if I'm becoming addicted to its power. That thought alone stops me. If there is anything I hate worse than being beaten to a pulp, it is being controlled.

I'm debating which way to go down the hall when I spot my backpack hanging up in an alcove just ahead of me. I practically leap to unzip the top. My bow and equipment belt are still inside, safely hidden. They probably hadn't had a chance to check my backpack yet. If they did, there would be no way they'd leave it in this hellhole. I slip the bow out, and out of habit, lightly rub its surface and the image of the Blue Dragon as I assess the area.

On closer inspection, the alcove has a small desk with a map pinned above it. The map doesn't make much sense without any idea of where I am. A walkie-talkie is clipped to the wall next to it, and a tiny television monitor in the corner of the desk shows four quadrants, each one displaying multiple locations.

I study the screen, but each location shows an empty hall just like the one I'm standing in—except the bottom right. That one shows four guards standing in front of a pair of double doors, two per side. They wear that same blue Triad Guardian uniform with the dragon crest across the top right of the chest.

There's a reason why a door needs to have four guards. I rip the map off the wall and storm back into my previous cell. The two guys are still lying on the floor, sprawled out, but the girl is just standing as I enter. Her eyes widen when she sees me, and she takes a step back.

At her expression, I cringe. I've seen people look at me in a lot of different ways, but never with that look. One of fear and hatred. Still, I don't blame her. After all, I'm bound by contract to a monster.

"Where is the Grand Council meeting?" I hold the map in front of her face.

"I will never tell you," she says in English, spitting out each word.

She whips out a side-kick, smacking me in the ribs. I stumble back and drop the map as she comes at me with another kick. I block her leg.

"I have to talk to them," I say, and jump-kick her. Her body hits the wall. I crouch before her, my body tense, ready for her to move. "You all assume I'm here for the wrong reasons, but the Tiger of Shinshi said I was the only one who could get this orb. There must be a reason why he said that."

"We assume nothing. We know you are after the orb for your dark lord."

"Some things aren't the way they look. I'm trying to save my country. You'd do the same thing."

She looks at the map and me, indecision flickering across her eyes.

"I don't want to hurt you," I say. "I never have. If I wanted to, I could easily have killed you a long time ago."

"The Grand Council is meeting at Xi'an," she says, her eyes shifting between me and the door. "But you are probably too late. Maybe if you hurry you can reach them in time."

She's totally lying. The answer slips off her tongue too easily. But I smile and say, "Thank you."

Then I exit the room and duck into the shadows of the alcove. I press myself against the wall and listen to the door open. I peer around the corner, watching her limp down the corridor and then turn right. I check the monitors and watch which way she goes. Once she's out of sight, I unzip my backpack and unscrew my water bottle, splashing water over my face so that it's somewhat clean. Then I strap my equipment belt and *goong dae* full of arrows to my hip and grip my bow tight. I check the monitor one more time and see she has come to the door with the four guards. She's speaking to them, waving her hands frantically. A smile reaches my lips. She's led me right to the Grand Council.

I slip my pack over my shoulder before taking off in a full sprint down the corridor. My boots pound the concrete floor, and my pulse starts hammering. I hope I'm making the right choice by going to the Grand Council. This could be a suicide mission. But the reality is, this whole operation has become too difficult for me to do on my own. I need their help.

Up ahead I hear yelling and footsteps. The guards are coming for me. I stop and prep my bow, waiting for them. They barrel around the corner, and I unleash an arrow. It hits one guard in the knee. I've already loaded and let loose another arrow by the time they realize what's happening. Both guards fall to the ground, grabbing their legs.

I run past them and retrieve both arrows before moving on. At the next turn, the corridor opens up to an entryway that leads to the double doors I saw on the screen. They bear the Triad dragon crest. The doors are opening, and the girl is strutting inside.

The guards' eyes widen as they see me sprinting toward them. They start shouting at each other, and the one on the right reaches for a lever on the wall. Still running, I release another arrow, pinning his hand to the wall. He cries out, while his partner comes after me, flipping through the air. I leap into a sidekick to meet his attack midair. His foot slams into my side. Pain shoots through me, but I push through it and focus on landing and prepping for his imminent second attack.

As my feet touch the ground, I watch in horror as the second guard, who's holding his bleeding hand, kicks the lever. An iron grate falls from the ceiling. There isn't time to think. Only react. I have to take the risk because I'm desperate to speak to the Grand Council. I dive across the threshold, praying the grate's iron teeth won't sink into my body.

The gate booms closed behind me. Its impact shudders the ground. I leap to my feet only to be met by five ninja-looking warriors, all dressed in black, their faces hidden beneath masks.

CHAPTER 20

I stand perfectly still, holding my bow in one hand and an arrow in the other. The orb has fallen out of my shirt and emanates a faint glow. No one moves. They eye me, poised in a crouch as if waiting for someone to order them to strike.

The circular room I've just entered is cavernous, with an arched bronze ceiling coming to a point at a red stained-glass window in its center. The walls are painted with Chinese scenes illuminated by floor lights that run around the edge of the room. It's hard to tell in the dim light, but I guess there must be at least a hundred men and women sitting on silk cushions around the low horseshoe table that spans the room.

At the front of the horseshoe rises a stage, where a man stands. He's wearing a traditional Chinese robe, and his long white beard falls down his chest to a point at the bottom. He's got bushy eyebrows, and as I study him, his eyebrows rise.

I've found the Grand Council.

Still no one speaks. They just stare at me, and I get the prickling sensation that I'm not wanted. I expect one of the ninjas to stop me when I stride toward the stage, but they don't. Instead they scamper after me as if they've suddenly become my escorts. I keep my eyes focused and chin up, refusing to let them hear my heart pounding against my rib cage.

"How dare you enter our sacred sanctuary?" the robed man asks.

"I've come to seek help," I say as I place my foot on the first step.

A man at the end of the horseshoe grabs my arm. "Don't take another step," he says in a low growl. From his fair complexion and thick lilting accent, I'm guessing he's from a Nordic country. He frowns down at me as if he'd like to rip me in half.

The others slowly begin to rise. I take in all their faces, their lined lips, their guarded eyes. There are no friends here. Then my eyes fall on Marc, flanked by Jung. They're both wearing their modern *hanboks*, Korean tunics and linen pants. Their swords hang by their sides, and a black band with *Shinshi* written in Korean is wrapped around their foreheads.

Marc nods, imperceptibly. It's enough. I shrug the Nordic man's hand away and start to step onto the stage. He withdraws a knife from his side and moves to stab me. I spin to fully face him and lift my palm as if to block him.

"Stop!" I command. Light shoots out of the orb, radiating on the hand holding the knife. He cries out, screaming out words in his own language, and his knife clatters to the ground.

I whirl around, trying to figure a way to control the situation. I just need a few moments for them to hear me out so they can understand that we need to work together.

Ninjas leap out of the shadows, screaming as they attack me. I've never fought Guardians from Japan, nor do I wish to. I hold up the orb, creating a force field to protect me. Light shines from my body. My hair whips through the air as the force of the orb's power builds within me. The ninjas bounce off the force field and fall to the ground, passed out.

The power rushes through me, filling every muscle and nerve. It's overwhelming and wondrous all at once. It takes all of my inner strength to slip the orb beneath my shirt before I lose control and land in a heap in front of them. I can't let them know that my humanity limits my power. They must believe I am invincible. Otherwise I'm doomed.

The room, which once was restless, now lies in utter silence. I'm not sure if it's from shock, awe, or horror. There isn't time to analyze.

"I request to speak," I say.

The head of the Grand Council eyes me under his brooding eyebrows. "You walk on shifting ground. One misstep and you will die."

"Die?" I laugh at this. He honestly can't be serious. Does he not know that death would be a welcome reprieve? If he could only know that it's the living that keep me from giving up. It's knowing my family and friends are in jeopardy. Everything I do is for them. "I am living my death over and over. It is not my life that I value. I lost that when I signed this contract."

I hold up my arm, and the bronze Chinese letters of my contract sparkle in the dim light, leaving behind a trail of smoke. The head grimaces, but nods.

"The world has changed," I tell the group as I stride up the stairs to stand beside the head Guardian. "The immortals have widened the bridge between our world and theirs. The lines have shifted, and one god in particular is no longer content with ruling his land alone. This is my master, Kud."

The warriors before me no longer hold that wariness in their eyes. Now all I see is hostility. Their knuckles whiten as they grip their weapons. Their anger washes over me in waves mixed with a hint of fear. It's so strong, so palpable, I can taste it. It tastes like blood.

"He has sent me to find the last hidden artifact of Korea," I continue. "The six Korean orbs of life were hidden a millennium ago because our Guardians of Shinshi knew that if one man or immortal held all of them, that person would have unlimited power. But now that Kud is actively seeking these orbs, they are no longer safe in hiding. They must be returned to the Heavenly Chest. Of the six orbs, all have been found except the Black Turtle orb. This is my mission. To acquire it."

"How dare you come to us with such blasphemy!" one of the ninjas yells out.

"This is where I need your help," I continue, ignoring the scowls. Instead, I focus on Marc. I see the intensity in his eyes, as if he's willing me to speak, and the almost-smile on his lips. *He believes me.* This thought alone spurs me on.

"I need to get this orb and return it to the Heavenly Chest before Kud can take it. He has created many beings that are partly human and partly from the Spirit World. These creatures can enter any dimension, and it's only a matter of time before one of them finds it. But more than that, war is at Korea's doorstep. Even without this final orb, Kud is right now planning on unleashing his power on our land. The balance must be shifted against him, and the only way that can happen is if we find this final orb and return it to the Heavenly Chest."

"I don't feel good about this girl," an Egyptian woman yells. "Her arm bears the mark of evil, and I can feel it dripping from her pores even from where I stand."

I swallow back the lump in my throat and straighten my back. The woman is right. I reek of evil. It oozes off the words of the contract in my arm, crawling over my skin like a virus. But I have to believe that my heart is desperately trying to do what is right. I may be forced to serve Kud, but he can't control my heart.

"You don't understand," I say. "Kud doesn't mean to just control Korea. If he can gain all six orbs, he will move to control all of Asia. And then the world. He won't be content until he holds it *all* in his palm."

"This sounds utterly ridiculous," someone says.

No, I want to say. *What's ridiculous is how utterly blind you are.*

"I can't do this alone," I say. "I need to know where the orb is located, and I will require your assistance in bringing it back to Korea, since every mythological creature in this country seems intent on killing me."

"Have you considered that there is a reason you are being hunted?" the head Guardian says.

"I am not an idiot." I clench my bow. "Of course I know that."

"You are right about one thing. You cannot do it alone," the head Guardian says, and for a moment I grasp for hope like

I'm dangling on the edge of a cliff with a rope inches from my fingertips.

But then he smiles. "The place where the orb is hidden has been guarded by those who have watched over it for thousands of years. They are strong and terrible. The stench of you alone will make them rise up from their resting places to destroy you. I doubt you will complete this mission at all."

"Why even take the orb from its hiding place?" one of the Guardians asks.

"Kud will find the orb one way or another," I say. "He is raising the dead to do his bidding. He sent me with two of his assassins to make sure the task is completed. If I fail, they will just step in next."

This incites a flurry of heated discussions.

"What if she's right?" Marc calls out. "What if this is our window of opportunity to stop Kud? And if we let it pass us by, we won't be able to stop him. We must save the orb from him before it's too late."

"The boy has a point," a man says. "But it should be a Guardian of Shinshi who seeks this orb out."

"But aren't we playing right into her scheme?" the Egyptian woman asks. "She wants us to take the orb out of hiding. Whether we allow her or the Guardians of Shinshi to have it, we are still doing exactly what Kud wants."

I finger my arrow, itching to set it into my bow and unleash it. But that is exactly the kind of thought that Kud would have. I shiver, realizing how I'm even beginning to think like him more and more each day. I peek down at the contract, flowing across my skin like bronze lava. Even now, I can't deny the fact that it's poisoning my heart, my soul. I set my jaw tight. Kud will never own me. Still, I hate how close this Grand Council is to the truth of who I am becoming.

"Shall we bring it to a vote?" the head Guardian says. "All in favor of helping this thing of evil gain control of a second powerful Heavenly artifact—as we can see, she already has one— raise your hands."

I feel myself sagging within. *Thing of evil.* This is what I am to them.

Evil is something that is so profoundly wicked that it lacks even the hope of goodness within. I may not be perfect, but I'm definitely not bent on destruction or malice. Every step I take is a step toward destroying evil, not creating it.

After everything I've been through and after coming this close to the orb, it nearly breaks me to see myself failing now. To allow the very evil they speak of to win. And to think that I will die by the hands of those who should be my friends and allies. Is this what it has all come down to?

I look around and see no hands raised. I have not sacrificed everything to stand here and face failure. To be called what I most despise. To be looked at as what I once hunted.

"The Grand Council has decided," the head Guardian says gravely. "You will be taken into custody and kept until a decision has been made on what is to be done with you. According to the Shinshi, if you are dead, your orb cannot be used. This may be another way to stop Kud."

They mean to kill me. How ironic that I've become more valuable dead than alive. I don't bother to explain to them that Kud has the power to control the dead, since no one seems to care to listen to me anyway. The orb may not have as much power in my lifeless fingers as in those of a walking dead, but Kud could still use it.

Dad's face comes to mind, and I think about that poster he's got hanging over his desk with the words of Martin Luther King, Jr.: *The ultimate measure of a man is not where he stands in moments of comfort and convenience, but where he stands at times of challenge and controversy.* Dad had always quoted it when I felt overwhelmed.

I hold out the orb. "Show me an exit," I whisper to it.

The orb's light radiates out in a long silky rope, whirling around and around the room, seeking a way out. But the light finally stops spinning and draws back into the orb. My heart sinks as I look down at the angry faces eyeing me warily.

I'm alone in a room full of the greatest warriors on the planet. And they are all desperate to kill me.

CHAPTER 21

My mind frantically scrambles as the ninjas and Triads stalk around the base of the stage like a group of lionesses circling their prey. The head Guardian leaves as a group of barrel-chested men creep toward the stairs.

There's no way I can overtake all these warriors. I could take down a few of them, but it would mean killing good and innocent people, and then I would die. I consider giving myself up and waiting for another opportunity to escape. I look at Marc and he's smiling. What the heck?

He looks pointedly at my equipment belt and then above. I follow his gaze to the glass window overhead. Now it's my turn to smile. I whisper a call for a force field to my orb. As the light surrounds me, I pull my tether and ascender from my belt. With a cry, the Guardians rush at me as one. Pressure hits the force field I've created, and I realize that someone here must have the power to break through my barrier. It's only a matter of time before I will weaken and be unable to withstand the attack.

Their movement is distracting, so I close my eyes, focusing on keeping the force field in place as I fumble with attaching the tether to my arrow.

Finally I fit the arrow to my bow and pull the string back to a full draw. The arrow flies, soaring up, and sinks into the wooden beam next to the window. I let out a sigh of relief and sling my bow over my shoulder. Then I grip the handle of the ascender with both hands and release the spring-loaded device. The sound of the ascender racing up the rope fills my ears as I try to block out the angry cries from below.

Sweat drips from my forehead, and dizziness washes over me. A shower of bullets skitters off my barrier. Halfway to the ceiling, I begin gasping for breath, and my stomach heaves. This is the longest I've ever used the orb's power without passing out.

There's shouting and running below. From the corner of my eye I see the grate lift. They must have realized I'm heading outside and are planning on stopping me there.

When I finally reach the top, I kick out the window. Red shards of glass rain down into the room below. Holding on to the beam, I swing myself through the new opening onto the ground above.

The air hangs heavy and thick around me, smelling of fresh-cut grass and flowers. I'm standing in a garden fenced in by wooden beams. I spin in a circle, trying to figure out which way to go.

Exit, I think to the orb.

A ray of light shoots across the garden and into a cedar forest. I leap over the fence and race through the cedar trees. Their branches hang low over the mist-draped forest floor. The scents of cedar and moss fill the air, and I wish I could stop and drink it all in. After a few minutes, I pause at a signpost and throw up. I've been using the orb too much. My hands shake as I tuck the orb inside my shirt.

The sign says the exit is just ahead, but I need to give my body a break. There's too much at stake for me to pass out. At the same time, I feel conflicted. I know it will be only a few minutes before they discover my location. They know where the roof of their meeting place is and that I can't have gone far.

I force myself to stand and take a step, then another. After each step I lean against a tree trunk until the dizziness fades. My pace begins to quicken, but I'm not recovering fast enough, because soon I hear the Guardians' voices shouting through the fog.

Then the roar of a truck rumbles through the air. I break into a jog and prep my bow as I run. Lights cut the fog, and I can make out the form of a box truck bouncing over the dirt road. The window rolls down. I drop to my knees and shoot.

The driver ducks and the truck swerves in the road.

"Jae! It's me! Marc."

I pause before I shoot my next arrow. Sure enough, that's Marc's head peeking out. He stops the truck and leans across the seat to open the passenger door.

"Get inside," he yells. "Hurry."

I hesitate, trying to read his face through the mist. Can I really trust him? I think about his note, which led me here, and how he pointed to the roof. He's been true to his word thus far.

Down the road, Guardians barrel toward me. A gun fires. I leap up and run to the truck, bullets ricocheting at my feet. As I dive onto the seat, Marc guns the engine, and the tires kick up dirt behind us. I pull myself to sitting and manage to yank the door closed.

"Where are we going?" I ask.

"Anywhere but here," he says. "We've been ordered to shoot you on sight."

"That's reassuring. So why are you disobeying orders?"

"They were tempting, I must admit." He shifts gears and careens onto the main highway. "But I'll pass. You're too darn sexy in that shirt."

"You don't happen to have a gun, do you?"

"It's against the code of the Shinshi. We only fight with our sacred weapons, unlike some of the other Guardian groups. I guess we never had to deal with crazy fighter girls like you before."

He gives me a lopsided grin.

"I've missed you," I say. "But you shouldn't have done this. You could get in a lot of trouble."

"They'll probably kick me out." He shrugs and then swerves around a slow driver. "But sometimes you've got to go with your gut."

He takes the first exit and slams the truck into overdrive. The truck bounces over potholes and belches out a cloud of black smoke. I grip the side of the seat.

"Where are we going?" I ask.

"See that big mound up there?"

A huge temple-like structure looms up within a valley of rounded mountains. We pass a road sign for the Mausoleum of Emperor Qin Shi Huang. Signs with his picture point visitors to a parking lot. But it's the line of black trucks—and black-dressed men emerging from the trucks and running up the long series of steps to the top of the tomb—that causes me to grab Marc's wrist.

"They're here," I say.

"Damn it," Marc mutters. "They must have radioed ahead and beat us to the tomb. We need to come up with another plan."

Marc skirts around the mound and veers down a dirt road into the fields of a neighboring farm.

"They're here because this is where the orb is, isn't it?" I study the massive hill as we edge around it. The mausoleum looks like a ziggurat or a Mayan temple covered with brush and grass, as if it's trying to blend in with the mountains but failing miserably. "Why are you taking me here? You know I work for Kud."

I'm testing him. I want him to believe in me, but I also want to know why and how far he will go. There's no doubt that he's changed in the last few months since he became a Guardian. His shoulders are broader, his hands are rougher, and he's got a thin layer of stubble on his chin. He's becoming a man. With every second we're apart, we're both changing.

Time and distance do funny things. They can tear you apart from those you love until there comes a point when you hardly recognize each other. I search his face for clues about how deep his decision to help me goes.

Marc drives into thick foliage next to a brick shed that looks as if it's ready to collapse. One side has crumbled, leaving a gaping hole. Branches scrape the sides of the truck until we're completely buried within the trees. An open field stretches on one side of us, ending at a line of brick houses, while the other side of the tree line ends at another wide-open field of tall, waving grass with the mausoleum planted in the center.

He switches off the ignition and then rakes his hands through his hair. He turns to face me with those green eyes of his that make me want to grab him and force him to stay beside me forever.

"I know you, Jae. I've been there with you through all of this insanity. We've had rough times. No." He shakes his head and laughs. "We've been through hell. Maybe we're still there, rattling around, trying every door to escape. But last night your words got me thinking. I'd do it all again—every second of it— to be with you."

"You would?" My voice cracks, and tears stream down my face. I reach up and trail my fingers over the scar along his jaw.

He grabs my hands, kisses my fingers, and whispers, "Absolutely."

The space between us feels too far, and I need him closer. I grab his shirt with both fists and pull him in, seeking his lips as if I'm starving. His mouth burns warm against mine, and I drink in his smell. His touch. His presence.

His lips kiss my forehead, and he whispers my name. I move my hands up to his neck and wrap my arms around his shoulders, clinging to him.

"I wish—" I swallow. "I wish."

"Shh." Marc kisses my lips. "We have everything we could ever want. Right here. Right now. After this moment, there are no guarantees for us anymore. Let there be no more promises between us except our love. Okay?"

I nod, unable to speak. My hands still shake as I cup his face and look into his eyes. What I see is the strength that I have lost somewhere in my darkness.

"Help me find a way, Marc," I say. "I'm so lost. And alone. And confused."

"I have something I've been meaning to give you. I bought it after Kud let us meet on the mountain, but you were taken away so quickly. I should've given it to you a long time ago." He withdraws a chain from around his neck. At the bottom is a square gold pendant. He shows it to me. Inscribed on the back are the words,

I'LL FIND YOU IN THE DARKNESS

I shake my head. "You don't understand. This is a death where I never stop dying. It's a darkness that is slowly eating at me, consuming everything I know and love until I'm nothing but a corpse."

I hand the necklace back to him, but he lifts it over my head and settles it around my neck.

"You're right. I don't understand. But I'm here and I'm not leaving. Will that be enough?"

I let out a long breath, the tension in my chest easing. I finger the pendant's smooth surface. "Yes. It's enough."

CHAPTER 22

The dense woods make it nearly impossible to open my door, much less slide out of the truck. The air around us lies in hushed silence. Through the branches, the skyline is streaked with reds and oranges as the sun escapes from the oncoming darkness. Despite the heat, I wrap my arms around myself and close my eyes.

I visualize what is about to unfold. Us entering the tomb, retrieving the orb, and exiting alive. It's the most irrational, idiotic plan I've yet to come up with.

"We should wait until the sun finishes setting." Marc rounds the truck to meet me. "Sneak in after dark when they're least expecting it."

"We'll never make it past all those Guardians, get the orb, and make it back out alive," I mutter.

Marc doesn't answer. Instead he stares at the tomb, his jaw tightening, and then he starts digging through the back of the truck. Soon he pulls out a blanket and his backpack.

"We should get a few minutes' rest. You don't look so good," he says, and then he tromps over to the shed. He yanks open the wooden door and peers inside. "This could work."

It doesn't take us long to make up a little camp inside the shelter. Marc withdraws two granola bars and a package of *kim* from his backpack, and we settle down to wait until darkness. For the first time since I stepped out of the airplane here in China, I allow my muscles to relax, and I ease deeper into the soft blanket.

"Maybe they'll think we've gone somewhere else," Marc says. "Like the Triad Headquarters or back to Xi'an."

"I seriously doubt it."

We eat for a few minutes in silence before Marc turns on his tablet and pulls up a picture of an ancient map labeled "Mausoleum."

"You sure your map is correct?"

He nods, and his body stiffens. This information has to have belonged to the Guardians of Shinshi, and by leaving the group and going rogue, he's just betrayed their trust and broken his sacred oaths. I pray his sacrifice will be worth it.

"It's hard to tell where the entrance is from this map," he says.

"This is all they gave you?" I ask. "No other instructions?"

"My instructions were to stop you."

"Right."

He touches the center of the picture. The screen changes to show a map outlining the layout of the tomb. "This is the only map we have of the inside of the tomb, and it was drawn by a Guardian based on secondhand directions from another Guardian."

"That's reassuring."

"The tomb has two courtyards." He points to the map labeled Outside Wall and Inner Wall. "Once we find a way through these two chambers, then we can enter the inner chamber where the burial coffin and all the treasures are. According to Shinshi legend, the orb is located there."

"This is good." I toss my crumbs onto the ground. For the first time in this whole trip, I'm feeling hopeful. "We can do this."

"Sure." He shrugs. "Just as long as we survive the booby traps and mercury rivers that are supposedly there. Look here." He points to a section of the map. "See how there are four passageways that lead down to the outer chamber? Well, only one of them actually leads you to the outer chamber. The others are death traps."

"You're just full of great news today." I moan. "Wait. Look at each corner of the map. It has the four guardians: the Blue Dragon, the White Tiger, the Black Turtle, and the Red Phoenix. These have to stand for east, west, north, and south."

Marc zooms in on each creature's symbol. I point my finger at the Red Phoenix's symbol and then pull out my compass from my belt. "If that symbolizes the entrance, then it's on the southern side, which would be there."

I point in the direction of the left side of the temple from where we sit.

"Nice work, Fighter Girl," he says.

"But once we're inside," I say, "it should be fairly easy to determine which direction to go, right?"

"The Council of Shinshi mentioned that things may not really be what they seem."

"What's that supposed to mean?"

"Legend speaks of walls lined with bows triggered to shoot arrows at any intruders."

"You're kidding, right? That sounds like something from a movie."

He pulls out two handheld breathing devices and hands one to me. "Considering that the legends have always had some truth to them, I figured it was best to be prepared."

"I'm supposed to hold that to my face *and* maneuver around flying arrows?"

"Wait. I thought you were invincible." He grins, but when I just frown at him, he clears his throat and slides the oxygen tanks and his tablet back into his backpack. "I'm hoping your orb can help us out if we get lost."

I take a deep breath. "It can, but it will tire me out. You'll have to do most of the fighting."

"We'd better get some rest, then."

Marc leans against the wall and pulls me closer until my head is resting on his chest. We don't speak. All that's left is the beating of our hearts. Through the open door, I watch the clouds drip with the ginger and crimson rays of the day's last light. The colors remind me of blood and pain, and I shut my eyes to block the images. Instead I focus on the warmth of Marc's body and the steady thrum of his heartbeat.

• • •

It's the warmth of the orb, pulsing warning beats against my chest, that drags me out of my deep sleep. I blink awake, trying to sort through the shadows around me. The door of the shed bangs against the wall in a steady thump, allowing moonlight to leak in.

A glint of silver catches my eye. I jerk to sitting and finally can make out the jagged outline of a sword. Sang Min's sword. There isn't another like it in this universe. Two forms loom over us, their outlines dark against the moonlit sky. My heart stops. Kud's goons have found us. I've no idea how. Not even the Chinese Guardians or the Shinshi have been able to track us, but somehow the Stiffs have hunted us down. Beside me Marc's muscles tense, and his hand snakes out to unsheathe his own weapon.

"Kwan!" I cry out, forcing my voice to sound pleasantly surprised. "You've found me! I'm so glad. I've had the worst time of things."

And then I start blathering nonsense about being chased by mythological creatures. *Truth*. Kidnapped in a taxi by a Triad Guardian. *Truth*. Escaping my kidnappers who had chained me to spiked handcuffs. *Truth*. And teaming up with Marc, who has promised to help us. *Truth!* Kwan and Sang Min don't respond, and it's too dark to be able to tell what they are thinking. If they had lie-detector sensors, I'm sure I would have passed with flying colors.

"Marc here thinks he knows where the orb is," I say. "We need him to lead us."

"I thought you had the White Tiger orb," Kwan says. "He is unnecessary."

I swallow, all my excuses piling up in the lame quadrant.

"But I have the intel on how to defeat each chamber we enter," Marc says. "No man has exited the mausoleum and lived to tell about it in a thousand years. You need me to survive. Remember?"

"The master must hear of this." Kwan withdraws his phone.

I leap up. "Are you sure that's the best idea? He doesn't need to know how we succeed, just that we succeed."

Sang Min spins his sword around his palm, a low growl rumbling from his throat. Kwan shakes his head no at Sang Min and hands me the phone.

"You call him," he says.

I stare at the phone and slowly accept it, my stomach knotting up. The plastic stings my fingers like it's covered with frost despite the humidity of the night. I don't know how to explain it, but every time I hear Kud's voice, he has a power over me. It makes me want to hurl the phone against the wall.

"You choose," Kwan says. "We kill you both or you speak to the master."

I weigh the odds of us fighting these two and winning. There's a good chance we could win, but we'd probably get injured. It's not worth the risk, so I push the dial button and wait.

Kud answers on the first ring. "My darling princess," he says in a thick voice. A burning sensation bubbles from the contract on my arm and slides its way up through my arm into my body. "I heard you have had difficulties. Tell me this is not so."

"Good evening, Master," I say, using my warmest voice. Then I turn so I don't have to see the fury passing over Marc's face. "Yes, there have been difficulties. The mythological creatures don't seem to like me. I haven't a clue why. And then the Triads kidnapped me. It's been rather challenging. But don't worry. Now that Sang Min and Kwan have found me, the three of us will be able to enter the tomb together. We should have the orb within a few hours."

"Excellent," Kud says. "It has been lonely here without you. I look forward to us spending more time together once you return."

I can't stand listening to him for another second. Somehow I manage a sweet good-bye.

The second he clicks off, I let the phone drop to the hard-packed earth. Kwan rushes to pick it up, gently dusting it off with a cloth.

"The two of you sound like good friends," Marc says in an annoyed tone as he begins collecting our items.

I widen my eyes at him, wishing I had telepathic powers. He's got to realize he needs to play along with this crazy-making game because if Thing One or Thing Two believes for one second that I'm double-crossing them, they'll slit our throats.

"Yes," I say in my most airy and non-me voice. "We are. I'm just so thrilled I can please him. It's been hard to be so far apart."

Marc looks up from his packing and scrunches up his face. He opens his mouth as if to say something, but then clamps his lips together and simply nods.

"Sounds like a blast." He straps his scabbard and pack to his back. "The four of us working together. A great team."

"Right." I sling my bow over my shoulder and check my belt and quiver, making sure all my supplies are intact. "Kwan and Sang Min, let me introduce you properly. This is Marc, an ex-Guardian of Shinshi. Marc, this is Kwan and Sang Min, two dead warriors from a long time ago who once were the fiercest warriors of their day. Kud gave them an almost-life, and now they are helping me find the orb."

"We should leave," Kwan says gruffly. "The night is aging."

"Party time," Marc says lightly, but his body posture and his hand lingering on his weapon speak otherwise.

"Do you think people will notice us?"

"What?" Marc says. "Two teens and two dead guys walking through a field with weapons? Nah." Then he checks his watch. "Besides. It's almost eleven. The tourists will be long gone."

I step out of the shed and push through the tree boughs. There in the distance the mound rises up like an ancient pyramid. Torches line the perimeter, and the place is blanketed in their glow. Music wafts to where we're standing.

"Looks like something is going on there." I twirl an arrow through my fingers.

"This does not look good." Kwan glares at Marc. "A trap, perhaps?"

"Trap? The place is riddled with traps." Marc grins as if he takes pleasure in making the Stiffs scowl. Then he shrugs and says, "It looks like a festival of some sort. Let's hope they are too distracted by Jae looking smoking hot to notice how weird you look."

Kwan turns from Marc and slips on his sunglasses, which is ridiculous since it's dark out, while I smack Marc on the arm.

"Come on, boys," I say. "Let's kick some Guardian butt."

We are totally going to die.

CHAPTER 23

A light mist drifts over the field, weaving in and out of the tall grass. As we draw closer to the mound ahead of us, the music grows louder. Torches flicker every few feet around the top of the tomb and up the steps.

"Definitely a festival," Marc says.

"And our friends are there, too." I eye the Triads positioned along the steps, which rise up the top. "We should go up the back."

As we move closer, we resort to crawling on our bellies so as not to attract the attention of the patrolling Guardians on top of the tomb. The Stiffs are silent as a *gwishin*, which is about the only thing we've got going for us. The full moon above is bright and plump and ringed with clouds, their wisps curling around it like barbed wire.

The moonlight was useful earlier, but now I'm wishing for darkness to cloak our approach. All a Guardian has to do is stare at the field long enough to see our moving forms.

Once we reach the wooded area, the ground begins to rise, and we scamper up the sides of the mound, darting from tree to tree. We hunker down on the outer side of the wooden fence that surrounds the courtyard at the top of the mausoleum. Marc was absolutely right. There's a festival of some sort happening. Dancers dressed in long white gowns and holding bowls of food move about on a large square mat that takes up most of the courtyard. Men in ceremonial dress line either side of the mat, holding colorful flags.

The musicians play in one corner while a crowd gathers around the dancers, videotaping and taking pictures. The dancers have the rapt attention of everyone except for the Triads, whose eyes scope the crowd like hawks. Even though they are dressed in solid black, they stick out like traffic cones.

"I count eight," Marc says.

"Ten," I say. "There are two more guards on the other side of that big plaque. Plus all those on the stairs."

"This is going to be difficult," Marc says.

"There's no way around it." I pull out my bow and prep an arrow, looking meaningfully at Kwan and Sang Min. "No killing, got it?"

As usual, Sang Min growls in frustration and Kwan gives no response. Marc takes a deep breath and adjusts his grip on his sword. The fence's beams are designed in an intricate pattern, so there's no way to slide through them. I vault over the top, but unfortunately I draw far too much attention. The guard a few feet away whips out a knife and throws it at me. I dive to the ground, releasing an arrow at the same time. As I roll across the brick-lined path, Sang Min swings his sword, knocking the back of the Triad's head. He slumps to the ground.

"This way," Marc says.

We scamper after Marc, through the shadows to the entrance on the west side, but we've now alerted all the Triads. While some race full force after us, four others stand in front of the entrance, blocking it. The four of us halt at the entrance. I glance around. We are now completely surrounded.

"Move aside." I lift my bow and aim it at the center Triad blocking the door.

Oddly, he bows and says something in Mandarin, doing exactly what I've asked of him. The others follow suit. Which is weird. Marc glances at me, his eyebrow rising. He's as surprised as I am.

"They say we may enter and die if we so choose," Marc says.

"Well." I flash a smile at them. "How considerate."

We shuffle down the sloping ramp, eyeing the Triads as they slowly step away. I'm trying to figure out why they would guard this tomb so heavily only to allow us to enter. The slope ends at a set of iron double doors. Two round knockers hang on either side of a dragon image. I grasp one knocker, which is cold beneath my sweaty palms, but I can't gather the courage to pull it toward me because everything about this moment is off-kilter.

"This is your chance to leave." I look over at Marc. "You know you don't have to do this for me. I love you no matter what."

"I'm not going anywhere," Marc says.

Just as I pull back on the knocker, a screech fills the air. I spin around as a massive flying horse with antlers and dragon-like scales dives through the cloudy wisps, flying toward us at a startling speed. It's a blinding sapphire blue, and the hair of its mane and tail burns like flames. I kneel and aim my arrow.

"It's a *qilin*!" Marc yells. "Usually they are considered good luck, but I think it sees us as malicious. Watch out!"

Just as I release my arrow, a blast of fire rains down on us from the creature.

Marc and I dive for the sides of the mausoleum entrance and cling to the stone walls, shading our eyes from the inferno. Kwan throws open the doors and dives inside. But Sang Min takes the brunt of the attack. His clothes burst into flames. His pantaloons flare into red and orange like torches until all I can make out of him through the blaze is his long hair burning, his empty eyes wide, and his mouth open in a scream.

His voice conjures terror through me, and I huddle against the stone. Dark black smoke gushes out of his open mouth, and the Triads watching at the top of the slope retreat, clamping their hands over their ears and backing away. The creature swoops back into the air, beating its long wings, and circles above. There's no doubt in my mind: it's preparing for another attack. If we're going to enter the tomb, we need to do it now.

Marc grabs my arm and shoves me around the screaming Sang Min and through the double doors. The moment our bodies pass through the doorway, Kwan slams both doors shut, drowning us in darkness.

"We're just going to leave Sang Min out there?" I ask, trying to catch my breath. "That creature will kill him."

"He was dead the second his body burst into flame," Kwan says.

"I'm pretty sure Sang Min is happy to be put out of Kud's service." Marc flicks on his flashlight.

"What exactly is a *qilin*?" I ask.

"It's a Chinese unicorn. They're considered good luck, unless you're evil and you're hurting someone who is pure. Then they're fierce in their punishment. I'm not sure if it was attacking all of us or just Sang Min."

"Let's avoid those."

"Agreed," Marc says.

I study the iron doors illuminated in the glow from Marc's flashlight. Sang Min's screams and the thumps from his fist pounding the doors echo against the walls. I shiver at the sounds as I take in the imprint on the iron doors. It's a monster with fangs and horns. Its mouth is gaped wide open as if eager to eat us alive. Goose bumps run up and down my arms.

"A *taotie*." Marc follows the lines of the creature and then the writing above with his flashlight. "A symbol of how we'll be eaten whole by the tomb."

Kwan grunts and holds his sword out before moving around the area. We're standing in a square entryway about ten feet across in every direction, with two more doors positioned directly in front of us. These two are more intricate, wooden and carved with all kinds of designs. Giant circular iron knockers with the face of the *taotie* on them mimic the image on the outer iron doors. I swallow the lump in my throat and step across the threshold.

"No time like the present." And I throw open the next set of doors.

A long stone passageway slopes down before us. Fire-lit brass urns line the base of carved walls, their flames flickering like snake tongues. I study the carvings. Monsters, dragons, lions, and all types of beasts are portrayed on the walls all the way down the slope.

"Do the Chinese Guardians come in here and light these torches?" I ask.

"No, from what I heard, none of them dare. It's believed that if you enter, you'll die," Marc says. "The builders of this mausoleum filled the candles with salamander fat blessed by the gods. It was thought to last for eternity."

The three of us pass through the double doors to stand on the platform at the top of the sloping corridor. It's beautiful, but there's something dark and magical in the air. I can taste it, feel it pressing around me and sinking into my skin. It's then that I notice how my arm tingles. I lift it up, and the bronze contract blazes bright in the murky light.

"This place is connected to the Spirit World." I say this in a whisper, afraid something lingering in the shadows might hear me.

"How do you know?" Marc asks.

"I can feel it," I say. "It's like breathing in mountain air on a winter night. It's cold and invigorating. Like I've been woken up after a long sleep. Plus, look." I hold up my arm for them to see the contract, its bronze liquid shining.

"Indeed the princess is right," Kwan says. "We must be vigilant."

Princess? Marc mouths.

I widen my eyes, trying to tell Marc to just go with it, and I start down the slope. Suddenly Marc yanks me back. The doors slam behind us, and a sizzling sound fills this second passageway.

"What was that noise?" I whisper.

"Whatever it is, it can't be good," Marc says. "And I don't like the look of those skeletons on the floor."

I squint through the torchlight. Sure enough, the path before us is littered with bones.

"I will go first," Kwan says. "You follow."

"Dude, be my guest," Marc says.

I strap my bow to my back and hold out my hands, ready to spring into action as I tiptoe in Kwan's wake. I hold my breath, hating the deathly silence of this passageway. We're about to reach the first bump in the path when a whizzing sound whirs through the air. Something spins from the long indent in the wall to my right.

"Watch out!" I scream.

But it's too late. A stream of arrows shoots out from the slot. One after another sinks into Kwan. He dives forward, clutching his arm and screaming in pain. Then, as he's about to stumble past the next indent, Marc yells out, "Don't move!"

The whizzing sound begins again. Kwan ducks back, only getting a few hits this time. The rest of the arrows fly across the other side of the passageway, burning up in the flaming urn.

"It's a trap," Marc says and squats down, rubbing his chin. "I've read that the emperor has this whole tomb rigged with them."

"You okay?" I ask Kwan. He's groaning and hunched over. Black blood drips from his hand as he rips out the arrows and tosses them aside.

"I hate it when you're right." I grimace at Marc.

"Honestly, I didn't think that, after a millennium, this tomb would still hold working traps." Marc runs his fingers over a groove in the floor. Dust cakes his fingers. "It doesn't make sense. It's not possible."

"But if this place is connected to the Spirit World," I say, "it makes perfect sense."

Marc eases up to the indent in the wall. He presses his face against the rock and shines a flashlight into the crack.

"Man," Marc says. "This is wild stuff. It kind of looks like a pulley system."

He takes out a granola bar wrapper and throws it in front of the crack. On cue, a stream of arrows shoot out, slicing a hole through the wrapper and slamming into the fire on the other side. Marc shakes his head and whistles.

"I think air currents rotate a rotor, made from what looks like butterfly wings, that triggers a pulley system. Then it releases a series of arrows."

"So, in order to pass, we can't create any air movement."

"Basically impossible," Marc says.

"Go on your belly," Kwan says from his squatting position. "All my arrows hit waist-high and above."

Marc and I look at each other.

"Try your backpack," I tell Marc.

He holds the strap and slides the pack across the space where the indent is. Nothing happens. I pull off my bow and slide it to the other side of the indent. Again, no arrows.

"Do you think it can discern living from nonliving?" I say.

"Only one way to find out." Marc drops to his belly and looks up at me. "You really want to do this?"

I let out a long breath. I didn't come all this way to chicken out now. I join him on the dusty floor, and together we both slide over to Kwan. I smile as I gather up the arrows that Kwan's pulled out of his arm. We've outsmarted this corridor. I just hope we're this lucky through the whole tomb.

"Give me a piece of your shirt," I tell Kwan. "These extra arrows might come in handy."

Kwan hands me a strip of his shirt, and I wipe away the blood. But as I do, I notice his black blood is mixed with a tinge of blue. Beads of sweat drip from the tip of Kwan's nose, and his mouth dips in a frown. He sways a little as he yanks out the last arrow. It's hard to tell if he's in pain, because he looks miserable pretty much all the time anyway.

"This blue." I bite my lips, wondering if I should say anything. "I think the arrow tips are dipped in poison."

"Then we must hurry," Kwan snaps.

He has a point. I clutch my bundle of arrows, and we inch our way down the rest of the passageway until we reach the last indent. My stomach feels sore from rubbing across the stone, and as I push myself forward, my wrists still ache from the shackles earlier.

"Stop." I hold out my hands, noticing something different about the ground.

Just on the other side of the last indent, the floor disappears. I grab Marc's flashlight and shine it through the gap. The light doesn't find a bottom. Then I point it to where the path should have gone. After about three feet of nothingness, the path reappears, levels out, and enters an arched doorway.

"We need to jump over that." I indicate the gaping hole before us with the flashlight. "But the arrow contraption makes a running start impossible."

Something slithers over my hand. A black centipede as long as my finger crawls over it. I shake the bug away. Then another one appears. I roll onto my back and shine the flashlight around me. My heart stops.

"Oh God," I say.

The once-smooth brick passageway is now swarming with black centipedes, creeping steadily toward us. Eyeing the slats in the walls, I slowly stand, making sure my body is between the areas where the arrows will fly out.

"We've got to think of a way across." Marc joins me at the edge, crushing the centipedes with the heels of his boots. "And fast."

Kwan takes his spear and slides it out so that it lands on the other side. "Hold this end," he tells Marc. "I will cross, then the princess, then you."

"Wait a second." Marc holds Kwan back. "How do I know you won't just get to the other side and take Jae with you?"

He glares at Marc. "Tempting as it is, the princess says you are needed to find this chamber. Your life is still a necessity."

"I don't care who goes first, just as long as we hurry." I kick at the centipedes climbing up my legs. There are too many. It won't be long before they cover every inch of our bodies. I can hardly focus as Marc bends down to hold the end of the spear while Kwan grips its shaft and swings out over the lip of the hole.

"Don't look down," Marc says.

Grunting, Kwan slides his way across the chasm. The muscles on his arms strain from holding up his weight, his legs swing over nothing, and his black cape swirls about him. When he reaches the other side, he palms the edge with one hand, but his hand slips. He is barely able to hold on, dangling with one hand gripping the spear. Marc lies down and pushes his weight onto the edge of the spear to keep it from rotating.

"I cannot find a place to hold," Kwan says.

"Use your axe," I say.

"Get these things off me!" Marc yells. Since he's lying on the ground, they have converged on him, covering his body like a moving blanket. "They're killing me!"

Frantically I use my bow to brush away the ones on his back, tossing as many as I can into the hole beside us. But there are too many of them, and within a few seconds they return in full attack. They crawl up my back and arms, biting me. I suppress my screams and focus on keeping them off Marc.

Meanwhile, Kwan grunts from the strain, blood pooling around his hand and probably making it slippery for him to hang on. Finally he reaches into his pouch and withdraws his axe. He swings the axe through the air and wedges it into a crack in the rock. The axe holds, and he swings himself up onto the shelf on the other side.

The spear shifts and falls off Kwan's end of the edge. Marc grabs hold of it, grunting under its weight, and heaves it up before it tumbles into the gaping hole. But the end of the spear must have swung too high, because a rain of arrows flies over our heads.

"Grab it!" Marc yells at Kwan and then to me, "Hurry!"

On the other side, Kwan holds the spear as I ease down to grab it. I know that it's far steadier than when Kwan was crossing it because both ends are being held down, but my stomach still churns as I clutch the spear with both hands and slip off the edge. My heart does a little dive as my body pulls at my hands, and then I'm dangling over nothingness.

I begin inching my way across the spear, wishing I'd spent more time on the monkey bars at school. My muscles strain at the pull, but Marc's cries prod me to move faster. The centipedes are likely eating him alive.

Kwan lifts me up on the other side, and Marc starts his crossing. I cringe when I see the centipedes have found Kwan's spear and are scampering after him like hungry little demons.

"Hurry, Marc!" I lie on the edge, my hands reaching out to grab him. "Just a little farther!"

The centipedes crawl up his hands, onto his arms, and onto his neck. His jaw is set and his eyes are focused on moving. Kwan reaches down and grabs him by the back of his shirt, lifting him up, and practically throws him next to me. I help pull him over the edge and rip his shirt off. The centipedes cover his back. They're everywhere.

He's panting and lying very still. Panic grips me like it never has before.

I start screaming. I can't stand the thought of them hurting him like this. I beat the bugs off Marc with his shirt, ignoring how his whole torso is swelling like a red balloon. Then I pull off his boots and pants, repeating my actions. I don't stop until every freaking bug is dead or thrown over the edge of the hole. Once I'm done, I roll him over and press my ear to his heart.

"He is most likely dead, or will be from the centipedes' poison," Kwan says in a flat voice.

Then I hear it. The steady *thump, thump* of the heartbeat that I love. I pull Marc onto my lap, bringing his head to my chest.

"He's alive." I glare at Kwan.

I rip open Marc's backpack and rummage through it until I find his stash of medicine and an EpiPen. I quickly pull off the cap and jam the needle into his thigh as hard as I can until it is empty. Using Marc's canteen, I pour water over his body and inspect his swollen bites. It doesn't seem like enough. I squeeze the entire tube of medical ointment over his chest and smear it everywhere. I kiss his forehead and whisper into his ear, trying to comfort him even if he can't hear me.

"We should leave him and move on." Kwan positions his spear in attack mode and scans the area. "This tomb will not let us relax. The boy has no connection to the Spirit World. He will not heal as quickly as we will."

Marc's eyes flutter open. He looks at his half-naked body and grunts.

"You could've just asked me," he mumbles, giving me a lopsided grin.

I hit him with his shirt and then pull him into a fierce hug, which makes him moan in pain. Then I shoot Kwan a told-you-so look. "See. He's fine. We wait until he's ready."

"Not fine," Kwan mutters. "But alive."

Suddenly I turn to him, needing to know his answer to the question that has been nagging at me. "Was your sacrifice worth it?" I ask Kwan. "The one you made at Kusong?"

He doesn't respond, staring off at the entryway, and I think he hasn't heard me. But then he says, "Maybe I was foolish to make a deal with the god of darkness. Maybe there could have been a better way. I do not know. What has been done is done."

There's such finality to his words that they sink heavily into me as I help Marc dress. It's a slow process because he can barely move, and his skin is so swollen that his clothing barely fits. All the while Kwan stalks in front of the entryway, growling into the darkness.

"What's wrong with him?" Marc asks.

"There's something waiting for us on the other side of this doorway," I whisper. "We can feel it."

CHAPTER 24

I force my fingers to work as I slide Marc's shirt over his head, but my eyes keep being drawn to the darkness. Just through the doorway a pair of yellow eyes glows, watching. But the moment I blink, they vanish, and I wonder if I've finally gone mad.

"Ow fwiends can't stay avay." Marc's words are slurred, as if his tongue is swollen. He nods to the walls on either side of the pit.

Sure enough, the centipedes are scurrying along the walls and inching their way toward us. I snatch up my bow and arrows and nod to Kwan. Whether we're ready to move on or not, we'll have to.

We creep to the arched doorway, each holding out our weapons. Marc struggles with every step, leaning on me for support. I'm tempted to have Kwan wait longer to let Marc rest, but relaxing by the pit won't help thanks to those horrible centipedes. The entryway leads us into another corridor, this one only about five feet in length. The memory of those yellow eyes makes each step nearly impossible for me. I prep my bow, aiming it at the ceiling, and then spin in a circle to check behind and in front of us. Eventually the corridor spits us out into a massive hall lit by torches.

Marc staggers and blinks, taking in the sight. "Wow," he says. "This place is incwedible."

"Are you okay?" I touch his arm.

"Doing betta." He gives a weak smile. "The EpiPen is the ticket."

"Maybe you should go back, take a rest."

"Naw. No way I'm leaving now."

The room is modeled after a Chinese palace. Before us are four towers made from stone, complete with wooden pagodas on top. Between each pair of towers is a closed gate, with the center gate being the largest. A massive bar stretches across it with dragon-faced handles. The walls are painted with ornate scenes of China: mountains, rivers, wildlife, and flowers.

Clay warriors line both edges of the room, their faces oddly lifelike with unique features and even hairstyles. Each figure is painted with bright pigments and a lacquer finish. Their plated armor is carved out in every detail, as are the spears, swords, and crossbows they hold.

"Amazing," Marc whispers beside me. "How is it that after all this time, this place has kept its original design all the way from the wooden pagodas to the paint on the terra-cotta warriors?"

"Another reason why I believe this place is connected to the Spirit World," I say.

"This must be the outer city," Marc says. "According to ground-penetrating radar, it's about four miles in diameter.

There are all kinds of chambers and rooms that were built for Qin Shi Huang's concubines and advisors."

"So we need to go through those gates," I say. "Seems simple enough."

The ceiling creaks. I look up to see trapdoors flipping open, and a loud roar fills the courtyard. Ashen-furred creatures that resemble a mix of a dragon and a lion swoop down from above. Each has a goatee and a single horn. Their wingbeats pump through the room like drums, and as they roar, I can see sharp fangs in their wide mouths.

"*Pixius,*" Marc says, holding up his sword. "Fierce and known for their prowess in war. I should have guessed. They are notorious for guarding palaces."

Their jaws stretch open, ready to rip us to shreds. A pang shoots through me because there's something about these creatures that reminds me of Haechi. I let loose arrow after arrow. Beside me, Marc swings his sword, while Kwan roars and stabs at the creatures that come within his reach. One snaps at my hair, ripping out a chunk, while another takes a large bite out of Kwan before I have a chance to send an arrow through its heart.

And then there's silence again. The three of us wait, watching the *pixius* depart, disappearing back into the ceiling. Marc sags to the ground, his knees buckling under him. I run to his side.

"Are you okay?" I ask, cupping his face between my hands. "You shouldn't have come. I should have listened to my instincts."

His fingers run along my shoulders and come away red. "You're bleeding."

"I'm fine."

"Then so am I."

I'm about to tell him how impossible he is when the walls behind the terra-cotta warriors shimmer. Kwan shuffles over to stand beside us. His arm is caked with blood as dark as tar.

"This is not good," he says.

I follow his gaze. The twin rows of terra-cotta warriors along the walls begin to move. Then, as each figure steps forward, another appears behind it. Rows and rows of them emerge as if they are appearing from a magical portal on the other side of the shimmering wall. Their feet clomp like a thousand soldiers marching, and their weapons rise as one to attack. Marc leaps to his feet while I hurriedly gather the arrows scattered among the dead *pixius*.

Then I start shooting. My arrows hit their marks perfectly but deflect off the lacquered armor.

"Your arrows aren't working," Marc yells over the clomp of marching clay.

The first warrior reaches Marc, and the two break into battle. It's disconcerting to see Marc fight against a clay figure with no expression or emotion. On the other side of me, Kwan's spear crashes through warrior after warrior, cracking them into pieces. I race toward the closest warrior and leap into a front-kick. The warrior totters, but its surface is stronger than I expected. My leg aches from the impact as I land. I spin around and take in the hundreds of warriors streaming through the walls. My chest sinks. There's no way the three of us will be able to conquer an army like this.

It's impossible.

Maybe Emperor Qin Shi Huang made a deal with the Spirit World to forever protect his tomb. But if he played with the supernatural, I'm okay with that. I race to the other side of the courtyard. Marc and Kwan glance my way, but they don't have time to question my actions or for me to explain.

I climb up onto a ledge, not far from the ground but high enough to give me some time away from the oncoming warriors. I close my eyes, take in deep breaths, and focus. It's been a long time since I've shape-shifted into a creature, and I'm not sure if it's even possible to do so here in China. But I have to take the risk.

I search my mind for an animal that could face this onslaught. Something that could crash and smash these warriors into pieces. The image of the *qilin* comes to my mind, with its sharp antlers and scaled body. Yes, it's perfect. I press my back to the wall and focus on the transformation. The antlers, the hooves, the head, the shimmering blue body. The room spins, and my insides feel as if they're exploding. I scream in agony, and it almost pulls me out of the transformation process. But I push aside the pain and focus on the image once again.

My head throbs and my insides twist in torture. It's as if my stomach is being squeezed into a pulp and my bones are snapping in half. Then everything settles, and my vision clears. Soldiers are surrounding me, and a sea of soldiers swarms Marc. He attempts to lift his sword, but he's too weak. He falters and stumbles, falling at the feet of a clay soldier. Fury wells up within my gut.

Destroy.

I paw at the ground and shake my mane; fire spits from my jaws. My antlers smash into the first warrior to reach me. He flies through the air, hitting the stone wall and shattering. I slam my ankles against the warriors on either side of me, flinging them through the air. Ahead of me, Marc's shoulders droop as he blocks a blow with his sword. I break into a canter, focusing on freeing him from the onslaught.

Fire blazes a path before me as I barrel through, and the soldiers shatter the moment my antlers crash into them. There are so many everywhere. Furious, I ram everything that comes into my path.

Destroy.

Swords slice against my scales, but this only angers me more. I run faster, crashing into everything in sight, my fiery tail sweeping in my wake. I lose track of time. Lose track of who I am. All I can focus on is one word:

Destroy.

Soon I paw at a pile of terra-cotta shards. Nothing moves. The anger surging through me dissipates, and the room blurs around me. I look for the hundreds of soldiers that surrounded me but see only broken shards. The adrenaline rush vanishes and is replaced with confusion. Something about me isn't right. Then I realize that I'm not *me*. I'm clutching a form that doesn't belong to me. I release the hold I have over the metamorphosis.

Once again the room spins, a whirlwind of dust and clay. My body spasms. The sapphire-blue scales transform into my own skin and clothes. My bow and arrows are gone, probably still on the ground where I shape-shifted. The contents of my stomach churn, and I lean over and throw up. I lie on the pile of clay and shake uncontrollably, unable to gather my wits or stand.

Finally I lift my head to scan the room for Marc and Kwan. I see neither, but I'm too weak to search for them. Tears roll down my cheeks as I take in the carnage before me. There's no way either could survive an attack like this. I may have even caused their deaths while I was swept away in the metamorphosis. The loss consumes me, and I collapse back to the floor.

. . .

I hobble through the piles of broken shards, not caring if I cut myself on the jagged edges. The air hangs in an odd silence, and orange dust balloons up from my footsteps. It takes me a good ten minutes to find Marc, and when I do, my heart stutters in my chest. Blood gushes from his forehead. His shirt is a mix of clay and dark red, which I assume is blood. He's lying beneath a large warrior. Unmoving.

"Marc!" I scream his name, run my hands over his face, and start digging through the wreckage. The clay edges slice through my shaking palms, but I'm so desperate to reach him, I can't even see straight.

Soon I clear away enough of the horrifying soldier to press my lips to Marc's. I kiss his eyelids and his cheeks, then caress his face. Once again, I press my ear to his chest. The thump of his heartbeat pulls my world back into place.

He's alive.

And that's when I lose it. I can't stop crying or shaking. The realization of how much he means to me hits me like a typhoon.

It's one thing to know that we can never touch or whisper silly things in each other's ears, that I'll never kiss him or feel his arms wrapped around me because we are separated by Kud, a monster.

But knowing he's gone—truly gone—would be more than I could deal with.

Maybe this is what true love is. My heart beats for him. Losing him would drive me to insanity.

"My fighter girl is crying," Marc croaks. "I've been waiting for this day."

"Oh God." I clutch him to my chest, not caring that my hands are bloody. "I thought you were gone. I thought you'd left me."

"I don't die that easily." He tries to sit up, cringing and rubbing the back of his neck. "That dude must have landed on top of me. Knocked me out or something."

"They're all dead." My voice shudders. I glance at the courtyard and the beheaded warriors. "Or broken or something."

"You used metamorphosis, didn't you?"

"Yes." I swallow and grip him harder. "I was right. This tomb is a part of the Spirit World. Every minute I'm here, I'm feeling stronger."

"I should be happy you just saved us there, but knowing you're becoming more connected to the Spirit World completely sucks."

I bite my lip and look away. He's right, and there's nothing else to say. Slowly I help him up, and he leans against me. We brush off the clay dust as best we can. My shirt is practically in tatters now, and my pants are torn—not that it matters anyway.

"If we have many more battles, I'm going to be half-naked." I laugh and stumble back to where I transformed to gather up my bow and quiver.

"I won't complain."

I roll my eyes at him and then freeze, grabbing at my chest. "Where's my orb?" I begin frantically searching the area where I shape-shifted. "It must have come off when I transformed."

Then I spot it glowing beneath a cracked head. I run, scoop it up, and put it around my neck. Marc doesn't say anything, but I see the wariness in his eyes as it settles on my chest.

"What?" I ask.

He shakes his head, but I know that look. He doesn't think I should still have it. Or maybe he fears its power will eventually kill me. He's not wrong often.

"Where's your deadhead buddy?" Marc scans the wreckage, tossing aside a breastplate and kicking back a set of legs.

"Kwan? Good question. He was here during the fight."

We search the entire area, and I'm about to give up when I find his spear. Nothing else. I kneel on the floor next to it. I'm not sure how I feel about him being gone.

"You think he bit the dust?" Marc picks up the spear.

"I hope so. For his sake and ours."

"We're free of Kud's grip now," Marc says. "You weren't attached to Kwan, were you? He was evil, Jae. You had to see that in his eyes. Besides, who knows what his real intentions were?"

Kwan was evil. Bent on destruction and death. The image of his mouth opened wide as he screamed and the terror he evoked won't leave me. But there was something about him that still held on to a piece of nobility and courage. I trace his name in *hangul* through the dust on the marble floor. He was created to be an instrument for Kud, who hated life and happiness. But I had found myself understanding Kwan better each day. I too gave myself over so my loved ones could be saved. The tug of Kud's bond is ruthless, unrelenting, and terrifying. The control he had over all three of us cripples me even now. Am I any different from Kwan and Sang Min?

Time will tell.

"You're right. It's just that after you fight alongside someone, it's hard to hate them anymore. Suddenly they don't feel like the enemy you once thought they were. The Stiffs were just as much victims of Kud's obsessions and greed as I am. I can't blame them for that."

"Everyone makes their choices."

I look up at him. A heaviness settles over me, and my throat constricts. "Yes, we do."

"Jae." Marc reaches for me, shaking his head. "I didn't mean you."

"No." I stand, brushing him aside. "You're right. We should get into the inner city before the Spirit World decides to send in reinforcements."

Marc tries to pick up Kwan's spear. "Man, this thing is heavy. Give me a hand."

It takes both of us to heave it up. We carry it over to the middle gate and use it to attempt to lift the bar holding the double doors closed. After about ten minutes, we finally succeed, and Marc collapses to the ground.

"What do you think is on the other side?" I lean over, hands on my knees, and pant as I inspect the gate to the inner city.

"The records say that once the emperor was placed in the burial chamber and the ceremony of his burial was complete, all the craftsmen and workers and all the concubines who didn't have children were locked inside the lower gates."

"That's horrible. And you think these are the lower gates?" At his nod, I grimace. "Fantastic. On the count of three, open the gate. I'll stand ready."

"*Hana*," Marc begins counting in Korean, gripping the knocker with one hand and his sword with the other. I notch in an arrow and draw back. "*Duel, set.*"

The gates fly open. I aim. But there isn't a beast to attack us. Or an army of clay soldiers. A mist rolls over the ground, seeping its way out toward us. And there, piled up before us, is a mound of bones. Sighs and moans fill the air. A chill slithers over me. The sound comes from the mist.

We stand still. I'm too shocked to move.

"'Like a green ridge is the ancient tomb,'" Marc recites. His voice is weary. "'Deep is the palace like a purple terrace . . . The soughing of pines can be clearly heard, / It sounds like the wail of the people.'"

"That's creepy."

"It's from the poem 'Passing by the Mausoleum of Emperor Qin Shi Huang,' written by Wang Wei of the Tang Dynasty."

"Right." I creep through the gate. The mist washes over me, smelling tangy and bitter.

This courtyard is even more spectacular than the previous one. The walls are decorated with exquisite, lifelike designs of mountains and rushing rivers accented by glistening gems. The stone floor is inlaid with mother-of-pearl in intricate patterns.

The bones crunch under my boots, and I cringe as I step through them. Beside me, Marc starts coughing. He pauses to rip a part of his shirt off and wraps it around his mouth.

"What is it?" I ask.

"That." Marc points to a rushing river before us. It's milky white and the source of the mist. "Quicksilver."

"So the records were true." I feel a burning sensation in my throat, but it doesn't seem to be affecting me like it is him. "Qin Shi Huang really did fill his tomb with poisonous mercury."

"Apparently. The emperor believed that mercury was the key to eternity. He just took the concept to a whole new level. No wonder no one leaves this place alive." Marc pulls out his gas mask, inspecting it. "I have enough oxygen in this for thirty minutes tops."

I turn to Marc and grab his arms. "Good. That's enough to get you out of here safely. You *have* to leave before the fumes kill you."

"I'm not leaving."

"Don't you see? You're coughing. It's killing you right now." I'm practically shaking him. "The gas has almost no effect on me. You have to go back and close that door."

"I can't do that."

"Then I can't go forward. I thought you had died back there, and I nearly lost my mind. Don't do this to me. If you love me, you'll go back and we'll close the gate. You'll be safe."

I somehow convince him. After I help him stagger back into the outer city, I slam the gate closed. Then I start running, leaping over bones toward the next set of doors. But I stop short of my goal because the river has wound its way directly in front of me. I eye its chalky surface. I doubt I can cross it without the mercury seeping into my skin and killing me. I'm stronger in the Spirit World, but even in this connected realm, I can feel my limits.

The rushing of wind draws my attention, and I spin around just as a red dragon dives from above, circling with its five-clawed talons extended. Its scales glisten like a river of fire as it bears down on me, and its antlers are primed to plunge into my body. I throw myself into an aerial to avoid its claws, and as soon as I land, I set my arrow and release. It sails just past the creature.

"You may not cross," the yellow-eyed dragon says. I recognize the narrow slits of its eyes. Now I know what has been watching us all along. "You come as a thief in the night. Your arm bears the mark of evil."

I grit my teeth. I'm tired of being told I'm evil and horrible. It's just getting old.

"I seek the treasure of my people." I aim my arrow and draw back the string. "It is not your right to protect it or withhold it from me. Let me pass."

The dragon snakes its body around and settles on top of a crevice in the wall. It cocks its head to the side and focuses on me.

"Look into my eyes so I may see the truth of your spirit," it says.

I swallow, not sure I want him to see that truth. Despite my good intentions, I know there is so much inside me that is selfish and angry.

"Why should I trust you?" I say as I lower my bow and search the river, hoping to find a way around so I don't have to waste my time with this dragon. "What can you offer if I allow this?"

"You already know. Or are you too afraid?"

I lift my chin, staring into the dragon's eyes, daring it to discover the truth. Its pupils grow larger, suns spinning in endless circles. My limbs weaken and I lose all control, which sends my pulse into overdrive.

I cry out, covering my eyes with my arms, but it's pointless. I'm falling through rivers of yellow and beams of sparkling light. I'm lost in the sun and a world of light. I try to reach out, but all I can do is burn in the sun-drenched glow.

CHAPTER 25

I blink awake. I'm lying on a cold floor smooth as glass. I try to move, but my muscles are numb. Above, a thousand stars stare down at me. I wait for them to wink like stars should. Not these. They're solid and bright and unblinking, casting an iridescent glow throughout the room. Soon I'm able to move a finger. Then my leg twitches. After a few minutes, I can roll onto my side to see where I am.

The wall before me is painted with images of mountains, rivers, forests, deserts, palaces, and gardens. Each setting features a man wearing a long robe and a pointed beard. His image is familiar, and I assume he must be Emperor Qin Shi Huang.

Treasures sparkle in the starlight, stacked along the walls and jammed into each corner. I wouldn't even know what these things were, but I'm sure Marc's parents would die to see this hoard. Gold statues, round platters, whole sets of bowls, and goblets. A large gong rests against another wall. The floor I'm lying on is beaten copper, and its bright surface shines like gold. My feet slip on the smooth metal as I try to stand.

The mercury river flows in from one end of the chamber, running through its center and then back outside. It's the only entrance in or out, which means the door I had been eyeing must have been fake. Any swimmers who braved the river would be dead before they had the chance to leave the tomb.

A golden coffin floats on the river. Could this be the emperor's coffin, endlessly riding on a river of quicksilver? As I watch it pass by, somehow it feels fitting. He tried to gain eternal life by ingesting mercury, and now his decayed body rides a river of the same poison for eternity.

The thought sends a shudder through me. As I watch the coffin disappear into a tunnel lined with torches and strange symbols, I see no difference between myself and the corpse inside. Living in Kud's land is no better. I'm rotting inside, riding a pointless river that just circles around and around.

I do a quick check of my belongings and realize my bow and arrows are still with me. So is the orb. I brush my fingers over it. A surge of warmth slides through the skin on my chest, comforting me.

"Show me the Black Turtle orb," I whisper to the White Tiger orb.

A beam of light shoots out of the orb and across the room. It settles on a pedestal against the wall. My legs wobble, still numb, as I cross the room. The dull pedestal is tucked back in the corner, a shadow compared to the treasures piled throughout the room. The White Tiger orb beams its light on a stone resting on top of the pedestal. Beside the jewels lining the tables and the bowls of golden treasures, the stone looks like a dirty rock.

My heart shudders as I realize this is the orb. I'm within arm's reach of it. It has remained hidden, tucked inside the bowels of this untouched tomb for a thousand years or more, and here I am, standing before it. Something catches the corner of my eye to my left and throws me off guard. I jerk up my bow, ready to shoot.

But it's only the coffin sliding past once again, making its way through the outer edge of the oval room. I let out a long breath and lick my lips. They're dry and peeling. I look down at my arm and realize all of my skin is peeling. It's like I have leprosy or something. Could this be an effect of the mercury fumes in the air? I think about Marc, hoping he's safe. I need to hurry.

I step closer and reach for the rock lit up by the orb dangling around my neck, but I hesitate, my fingers hovering over it. I notice a plaque just under it.

路遥知

It's written in ancient Chinese, just like the inscription on Haemosu's tomb. I squint at it and realize with a shock that I'm able to read the characters. Perhaps it's because of my connection to the Spirit World, or maybe the words are being revealed purposely to me.

It says, "As distance tests a horse's strength, so does time reveal a person's real character."

Suddenly memories race through my mind: golfing with Dad, entering Grandfather's ancient cave by the ocean, watching the dragons carry Grandfather away, seeing Kud engrave the tattoo on Marc's arm, and holding Komo's hand as she lay in a coma at the hospital.

Too much pain.

Too many horrible memories of the people I love getting hurt over and over. I'm tired of the suffering and not being able to stop it. This orb is my chance to tip the balance in favor of Palk and the light.

I wrap my palm around the flat rock's surface, holding my breath. I half expect something horrible to happen. I brace myself, ready for a sensation to race through my body. Instead, I feel nothing but a smooth flat rock. I cup it in my palms and hold it up closer, searching for marks or engravings.

Hope trembles in my chest.

But there are no marks. And no peace for me. This stupid rock was my hope for life. My hope for love. My country's hope for unity. And now, there will be no reprieve from the endless hate and darkness of Kud's ever-hungry arms. A weight like a thousand pounds hits my shoulders, and my knees buckle from the burden of it all. I kneel on the coppery floor, despair rushing through my veins. Perhaps the orb was already claimed or owned, maybe even by the dead emperor. An orb may only have one owner until it is passed to the next person.

"Please," I whisper to the rock and lean forward. The necklace Marc hung around my neck comes loose from its place inside my shirt. The gold inscription sparkles in the dim chamber.

I'LL FIND YOU IN THE DARKNESS

I stare at the rock and lick my lips. Here I am in a forbidden tomb filled with poisonous gases, and I'm talking to a rock. It's completely ridiculous.

"I claim you."

The rock remains unchanged. I feel foolish. I'm about to hurl it across the room when the shape twists and contorts. The rock vibrates, and the smooth surface explodes, red dust bursting into the air and falling about me like ash from an erupting volcano.

The sparks swirl around me in a whirlwind, burning the contract on my forearm. I press my arm to my chest, protecting it from the embers that seek to sear it. The fire sparks sharpen and elongate into long, knife-like lightning bolts, climbing toward the unblinking stars.

I'm caught in a firestorm. The flames feast on my clothes and lick my skin. I scream in agony.

And then it all disappears.

I'm lying in a bank of snow, fresh and cold. It coats my skin and cools the memory of the fire. Slowly I sit up and trace my hands and arms with my fingers, searching for burns. There are none.

A breeze kicks up around me, swirling the snow and whispering in my ears. It's a music I've never heard before. Wind and snow sing together in a breathless dance. Jagged mountains rise up around me as if the peaks ache for the stars. A crescent moon hangs above, lingering in the breaking dawn.

I rise and look around, my tattered clothes whipping about my body. I'm standing on a peak similar to those around me.

Clouds drift below me, and beyond that is a descent that makes my stomach dive. I must be ten thousand feet high.

The sensation of something watching me causes my skin to prickle. Slowly, I turn. Before me looms the Black Turtle, as large as a car. Its black armor is such a contrast to the blinding white of the snow. A snake curls around its body, twisting and coiling over the massive shell. The turtle's claws dig through the snow, knocking loose a burst of snowflakes. It lowers its long neck, and its piercing white eyes assess me as if deciding whether I'm worthy of its presence. The bronze liquid glare of my contract stands out in this world of pureness.

"Great One." My voice rings strong across the crisp air. "I come in peace."

"Who speaks to me as such?" the turtle asks in Korean.

The ground around me shakes, and I fall back into the snow. But once again I rise, my pulse racing even faster as I stare up at this great beast, each leg as large as my body. I clench my fists and focus on my words. They must be perfect.

"I do." I lift my chin. "Jae Hwa, daughter of Korea, bearer of the Blue Dragon bow and the White Tiger orb. The girl who saved her family from the curse of Haemosu and now seeks freedom from Kud's bond."

"Yes. And so you are. Not a stranger, but still a wanderer. Why are you here?"

"To claim your artifact. It must be returned to the Heavenly Chest so the balance can be restored."

"Listen to the music of the wind." The Black Turtle inclines its head to the left. "It is full of pain and aching, but with it comes a completeness. There is no fulfillment without that journey. Do you understand?"

I nod. *Yes.* Oh yes. A tear trickles down my cheek and freezes on my face.

"Jae Hwa, descendant of Princess Yuhwa. Your legacy will be ours."

Its mouth opens wide, revealing a long tongue and jagged teeth, and then the creature flies at me. Its claws grab my shoulders; the snake wraps around my waist. I'm unable to resist the turtle's hold on me. I scream as the mouth sucks me inside its jaws, and it swallows me whole.

CHAPTER 26

I wake to milky white water rushing over me. I'm lying in the exact place where I first held the Black Turtle orb. The cold iciness of the water snaking over my skin causes me to bolt upright. I gasp as the memories of the Black Turtle swallowing me flash through my mind. Then I shudder and run my hands over my body, checking to see if I'm still myself. Something feels different. I can't explain it or place what that is.

The water rises so that my shirt billows up around me. Frantically I stand, my drenched hair dragging around my shoulders. My bow bobs in the water at my feet, and I snatch it up and take in my surroundings. I don't know what has happened, but the mercury water is rising from the riverbed that once circled the room, gushing across the floor, and drowning the treasures.

I don't have much time, but I can't leave this chamber without the orb. I splash through the poisonous quicksilver in search of it. Then, as if it's once again reading my mind, the White Tiger orb shoots out a ray of light into the water at my feet. I dig through the water, which now reaches my knees, and grope through its murkiness until my hands clasp something hard.

Lifting it up, I study it in the dim torchlight. The black rock has flattened and stretched into an arched shape, almost like a bracelet. Inspired, I slide it over my wrist. A tingle skitters across my skin around the bracelet. It fits perfectly, as if it's made just for me. The surface shimmers, and for a moment I believe I can see the Black Turtle's eyes, its expression once again reminding me of legacies. But no, that must be my imagination.

Everywhere the water touches my skin, it burns, which drags me away from staring at this new bracelet. The water is rising at an alarming rate. If only I knew why and how to stop it. There's no way I can swim through this water for long. I grab a torch off the wall and wade through the room in search of an exit.

I call to the White Tiger orb for a way out, but its light just circles the chamber. I burst into a hysterical laugh. Here I am, clutching three of the greatest weapons Korea has ever known. I've managed to defeat all the booby traps the masters of the past have set, only to drown in this tomb.

And then I see the answer to my problems. Qin Shi Huang's coffin is floating through one of the two openings. It gleams a brilliant gold in the torchlight. For a moment, the shine of it yanks me back to another time, when Haemosu gilded my wrist with his five-dragon bracelet. I reach to rub my wrist and my fingers find the Black Turtle orb there in its place. Somehow this doesn't settle me. I seem to have replaced one Spirit World artifact with another.

I trudge through the water, shoving aside the burning sensation, and reach a space just ahead of where the coffin floats.

I have to time this perfectly, or I'll miss and the coffin will slip through the narrow opening before I have a chance to grab hold of it. The water rushes around me as if it's picking up speed by the second. I leap for the coffin and land on top just as it slips through the opening in the wall. I duck my head, but the top of the ceiling still scrapes my scalp. If I had waited until it had come around again, the coffin wouldn't have fit back into the tunnel with the water rising so quickly.

The water carries the coffin and me out into a narrow canal. The ceiling yawns above so high I can't see the top. Torches line the walls, just like the rest of the mausoleum, but the engravings here are of horrible creatures that seem to twist and contort in the firelight. Then I realize these aren't just engravings sculpted into the stone thousands of years ago. They are alive, slithering over the walls.

Demons with bulging eyes and slobbering mouths raise their claws as if to scratch off my skin. Snakes writhe as if eager to strangle me. I shudder as I pass each one, clutching the sides of the coffin in case a talon should reach out to drag me under the water.

Inch by inch, I reposition myself on the top of the coffin, trying to keep it from tipping as I move. Finally I face forward and grip the sides with my hands. The skin on my arms continues to flake off, leaving behind a raw redness. I can't even imagine how the rest of my body must look. My eyes burn, and tears stream down my cheeks. My chest squeezes tight, and I start coughing.

As I float on my coffin-boat a new realization hits me. I'm slowly rising. Whatever I did with the orb must have unlocked the floodgates of this tomb, a final deathly trap. If this flooding continues, it will take me up to the top. Which would be great, except who knows what's on top? My guess would be a stone ceiling: my own coffin.

And then there's Marc. *Crap.* I bet the entire tomb is flooding. My pulse hits overdrive, and I forget about my body screaming in agony. All I can think is that I need to find him and fast, before this place becomes our tomb. There's no way I will leave this tomb without him, even if it means I die trying.

I call Marc's name over and over, my voice shrieking frantically. Light from the White Tiger orb skitters over the walls and the water, searching for a way to him. Meanwhile my coffin twists around bend after bend. I realize it won't be long before it will hit the burial chamber again, and I sag against the coffin in despair.

Then I drift up to a wide arch, and the river spits me out into a huge room. At first I don't recognize the place with all of the extra water, but then a series of bones floats by me. This is the inner city. I had been right in thinking that the entire area has flooded. I have no idea how deep the water is, but when I see the gate and that the water is halfway to the top, the full impact of the flooding hits me.

This is happening fast. In just under fifteen minutes, this entire cavernous space has filled with water. I grab a floating board and paddle my way over to the double doors, grunting with each stroke. Once I slide alongside the gate, I balance on the coffin and grasp the bolt, lift it up, and toss it aside. It takes all my might to shove the gate open. Water surges out of the doors, and my coffin and I go flying forward. I tumble and roll across the hard floor, water shoving me forward and down. I sputter and gag as I swallow the poisonous liquid.

"Jae!" Marc calls to me from the tunnel we first entered from. A beam of light from the orb glows on him.

He's holding one of the gas masks to his mouth. He can't know how just seeing him standing there makes everything right. I snatch up the board I was using as a paddle and struggle through the oncoming water to reach him. Each step is agony as my chest constricts and my skin sears, but when I reach the stairs, I practically run to him. If I'm going to die, I want it to be in his arms.

When I collapse into his arms, he's shaking. Then he takes off his mask and kisses me, and even though I know the water is ever closer and the poisonous air is choking us, I don't care. Then he shoves the other breathing device onto my face and wraps the strap around my head to keep it in place.

"Don't die on me, Fighter Girl." But he's coughing, too. "We're going to get out of here. Just hold on to me."

He places his mask back on his face, and we race back through the opening and enter the sloping corridor riddled with traps. I slap the board over the gap we once used Kwan's spear to cross. Water now rises below in what used to be an endless gaping hole.

We work as a team. He holds the board as I crawl across, and then I hold the board for him on the other side. Once both of us are back on solid ground, we drop to our bellies and begin the slide back up the corridor. I scream out with each movement. A layer of my skin has flaked off, and sliding feels like rubbing my belly over sharp rocks. Beside me Marc coughs and grunts. He can't be doing much better.

It's as if the tomb knows we're about to leave and it can't let us escape, because halfway up, I spy water rising just above my boots. My body is at war. The part of me connected to the Spirit World is fighting to heal my body, while the humanity in me weakens my every step.

"Jae," Marc says with a gasp, his voice muffled through the mask. "Go ahead without me."

"I'll never leave you."

"Do you have to be so stubborn? You sure know how to tick off a guy."

"I feel great." I burst into a coughing fit. "The Spirit World heals me faster than you."

"Not fast enough, apparently."

I claw at the ground to force myself to keep moving. I scream in agony. My vision blurs. But I push past the pain. Once I reach the entrance, where it's safe from flying arrows, I turn and grab Marc's hands and pull him the rest of the way up the ramp.

Torches swirl around me. Water rises ever closer. Wind rages through my ears. Pain burns through me like an inferno. I can't see through its burning fire. I'm choking and running.

I'm dying, and this time I can't be saved.

• • •

My spirit pulls away from my body. I'm desperate to leave this pain behind, but then I remember how Kud raised the dead to walk again and do his bidding. I don't want to ever be helpless, subject to his whims. And now that I possess two orbs, he'd find a way to seek out my bones. He'd find a way to use my dead body to follow his commands. I'd be no different from Kwan and Sang Min. As it is, the lines are thinning to the point that it has been a daily decision to be the person I want to be.

And if Kud had the power of three orbs, the balance would be tipped. This can't happen. I can't let it happen.

I grab hold of the pain, embracing it, soaking it in until I feel everything. I draw in a deep breath of fresh night air and know instantly that we've left the Spirit World. I open my eyes and find myself in Marc's arms. He's got me pressed against his chest. I can hear the steady rhythm of his heartbeat. It's a beautiful song to my ears. Above us, wispy clouds curl around the full moon.

I think back to when I first battled Haemosu. He shape-shifted into a bird and nearly killed me by slicing his talons down my back. After I escaped his clutches, Marc found me sprawled in the school hallway, my skin bloodied and ripped to shreds. Yet by the time we entered Nurse Lah's office, my wounds had nearly healed.

I pray our bodies heal as quickly tonight.

Gazing about me, I realize we're outside of the same door we used to enter the mausoleum. The air is full of stillness, so the ceremony that was going on below must be finished. Kwan and Sang Min are gone. For a moment, I believe we are free. Then I see the shadows moving.

"I did not think it was possible to escape the horrors of the emperor's tomb," one of the shadows says. "But that is why we are here: to kill any who might have escaped death."

CHAPTER 27

In the moonlight, the Triad Guardian studies us as if he's unsure of what to do. Then he calls out for the others.

Great.

Marc groans and shifts as a group of them forms before us. He says something to them in Mandarin. They eye us suspiciously, still keeping their distance.

"I told them our bodies carry poison and not to get too close," Marc whispers to me. "The only nice part about leaving the Spirit World is that my wounds are healing quickly. Guess it's the bonus of still being human."

By pure brute determination, I manage to stand and point to Marc. "He's my prisoner," I say.

"Like they're going to buy that one," Marc mumbles under his breath. His lips curl in a smile and his eyebrows lift. "They know I stole their truck and rescued you."

"I forced him to do my bidding," I say, loud enough that the other Triads can hear me. "I put a spell on him. He has no control over his actions."

Marc shrugs. "Now *that* might be true. I wondered why I couldn't say no to death traps and continuously put myself in danger when you're involved."

"This isn't the time for jokes," I mutter, rolling my eyes. "You're not helping. They're going to kill us. Better if it's just me instead of both of us."

Marc laughs then. Really laughs. As if this is the funniest situation he's ever been in. He rolls his body over and, with a grunt of obvious pain, pushes himself up to lean against me.

"You sure have an interesting way to party, Fighter Girl." A sly grin crosses his face. To the Triads he probably looks relaxed, calm. But I see how his hand slides over the hilt of his sword. How he clenches it until his knuckles are whiter than snow.

"You sure?" I ask him.

"Never more."

"Hand over your weapons," the head Triad tells us. "Toss them on the ground, and we will all walk down together like civilized people."

"I've just fought demons, poisonous gases, and booby traps set two millennia ago," Marc says. "I've survived the impossible, all in the pursuit of saving a country from death and destruction. What have you done? What right do you have to stop us? What ultimate purpose do you have to stand in our path?"

With each word, Marc stands taller. He raises his sword. Moonlight glints off it, revealing the gaping mouth of the dragon on the hilt. I can almost imagine its roar, lifting from the far shores of home. And as Marc lifts his head, focusing his eyes on the men surrounding us, a rush of wind cuts past, rustling his hair. It's as if the Spirit World has heard his words.

And the air strengthens me. The weakness that pulled me to the ground falls away, and my skin no longer burns. I realize that the doors to the mausoleum still gape open.

"The world hangs on the brink of darkness," Marc continues. "I can see the dark hovering on the horizon each morning. It's biding its time until we are most unsuspecting, and then it will drown us. I won't stand aside and let it rule those I love. I won't let it destroy my family or my home."

Marc begins to pace, and I see the unease on the Guardians' faces. They look to their leader for direction, but he doesn't move. His expression looks as if he, too, feels the horror that we all stand on the brink of.

"Korea may not be the land of my birth," Marc says. "But this doesn't mean it hasn't become what I now call home. I cannot allow a power to grow so that it can destroy everything. So I ask you, from one Guardian to another: stand down."

A silence hovers over us. For a brief moment, I think the leader will cave and that Marc has actually convinced him to allow us to run free. The head Triad lowers his sword and whispers to his right-hand man.

The bronze on my arm burns bright in the darkness, a constant reminder of my failure. My bondage. I dare to try to cover it.

Which was a bad idea because the Triad leader's eyes follow my gaze to my arm. I've reminded him without a single word or action who I really am. What I represent.

"Did you find what you once sought?" he asks conversationally, yet his lips press together and his face becomes closed as he grips his sword tighter. We are lost to him. To everyone.

"No," I say. "We failed. The tomb flooded before we could come across any signs of it."

I cringe inwardly, hoping he'll believe my lie. He can't possibly know what the Black Turtle orb would look like because it took on a new shape after I claimed it.

"How unfortunate."

"My thoughts exactly," I say.

The Triads raise their swords as one. We are so doomed.

"She's bewitched you," the head Triad tells Marc. "But me and my men, we will stand strong against her."

Marc wastes no time. He dives into the throng, screaming at the top of his lungs like an ancient Nordic warrior and cutting a path for me to race through, all without hurting any one of them. Then I call to the White Tiger orb. Its light blazes out and I don't hold back, drawing from all of its power. I create a barrier so that we can run away.

But as we sprint across the courtyard where earlier the dancers stood, one of their men rushes to a large stone pedestal before us. He slams a narrow tube into the stone, and a series of flames shoot into the air, some red, some yellow, others blue. They burst above us in a cloud of fireworks. But there's something different about these flames. I trip over a crack in the stonework as the colors merge into shapes.

Dragons. Lions. And beasts I have no way to identify.

"Are those real?" I scream at Marc.

He slows down to take a look, and his mouth gapes open in shock. "Yeah. Run!"

We fly down the long series of steps that trails from the top of the mausoleum to the parking lot below. My feet barely touch the ground, and it takes all my muscles to keep myself from rolling forward and somersaulting down the staircase.

Triads run up to meet us. I kick and knock them backward while Marc does the same with his sword until we reach the parking lot. As our feet hit the gravel, we are met by a throng of warriors from the Grand Council blocking our path. The Triads must have alerted them.

There's only one way left to go. Marc jerks right and out into the field that we crossed what feels like an eternity ago. I release the power of the orb and immediately feel my strength depleting. With each step, my legs drag like wooden blocks. Still, if we are to have any chance, we have to press on.

Then Marc jerks to an abrupt stop. I ram into his back.

"What is it?" I ask, but as I step around him I understand.

There before us stands the rest of the Grand Council. Somehow, they've led us out here. The Triads race down from the top of the tomb to flank us on the right, while the ones we met at the parking lot fill in behind until we are completely surrounded.

"This isn't looking so good," Marc says.

That would be the understatement of the century. There are all kinds of men and women surrounding us. Some wear sleek black pantsuits, while others are dressed in old-fashioned pants and tunics. They hold an assortment of weapons: spears, bows and arrows, swords, and even some objects that I'm sure possess magical powers. These fighters are the best that our world has to offer.

There is no escape.

"Hand over the heavenly objects," Jung says, taking a step toward us. He's still wearing his loose black pants and the sleeveless black shirt that shows off the tattoo of the Tiger of Shinshi. The sword at his side gleams with a silvery sheen, and the ends of the black band flutter out from the side of his head. His jaw is tight, and the muscles on his arm are flexed as if he's ready to defend himself at any second. "Those belong to the people of Korea. They are not meant for Kud or his servants."

I swallow back the bile that rises to my throat. My chest tightens and my resolve dissipates as his words sink in. He's right. I am a slave of Kud. I may not wish to be, but that is irrelevant. I bear his mark on my arm. And who am I to stand against these Guardians? They are trained and prepared for crazies such as me.

Why am I even bothering to try to return the orbs to the Heavenly Chest in Korea, where I'll be under Kud's grip?

My hand brushes over the necklace Marc gave me, and suddenly its words take on new meaning. I may be in the darkness, lost and wandering, but I don't have to stay there. Not even death will stop me from keeping true to what I believe.

"Kud may have my body," I say, holding up my arm. "But he can't have my heart. And my heart lies with Korea."

"You are making a mistake," Marc says to the assembled Guardians. "The Tiger of Shinshi asked for us to assist her. No one could have gotten the orb without having power in both the Spirit and the human worlds. She had to go. And now she needs to return to Korea. Help us."

"No. *You* made the mistake of betraying us." Jung nods to Marc. "You are dead to us now."

Marc's head jerks back as if Jung's words have literally punched him in the face. His chest rises and falls. I can tell that it's taking every ounce of his energy not to leap at Jung.

"If you don't turn yourself in, we will fight to the death," Jung says, his jaw set.

"It does not have to be this way," Marc says. For the first time, I see a crack in Jung's resolve.

"Please," I say. "We don't want to hurt anyone. Just let us pass."

Regret flashes through Jung's eyes, and he sucks in a deep breath, steeling himself.

Marc gazes down at me. His eyes have never looked greener. That dimple, that wild hair. It leaves me breathless. I love him more than I could ever have imagined. Maybe it's when you are about to lose everything that you understand true love. Maybe it's when you have nothing that you recognize love in its purest form. I wish we had more time together. I wish I'd chosen the movies rather than seeking out the White Tiger orb. I wish I'd hung out at his house and watched reruns instead of spending extra time at the archery center.

I wish for us.

My lips almost smile. "Thanks for choosing me."

"I will always choose you," Marc says.

Within seconds I hear an arrow whooshing through the air at me—a sizzling sound, laced with magic that I'm sure carries poison of some sort. I lean back. It flies across my chest, missing me by centimeters. Jung leaps at Marc, and the two clash in an enraged fury, swords clanking and crashing in the midnight air. I barely have time to unleash my first arrow before more are flying right back at me. I flip across the grass, kicking and spinning.

It isn't enough.

There are hundreds of them and two of us.

We have no chance.

I call upon the White Tiger and Black Turtle orbs. It's not hard to find the White Tiger orb's power. It's waiting for me, eager and ready. In a burst of white, it stretches across my skin and radiates out, creating a barrier. But the Black Turtle orb is elusive, just as it was in the tomb.

A bloom of fire erupts at my feet. It shakes the ground, splintering the grass in front of me, and I stumble, nearly falling into the gaping pit before me. I lose my hold on the White Tiger orb, and the shield protecting me vanishes. I search for Marc, but he's nowhere in sight. Panic causes my heart to race faster than I thought imaginable.

I have to find him. I must keep him safe.

Another arrow flies at me. I twist, just missing it. A burst of blue fire hits my arm. I scream out in agony. *Black Turtle! Where are you?*

I pull deep within myself to find its power. I'm desperate, frantic. And then it appears, rising out of the deepest corner of my mind. I hold out my arm where the bracelet is twisted around my wrist. The edges of its black surface sizzle like an electric storm. A burst of light pulses out of the bracelet, creating a sonic boom. Its glacial blue floods the entire plain, every inch that my vision reaches.

And freezes every man, woman, and blade of grass like ice.

My heart stops in shock. I'm not quite sure what I've done, but seeing everything frozen, my mind is blown. I turn as a sword arcs above my head. If I had waited a second longer, I'd have been headless.

I start running, and it's like I'm pushing through thick sludge. I can barely move. But all I can think about is finding Marc.

And then I spot him. A man with a thick beard, braided hair, and a strange button-down suit has his sword partially plunged into Marc's side. I scream and push all of my energy into reaching Marc. When I finally make it to him, I'm panting. I'm so exhausted that I can barely stand. Sweat drips from my forehead and down my back.

I grab the man's sword and pull it out of Marc's side. Inch by inch. Until it's free.

"How dare you!" I scream at the man, rip his sword out of his hands, and fling it into the forest. But that isn't enough so I kick him in the crotch. *Scoundrel.*

But then it all becomes too much, and weariness sets in. I need to release the power of the orb; its energy draws too much out of me. The moment I let it go, the blue air rushes back to my wrist like a wave of gushing water.

Everything unfreezes, and chaos erupts once again. The surprise on the faces of those around me almost satisfies me. Everyone is shifting and glancing about in confusion. I grin. If I wasn't fighting for my life, I'd be laughing at them.

Those beside Marc stand still, watching the warrior fall to the ground, doubled over. Before they can orient themselves, I've kicked two of them, knocking them out cold.

"Marc." I pull him to me. "Are you okay?"

He grunts and slides one sword into a sheath. Then he shoves his hand to his side.

"Still kicking." He grimaces. "What did you do back there? How did you move so fast?"

But there isn't time to talk, because the Guardians are attacking us again. I need to rest so I can use the Black Turtle orb again, but there is no time for rest.

Time, I realize as I block one blow and side-kick at another attacker. That is what the Black Turtle orb does. It stops time. But how can I use that to escape without leaving Marc? Beside me Marc fights with his left hand, but he's sagging. A giant woman with long, wild hair and saucers for eyes jumps over my current attacker and looms above me. She's holding a strange-looking rod. She lifts it up, and as she does, the core of the rod glows and a thin curl of smoke snakes out from it. A muttering sound rumbles from her throat, and her eyes dilate. I back away as the smoke takes the form of a strange-looking beast with bulging eyes and a wide-open mouth. *Oh God.* It's the same as the creature on the outside doors of the mausoleum. The *taotie.*

I just can't.

I can't handle any more beasts. Or swords. Or magic traps or blasts.

I dig deep within myself for every last ounce of my strength and call upon the Black Turtle orb once again. I need it all to stop.

Just stop.

The burst of glacial blue blooms out from my wrist once again. And just in time, because a stream of red snakes is caught in midair, falling from the wild-haired lady's stick. Their fangs are open, inches from my nose, ready to take a chomp out of me.

I spin around and pull on Marc. We move an inch. Then another. It's pointless. I don't have the strength. Pulling him is like hauling a dead horse. If I could just have a little more time, maybe I could think of a way out of this mess. I sag to the ground, exhausted. I pound the earth, knowing I'm wasting my extra strength, but I can't leave without Marc.

The thump of my heartbeat pounds against my ribs, vibrating in my ears. I'm kneeling, but my body feels as if it's running up a steep mountain. In a desperate act, I clutch my bow and arrow. I let loose one, two, three arrows, aiming for the legs of those near me, hoping to slow them down. But the effort kills me. I feel my hold on the orb's power slipping away.

"No!" I scream to the Black Turtle orb. *"No. Don't leave me. I need to save my people."*

And then the ground shudders. A burst of iridescent green light fills the sky, and a cloud funnels down from above, sparkling like emeralds. Wind rushes across the plain. No one in my ice hold moves; only my long hair and clothes are caught in the breeze. The air tastes sweet, and as I breathe it in, it's like drinking springwater. My heartbeat slows, and I rise, my muscles renewed.

The spinning cloud slackens until I can see through its green haze. A man stands in its core wearing a traditional Chinese silk tunic with a jade robe and canary-yellow pants. On top of his head rests a straight red hat, and long black hair falls over his shoulders. A thin mustache curls down on either side of his mouth. I'm not sure who this man is, but I'd be an idiot not to recognize his power. This man must be a Chinese immortal. A great one at that.

I shift back and forth, unsure what to say, what to expect. Finally, I resort to a low bow. When I dare to raise my eyes back up, his face hasn't registered any change. I'm not sure if I've pleased or displeased him. Probably the latter, knowing me. This is another time when it would be helpful to have Marc standing beside me. He'd know who this man is and how to act.

The immortal clasps his hands before him and stares at me with deep brown eyes. "You have stirred trouble like a sand-storm. You sting the eyes and choke the throat."

Being compared to a sandstorm isn't a good thing. Still, stinging and choking are minor infractions compared to what I've actually done.

"I came to recover my people's treasure."

"And in exchange for your treasure, you give pain and death? Interesting."

Crap. I glance around. The faces surrounding us show open mouths, angry eyes. Weapons are raised, and injured warriors are scattered about on the ground. He is right. I've brought pain and war. I cannot deny this. I hang my head.

"I never meant for this to happen," I say. "The immortal who rules me wishes for this orb so he can control not just Korea, but every land on the planet. I am determined to bring it back to the Heavenly Chest. It never was my intention to hurt anyone. But with Kud's contract blazing brighter than a star, no one will believe me. So they are determined to destroy me instead."

"Yes. This I know."

I jerk my head up, surprised he already knows this. "Then you know what is at stake. You have to believe me. All of these other Guardians are trying to stop me, but if they kill me, Kud will just gather up my bones and resurrect me into one of his awful creatures to do his bidding. I have to trick him and stop him. I beg of you, if you have any respect for peace, help me."

"I was sent to speak to you, yet I now see your path is not with me." The air shimmers, and for a moment I'm afraid he is preparing to leave, but there's a look of worry—or is it concern?—that crosses his face. His forehead bunches up.

I'm not about to argue with an immortal. That has never worked well for me. Obviously. But there is one thing I do know: they all have their soft spots. They have their needs and desires, just like we humans do. And as I stand in his presence, I feel my body drawing on his power. There must be something in his cloud that is connected to the Spirit World.

"I don't want any part of this destruction," I say. "The boy I love has been stabbed. He will die if I don't take him to a hospital. Do you think I want to lose him?"

Still, he hesitates. I know there's something in my words, in my humanity, that has found a place in his heart.

"Look at me," I say. "Search me. Am I lying to you? No. I've made a promise to bring the orbs to the Heavenly Chest. Don't make me break it. Let me return to my home and make it a land of peace."

It's that last word—*peace*—that causes his eyebrows to rise. He believes me. I think.

The wind changes and begins to spin. Emeralds sparkle around me until the man is lost once again in an endless funnel. It lifts into the air, disappearing into the clouds. I frown as I watch him leave, and I kick at the ground. He did nothing. Nothing. Immortals are selfish beings, I decide.

But then I freeze, realizing how strong my body has become. I've been foolish. He didn't give me much, but he did give me something. Strength. And, in turn, time. What will I do with it? Kill each of those around me? Or run? Around me everyone is still frozen, and still I'm not tired. I take in each of their faces. They are innocent. They are the good guys. Death doesn't belong in this moment.

I have a few minutes at most before his leftover power fades. I start running in very slow motion to Marc.

I wrap my arm around him and drag him to me. I focus on separating him from the others. I close my eyes. A searing pain stabs my brain, but I ignore it. Finally I'm able to pull him out of his immobile state so that we're together in this frozen world.

I want to memorize this moment. It's just the two of us, alone, separated from the madness that presses on us, desperate to rip us apart from each other. But Marc's eyes clear, and his head whips around, taking it all in. He moves in slow motion, even slower than I move.

"What is going on?" he asks.

"I'm using the Black Turtle orb." I start the slow process of moving, pulling him after me, away from the angry faces and raised weapons. "I've stopped time for everyone but us. We must hurry. My strength is fading."

He doesn't move at first, and his resistance is almost more than I can bear. I feel my hold on him slipping.

"I can't hold on much longer." My voice trembles, and I look at him, begging with my eyes.

He nods and steps after me. Each step lasts a lifetime. It feels as if I'm carrying a load of bricks that weighs more as each second passes. At last we pass by the last of the Guardians. The field spreads before us, and yet I know we haven't gone far enough. I'm now stooped over. Marc has his arms wrapped around me, holding me up, but his grunts tell me he's in pain himself. I can't think of that or of how much blood he's lost. All I can focus on is one step. Then the next.

"The tree line," I whisper as I focus on the trees, their boughs frozen. "Must get there."

My headache now has become a full blazing-fire migraine. My vision is so blurred that I'm not sure which way is which. But I grip the orb. I can't let go of it. Just a little longer.

And then sharp briars cut into my legs and arms.

"We made it." I collapse into the brush.

I release my hold on the orb. The rushing sound pulls back into my wrist. The icy blue sky flushes away, leaving behind the moonlight and the torches. I roll over onto my back, watching the world waking back up. The wisps of clouds snake back across the sky, oblivious to our pain and agony. A shout rises up from the group of warriors in the middle of the field. A smile curls on my lips.

It's not enough. I know this. They will find us soon. But I have to savor the moment when Marc and I disappeared from before their very eyes.

Something grabs my wrists, and then I'm being dragged across the ground and through the brambles. A vague thought crosses my mind: Marc must be pulling me away. But I don't care that my back is being jabbed by rocks and sharp sticks. I want to memorize that vision of chaos on the field. The cries of panic still fill my ears, and I love it. If I could move, I'd throw my head back and laugh.

"Come on, Fighter Girl." Marc's pleading cuts through my maniacal thoughts. "You gotta help me here."

But the thing is, I don't want to help. I want to close my eyes and forget everything. Why does living have to be so freaking difficult?

CHAPTER 28

Marc heaves me against the side of the truck and tosses my bow and quiver to the ground next to me before staggering to the driver's side. I'm too tired to yell at him for lifting me. But the blood that soaks his shirt terrifies me. I grip the sides of the torn vinyl seat and pull my body inside. Before I have even adjusted myself into a sitting position, Marc turns on the engine and slowly rolls the car down the dirt road without the lights on. The truck creeps by the village houses, silent and still except for the laundry waving under the moonlight.

Beside me, Marc grips the steering wheel as if he's about to rip it off. His shirt is dark and wet. Blood pools on the seat next to him. With shaking hands, I rummage through his backpack until I find a large bandage and an Ace wrap. I tie the bandage tight against his side with the elastic wrap and then kiss his cheek.

"Stay alive," I say.

Ahead of us a line of trucks blocks the road. Marc swears under his breath. As soon as we rumble into view, they flick on their lights. I cover my face from the glare.

"So much for sneaking about," Marc mutters.

He jerks the truck to the right and guns the gas. The tires spin, dust flying up, but we take off around the last truck, scraping my side of our truck against a line of pine trees.

Pings of gunshots fill the air.

"They're shooting at us!" I say.

"No. They're shooting at the tires, which is worse."

Marc slams his foot on the gas as we swerve back onto the road. The tires screech. I grip the dashboard as we skid up the ramp onto the main highway.

"Do you know where you're going?" I ask.

Marc flips open the glove compartment, digging through it so that most of the junk falls at my feet. The truck zigs and zags over the empty road. Finally he procures a map.

"No." He slaps it against my chest. "But this should help."

"They will alert the entire police force and the military," I say. "You saw how tight the Chinese Guardians are with them."

"Got a better idea?"

I glare at him, but he's too busy checking the rearview mirror to notice. I snap open the map and squint in the semidarkness, trying to read the Chinese characters. I'm so tired that nothing really makes sense. I flip the map around.

"Don't tell me you can't read the map." Marc lets out a frustrated growl and tries to grab the map. I hold it out of his reach.

"You drive while I try to figure out this GPS system." I stuff the map into the crevice between the door and the seat and begin pushing buttons on the panel. "This truck has all the bells and whistles. I'm sure I can figure it out."

"We don't have time for you to figure things out."

"Impatient, are we?" The system lights up when I touch the button on the right. A girl's voice starts talking to us in Chinese.

"She wants to know where we want to go," Marc says.

"Right." And we have no clue.

"We just passed a sign that says we are on G30 heading toward Xuzhou," he says.

"Which means we are going the exact opposite direction from Xi'an." I sigh.

He rakes his hand through his hair and shrugs. "Could be a good thing. They will be expecting us to head to the airport in Xi'an."

"Which is what we should be doing." I bite my inner lip as I study the map. "This road will eventually take us to the coast."

I type in the characters of the city and push Enter.

"Lianyungang," the electronic girl voice says. I push another button and the lady's voice continues, this time in English. "Lianyungang is well known for its foreign trade port, which has been prominent since the 1680s during the Qing Dynasty. The name comes from Lian Island, located off its coastline."

"Lian Island." Marc slaps the steering wheel. "That's the one."

"Lianyungang," the girl continues, "is located approximately eleven hours and twenty-three minutes from your current location."

"What? Eleven hours? We need to turn around. I'm not driving across all of China for that."

"There's just one problem," I say, rummaging through my backpack. "My passport is missing. I don't know how we'll get back to Korea."

Marc is silent at that. He presses his lips together and his eyebrows rise, and I know he's thinking that we are so screwed.

"The Triads must have taken it when they kidnapped me. We could go back and get it."

He shakes his head. "That's suicide."

I lean back in my seat. It's too dark to see much, but the road stretches before us like an endless path. A light drizzle of rain begins splattering across the windshield. There are hardly any cars on the road. Mostly just large service trucks.

The truck rumbles forward. We sit, listening to the rain and the electronic lady giving us random updates on our progress. All I want to do is close my eyes and sleep for eternity. But I can't, because Marc is bleeding to death. I rack my brain for a way to solve this mess. Maybe I could steal a passport or threaten someone's life. I've gotten good at that kind of stuff lately.

"I don't think they're following us," Marc says. "They must have assumed we went toward Xi'an. Which, granted, would've been the smart move to make."

"We'll find out soon enough."

"We've always wanted to take a road trip." Marc attempts a smile. "Looks like we finally got our wish."

"Yeah. Guess we did." I check his bandage. The bleeding has slowed down. I replace the bandage and rewrap him, and then I pull out the ibuprofen and make him take it. He washes it down with a swig of water.

"You should get some rest," Marc says.

"No. We should stop and get better bandages for your wound, and then *I* should drive."

"Not until I've created more distance between them and us. Besides, I doubt anything is open at three in the morning. You should rest and get your strength up."

"Look who's talking," I say. But then he gives me this adorable look, with his eyebrows raised and his dimples showing. I roll my eyes. "Fine. I'll lie down, but I'm not going to sleep. Someone needs to keep you in line."

I stretch out on the seat, resting my head on his lap. He smells like sweat and blood, but I don't care. He's real and alive and we're together. I clutch the material of his pants leg.

"We should've done one of these road trips a long time ago," I say.

The swaying of the car lulls me into a peaceful rest, and my eyes close of their own accord.

• • •

The truck isn't moving when I wake up. A groan escapes my lips as I lift my head off the vinyl seat. I should never have closed my eyes. Stupid, stupid. Every muscle screams at me as I swing my legs to the floor and sit up. I've got a raging headache that makes my vision swim. Outside, a light haze hovers over the parking lot. We're stopped at the pumps of a Sinopec gas station.

I search the lot and then squint at the glass windows of the convenience store, but Marc isn't anywhere in sight. My heart starts its crazy beating, and even though it hurts to move, I push open the door and slide out of the truck. My knees buckle as my boots hit the pavement, and dizziness causes me to stagger for a moment, but I push away those feelings. Rain drizzles around me, but since we're parked under a flat roof, I stay dry.

A bell rings as I enter the store. The place has a strange feeling. It's similar to a convenience store in the States or Korea, yet not quite the same with the rows of Chinese packaged foods. A clerk with gaunt cheeks and wrinkles radiating from his eyes nods at me as I enter. I can tell by his lack of smile and the tightness around his eyes that he's wary of me. He combs back a strand of greasy hair and returns to reading his newspaper.

Then I spot Marc by the coolers, pulling out bottles of water and waving one in the air to get my attention. I run to him and latch on to his arm.

"I didn't know where you were," I tell him as he piles up bottles in my arms. "I—I kind of panicked."

"I don't know why." He grins down at me and kisses my forehead. "It's not like we've nearly died multiple times or been hunted by strange creatures."

I smile. I could drown in those green eyes of his. A rack full of touristy clothes catches my eye. I grab a T-shirt imprinted with a panda and the words "I love China!" and a pair of black leggings. "I'm going to wash up and change," I say. "That mercury may have belonged in the Spirit World, but I'm not taking any chances of the possibility of it lingering on my skin and clothes."

"True." Marc grabs a black shirt. It has terra-cotta warriors across the front with the words "I am a WARRIOR."

"Suitable?" he asks.

"Very."

After we wash up and change in the bathrooms, we roam the aisles, grabbing armfuls of packaged noodles, snacks, bandages, and water bottles. The phone beside the clerk rings, pulling us back to reality.

"We should hurry," Marc says. "I don't like the way this guy is looking at us. Let's hope he isn't talking to the police."

The clerk now has the phone pressed against his ear, listening.

"It doesn't help that we strolled in here with bloody clothes."

We pile up our purchases on the counter. Marc pulls out some *yuan* and hands the money to the clerk.

"Jae Hwa," the clerk mutters, the phone still pressed to his ear.

I freeze as he utters my name. Marc's outstretched arm stops; the bills sag in his hand. Then Marc snatches the phone from the clerk and snaps it shut. From the corner of my eye, I spot a police car driving into the gas station's parking lot, followed by a black truck, a replica of the one we stole and have been driving.

The cell phone rings on the counter. It shakes and moves with each buzz. The room fades around me, and it's as if I'm looking through a tunnel as I stare at the phone. It's calling for me. I have to answer it. It must be answered.

"Don't." Marc touches my wrist.

But it's too late. I'm reaching for it, flipping it open, and pressing it to my ear. Meanwhile Marc hurtles over the counter, pushing off it with one hand and grabbing a can of vegetables with the other. He smashes the can over the clerk's head, the money flying into the air. Outside, sirens erupt from the parking lot, but all I can focus on is the voice on the other end of the line.

"Jae Hwa."

"Kud," I say.

His voice sends a wave of cold fire through me. My arm flares up as his words reach my ears, the bronze swirling like the flickering of flames.

"Have you found it?" Kud asks. "I hope so, my dearest. Because I thought you should know that I have decided your father will be the first to die."

"No." My body trembles. The memory of Dad's face sways before me.

"You must hurry, Jae Hwa. My princess."

My princess. It's as if he's slapped me across the face. Those words snap me out of my stupor.

"I am not your princess!" I scream, and then I hurl the phone at the window. The glass shatters as the phone crashes through it. The phone sails through the air until it bounces on top of the police car's hood. The policeman leaps from his car and aims his gun at the store's entrance.

Crap.

"Duck!" Marc yells at me.

I dive behind a row of Nongshim instant noodles. Bullets ricochet across the glass, sending shards flying through the air. The clerk groans from behind the counter, and then his hands slap on the countertop, sending the newspaper flying. His head emerges. A giant purple bruise is blossoming on his eye.

"Why did you hit that man?" I ask Marc as we run down the aisle.

"That's not a man," Marc says.

I glance back, and the clerk bares his teeth at me like a rabid animal. "Right."

"I'm not sure who or what he really is," Marc says, "but I'm not sticking around to find out. I think Kud's little phone call did something to the creature."

We peer over the rack to stare out the window. The police officer is talking into his walkie-talkie as a Triad Guardian opens up our truck and pulls out my bow and Marc's sword.

"No way he's touching that." I take off in a running start and dive through the shattered window.

I flip through the air and land in front of the officer. I kick the gun and walkie-talkie from his hands before he even has time to process what has happened. He has this startled look in his eyes. His mouth opens, but nothing comes out. It dawns on me that he's probably never experienced someone like me before. I give him a front-kick to the jaw. Something to remember me by. He crumples to the ground. I nod in satisfaction as his eyes close. It's better that he isn't aware of what's about to happen, because the otherworldly creature in the gas station is now roaring.

Marc races to our truck, but the Triad pulls out a long whip and snaps it, slicing Marc in the shoulder and ripping his shirt. Then I notice that the Triad has shot out our truck's tires. We aren't going anywhere anytime soon.

The clerk or creature or whatever it is stumbles out of the store. He shimmers once, and I get a glimpse of leathery skin, bulging eyes, and two horns protruding from his head. I stand indecisively. It's one thing to deal with these kinds of creatures in the Spirit World. But here in the open, with my body weak and Marc injured, I'm not sure what our options are or where we can go.

"Get in!" Marc yells from the window of the other black truck.

The Triad Guardian is rolling on the asphalt, hands pressed to his stomach. *Good one, Marc.* I snatch up my bow and quiver from the ground next to the Triad and jump into the truck. Once again, we're racing away, tires squealing as we take off down the highway.

"We won't have much time before the police and the entire Grand Council are on our tails," Marc says. "I'm sure he alerted them to our location."

"We can't go to any airport." I bite my lips. "They know who we are and where we're heading."

"You shouldn't have answered the phone."

"You shouldn't be driving. It's my turn."

He doesn't say anything and grips the steering wheel tighter. I look out the window, refusing to have this conversation. I can't face the truth, not out loud.

How can I explain that I couldn't stop myself? That the pull was too strong? This thought alone terrifies me. The weight of it settles into the pit of my stomach like a giant rock. I rub my hand up and down my bow, focusing on its smoothness and the grooves where the notches are located. What if I can't say no to Kud once I enter Korea?

I know Marc is thinking these very same thoughts right now. Is he second-guessing his choice to be with me? I peek over at him. His jaw is set and his knuckles are white.

Deep breaths, I tell myself. I can't panic at this point. Still, it's hard to control the thoughts flying through my mind, because Kud said Dad was next.

Dad.

Wearing his perfectly pressed suits. Searching through the forest for a tiny white ball just because he's never lost one of Mom's precious golf balls. Tears falling from his eyes when he waved good-bye to me at the bus terminal when I went to North Korea.

I wonder what he's doing now and where he's at. His tie is probably crooked. I hope he's not drinking too much. That he hasn't drowned himself in work. That he's sleeping and not making a million paper cranes.

What does Kud have planned for him?

"We will find a way." Marc finally breaks the strained silence, eyeing me. The worry hasn't left his face. "We can do this."

"I'm glad you came to China." I run my finger over the edge of my tortoise bracelet. "You've gotten pretty tough out there."

"Training paid off, I guess. Nothing else to do after you left."

"What about that girl who was with you?" The question just pops out on its own. It's one I've been dying to ask but have been too scared to face. In fact, I hadn't planned on saying anything at all because I didn't deserve to have him waiting for me.

"Hana? She's a friend. She doesn't even compare to you."

I pull out a bandage and lift Marc's shirt. I pour some water on his wound, and then I dab some antiseptic on it and apply another bandage. At least the bleeding has stopped.

"She didn't look at you like a friend."

He shrugs, and then a smile creeps across his face, his eyes twinkling. "You jealous? Yes, you are. Jae Hwa Lee is jealous."

I glare at him. "Maybe a little. I'm surprised the Council sent you, given your relationship with me. And you are pretty new."

"They didn't at first." He lets out a sigh. "Your grandfather made me promise not to tell you, but I think you deserve to know."

I frown. "Know what?"

"His fighting abilities aren't like they once were. He said he was too old. So he asked me to go and keep an eye on you. At the last minute in the airport, he added me to the team. Jung was against it. Said I was too involved, which was true, but your grandfather insisted. I've no idea what the Council of Shinshi will think of this when we get back home. They'll probably kick him out for insubordination or something."

"Who would ever think that my family could cause so much trouble?"

"My dad is going to kill me. But it was worth it." Marc glances in the rearview mirror. "I think they're following us."

"That's crazy. How did they know where we are?"

Marc taps on the console. "There must be a tracker in these trucks. It's the only thing I can think of that would explain how they keep finding us."

"Great. We'll need to ditch this soon." I see a sign for the port, and a new thought hits me. "The port. It's perfect."

Marc nods slowly and takes the next exit. "It's worth a try."

CHAPTER 29

We park the truck in an abandoned grocery store parking lot, load up our belongings, and take off in the direction of Lianyungang Port. Every alley and person we pass on the street causes me to wince, especially since everyone openly eyes us. I can't blame them. We're sporting our new tourist T-shirts, but our shoulders are hunched as we shuffle along, and we've got our weapons strapped to our backs.

"If anyone asks"—Marc's voice sounds as if each word takes effort—"we're on our way to a costume party."

"Either that or the loony bin."

"That might be closer to the truth."

As we hike down the quaint cobblestone sidewalk lined with trees, I keep a sharp lookout for the Triads. Once they discover our discarded truck, it won't be long before they find us. Between Marc's injury and my lingering fatigue from using the orbs, we're both having trouble just walking.

Most of the houses we pass by are bordered by shoulder-high concrete walls decorated with geometric cutouts, which I would consider pretty in any other situation. But as things stand, the streets begin to feel claustrophobic. If a Triad truck were to come barreling down the road, there's nowhere for us to run.

The mountains rise up behind us, covered in lush, vibrant greens that seem to call me away from the bustle of the city. But I press on, focusing on the tall cranes and ships in the distance. As we near the port, the smells of fish and the brine of the ocean reach my nostrils. The houses turn into box-like concrete buildings. They are devoid of shutters and washed of color, leaving behind a mix of browns and grays. Only a blue-and-yellow umbrella at a fruit stand resists the bland world of concrete.

Soon we come out onto the docks, and the quietness of the town vanishes. We're immersed in the clanking of cranes, the rumbling of trucks, and the honking of boats. Containers, labeled "China Shipping," are stacked up on the docks like Lego bricks.

"We need to find a boat heading to Korea," Marc says.

The docks are overwhelming, and I don't know where to begin our search. Crane after crane lines up along the docks, their orange and blue structures reminding me of storks as they reach to the sky and then dip down to pick up containers before loading them onto container ships. A sea breeze washes over me, whispering in my ears to hurry, hurry, hurry.

I eye the road and spot a truck with the emblem of the Triad Guardians on its side. I shove Marc behind a building. The once-white siding is now yellowed and splattered with mud, but I don't care as I press my back against it.

"They're here," I tell Marc. "I saw one of their trucks."

"If only it were darker. We'd have an easier time blending in."

We dart from structure to structure and then slip behind a row of containers in a myriad of colors: brown, orange, green. We pass by a giant sculpture of an anchor set on top of a rectangular platform. A tourist group circles the structure, snapping pictures of it. Marc pauses and then joins the group to gawk up at it.

"This is the symbol of the Eurasia Continental Railway that spans two continents, all the way to Europe," Marc says.

I drag him to me. "We don't have time to admire architecture."

"If we make it out of this mess alive, you've got to promise to travel the world with me."

"We don't have time for this. Come on."

"Promise?"

Sweat coats Marc's brow, and he sways slightly on his feet. His shirt looks wet near his injury. I touch his side. Blood covers my fingers, causing my heart to kick up a notch.

"Yes, I promise. I'll go anywhere."

Satisfied with my answer, he grabs my hand and we take off again. Once we come to a secluded section where we can hide behind a shed and a stack of containers, I force Marc to take off his shirt and blood-soaked bandages. Then I pour fresh bottled water over his wound and apply the last of the antiseptic cream to it. I bandage him up again, and we take off. We wander through the containers, and soon Marc finds a Hyundai container ship.

"Bet you that ship's heading to Korea," Marc says.

Not far away, we find a guy with a clipboard barking orders into his walkie-talkie. It seems like he's talking to a crane operator above.

"You distract the foreman and find a way to get him to put down the clipboard." Marc points to the clipboard guy. "Then I can check to see if the destination is mentioned on the manifest."

I smooth down my hair and adjust my wrinkled panda shirt. I can't even imagine what I must look like at this moment, but *homeless*, *vagabond*, and *crazy lunatic* are all words that come to mind. I plaster on a smile and sashay over to where the guy stands. He's wearing a bright orange jumpsuit, the zipper trailing the length of his torso. An insignia patch is stitched on to the right side of the uniform. Most of his dark-colored hair is hidden beneath his orange helmet. From the hard set of his jaw and the way he clutches his walkie-talkie, I can tell he means business.

"Hello," I say, hoping he speaks English. "I'm kind of lost. Can you tell me where the closest place is to get some food?"

"Misses," the foreman says, and then he frowns as he takes in my clothes. "No English."

I wave my hand in front of my face and sigh. "Please. You must help me. I think I might faint."

Meanwhile Marc has slipped up behind him, trying to crane his head over the guy's shoulder to read the clipboard. There's no way this is going to work. I decide to speed things up. I throw myself at the guy, pretending to faint. He drops the clipboard and manages to catch me.

"Oh, sir." I clutch him tight. This way he won't be able to turn and see Marc pick up the clipboard. *Come on, Marc. Hurry it up, already.* "Thank you. You saved me."

The man starts rattling off something about how I'm not supposed to be here. Marc lifts up his head, and his eyebrows rise. The guy calls out to someone in the construction trailer behind us and then wraps his arms around me, as if to carry me. He smells like a mix of fish, sweat, and beer. Gross.

Finally Marc slips the clipboard back down at the guy's feet and walks around to stand in front of the foreman.

"There you are, baby." Marc lets out a relieved sigh and holds out his hands as if he's been searching for me all day. "I've been looking everywhere for you."

I bite back a laugh. Who knew Marc could be such a good actor? "About time," I snap. "I'm dying of hunger."

Marc thanks the foreman in Mandarin and hugs me close to him as we stroll away.

"This is the boat we want to take," Marc whispers into my ear. "It leaves for Incheon in an hour. We have to figure out how to get on it ASAP."

We hunker down behind a set of crates as a light drizzle begins to fall. Crewmen move about the docks, hauling ropes and calling out for the last containers to get settled in. Around us the port is full of sounds of honking and seagulls. Ships are pulling in and out of the docks. Finally, the area is clear and no one seems to be walking about. Marc nods at me. We sprint across the slick concrete, cross the gangplank, and slip onto the ship's deck.

We slink about the narrow passageways until Marc finds a map of the ship printed on the wall.

"We'll need to find a place that isn't busy." He traces his finger across the map. "Let's go to the cargo hold. Seems like our best bet."

A crewman strolls by, puffing on his cigarette. We duck into an alcove and wait for him to pass. Then we take off down the passageway. We can't mess up or let ourselves be seen. This is our only chance to get to Korea and get there quick.

When we get to the hold, the smell assaults me. It's a mix of sewage and dead fish.

"How long do you think we'll be down here?" I ask Marc. "Because I'm not sure I can stand this stench."

"Hopefully we'll be out by tomorrow morning if all goes well."

We find a dark corner far from the doors and settle down. My stomach growls, and I kick myself for not grabbing those snacks and water bottles at the convenience store. I check Marc's wound one more time. All this running around is making it nearly impossible for him to heal.

"I'll go scavenge some food once things get settled," I say. "You should rest that wound of yours."

I have to admit, I'm exhausted. My muscles ache. My head pounds. It hurts to even think about moving to stand. My body has been living high on adrenaline for the past twenty-four hours, and now that we're safe, it's crashing.

Before I know it, I'm lying down on the cold floor next to Marc and my eyes are shutting. He pulls me closer so that I'm leaning against his chest, and I fall into a sleep filled with the sound of his heartbeat, steady and strong.

. . .

I wake to the sound of loud clanging and honking. I check my watch. We've been sleeping like the dead for at least twelve hours. Marc sleeps heavily beside me, oblivious to the commotion above. I stare at him, his face so smooth except for the light stubble. His hair is wild, as usual. I itch to run my hands through it, but I don't dare wake him. He needs every second of rest. Even his lips tempt me. He's got a cut on the right side of his bottom lip, probably from one of the fights we got into. God. There have been so many battles.

So much pain. So much separation. I tuck my knees to my chest and cover my face with my palms. I know I should be checking to see what is going on, but I don't need to be told where we are.

We're in Korea. I can feel it all the way in my bones. It's a good feeling, as if I'm breathing in the air I've been meant for. Yet at the same time, that sense of dread fills me. Because everything I've fought for these last few months will come down to these next few hours.

I think about how I couldn't resist answering that stupid phone, and goose bumps trail up my arms. I want to be strong. I want to have enough strength within me to complete this task and save my family, my country.

I look over at Marc and I almost smile at his peacefulness. I want to save *us*.

A shimmer of light illuminates the cargo hold, golden and warm. Curious, I squirm out from behind the container that Marc and I have made into our haven for the last twelve hours. Peeking around the corner, I see Haechi standing before me. He's beautiful and terrible all at once, and his lion-like body seems even more massive than I remembered. His golden hair shifts with each breath he takes. His eyes are fiery and alive, yet there's the deep wisdom showing in them, too.

He bows his head. I edge out from my hiding place, which is silly, really. He's here because he knows I'm here. I bow in return.

"Daughter of Korea," Haechi says. His rumbling voice reminds me of thunder on a summer day. "You have returned with the treasures."

"Yes."

I open my mouth, but I don't have words. Technically, Haechi and I are now enemies. He's on Palk's side, and I'm on Kud's. Light and darkness. Good and evil. But does it have to be that way? It's as if a gap looms before us. I feel the shove of Kud's anger at Haechi's interference, and at the same time I feel the pull of Haechi, the defender of the weak, the homeless, the hopeless. The hopelessness in me overcomes my other emotions and draws me to him.

"And what is your will in this?" He tilts his head to the side, and I still can't decide if he's a lion or a dragon.

"I am bound to Kud." I hold up my contract, and it shimmers and flickers, stronger now that I'm standing on Korean soil. And yet my voice is weak and my head hangs. I'm full of hatred at myself for every mistake, every battle wound.

At what I've become.

"Yet the choice still lies within you," Haechi says.

"This is true." I hold up the Black Turtle orb. "I know what needs to be done. But I need your help. Can you take us to Palk?"

"I will do what I can. We must hurry on the wings of the crane. Danger is near."

At his words, panic sets in. He's right. We've wasted too much time sleeping. Kud has probably been able to regroup to meet me. I rush to wake Marc, who startles when he sees Haechi. Marc nods and bows. Haechi takes off across the room toward the door, bounding around the crates and containers as if they are merely cones in a maneuver he's practiced every day. Marc and I sprint around the obstacles and follow him up the stairs, our boots clanging on the metal grating. Then we run through the smooth-walled corridors until we are out in the open air.

I stop at the view that greets me: the mountains in the distance rising up like sleeping dragons, the churning dark waters, the port lined with cranes in neat rows. The sky above is full of rolling gray clouds streaked with oranges and purples as the sun begins its descent over the mountains. A deep sadness rolls over me. I don't want to lose any of this.

But Haechi bounds ahead and we follow. We come to the gangplank, and the dock is full of workers shouting orders and unloading cargo. They might not be able to see Haechi, but they'll definitely be able to see Marc and me.

Haechi stops and lets out a long roar. A gust of wind blows from his jaws, streaming out across the gangplank and down the dock to the street.

"Come on," Marc yells, grabbing me. "He's making an invisible path for us. Cloaking us from the workers."

The two of us take off, sprinting across the docks and down the street into a marketplace. Lanterns illuminate the market into the evening, casting an orange glow on the carts stacked with fish. We duck and squeeze through a throng of people. A scooter nearly runs me over. I leap out of the way just in time, the heat from the engine hot on my skin.

Ajusshis and *ajummas* sit on their stools, focused on the miniature television screens set up in their shops. I stop at one shop as the images on the screen catch my eye: tanks rumble down dirt roads, and then rows and rows of soldiers flash across the screen. The announcer comes on, and as he speaks, the image of the North Korean president pops up in the top right of the screen.

"We are on the brink of war," the announcer says. "The UN has been called in for peace talks, but from the movement we are seeing in the North, it looks like peace is not on North Korea's agenda."

Marc runs back to find me and grabs my arm. "We need to go now. A group of wild hounds is chasing us."

"We need to find the bus station," I say. "Unless you know a way into the Spirit World."

Haechi catches up with us. Blood is splattered over his golden fur and horns. "There is an entrance to the Spirit World this way," he says with a growl.

But when we come to a wide-open courtyard, we stumble to a stop. There before us stand nearly all of the Guardians that we had just left in China yesterday. A stone lantern rests directly behind them, and wavering light from it engulfs the area. It's an entrance to the Spirit World. It has to be.

CHAPTER 30

I look at Haechi. He's eyeing the group and pawing at the ground. I realize that no one other than Marc and I can see Haechi. He's kept himself shrouded.

Jung strides forward, his sword clenched in his fist at his side. "I told you they'd come here. They need an entrance to the Spirit World."

"You were right," the head of the Grand Council says. "She's got determination, if nothing else."

"Hand over the orbs," Jung says. "I will make sure they are placed safely in the Heavenly Chest. You can't be trusted. You are a servant of Kud. I bet you don't even know how much he controls you."

"I may be his slave, but he doesn't control my soul," I say, but I feel myself wavering. Is he right? Do I have enough control over myself to return the orbs to their rightful place? And what difference does it make if I give the orbs to Jung or anyone here? Still, I find myself unable to trust anyone with these treasures.

"You will have to trust us. We are close. So close to achieving our goal. How about you come and escort me?"

"Are you really that foolish?" Jung shakes his head in frustration. "Jae, I have to admit that I was wrong about you. I believe that you're innocent. But I also believe you're living in a delusion. Let's just say you're telling the truth. You enter the Spirit World, and then Kud shows up. When he appears, you will be helpless, and you'll hand over the orbs even though you don't want to. Then we will all die."

"The Guardians mean well," Haechi says. "And perhaps they are right."

I turn to Haechi, and suddenly I'm unsure of everything. If he thinks they are right, maybe I've been warped. Maybe Kud has affected my judgment. Maybe I am completely delusional. I rub my hands up and down on the Black Turtle orb bracelet, wishing someone would tell me the right thing to do. I remember how Kud pulled me away from the Tiger of Shinshi and how Grandfather had been unable to stop me.

"What should I do?" I ask Haechi.

"The Guardians are right. It is a great risk," Haechi says. "You must do what you believe is right. I will go and alert Palk."

"But—"

"Stay strong." And with those words, Haechi dives over the Guardians' heads into the wavering light and vanishes in a swirl of wind, gold, and magic.

"Who are you speaking to?" Jung asks, raising his sword.

"Haechi," Marc says. "He's going to ask Palk for help. The reality is Jae is the only one strong enough to stand up to Kud.

We must tread carefully. He's raising creatures from the dead to do his bidding. If we're not careful, we'll all become his slaves."

"You're both crazy, man," Jung says. "Us getting defeated is minor in the full scheme of things. Haven't you heard? North Korea just invaded the eastern provinces, and their nukes are aimed right at us. We are at war. The time for wishful thinking is over."

What if Jung and the Guardians are right? Now that I've reclaimed the orb and brought it back to Korea for the next stage in its journey, maybe I need to let someone else take over the task.

"Fine," I say. "I just hope you're right."

Everyone stares at me, holding their breath as I pull the chain from around my neck. The White Tiger orb's glow is muted, and just taking it off sends an ache through my body. I hold it before me, suddenly desperate not to part with it.

"Are you sure?" Marc says.

"No."

Jung's eyes widen as he realizes what I'm doing. Quickly he pulls out a black pouch from his side. "This is the very pouch the original Guardians used to transfer the orbs to their secret locations a thousand years ago." He holds out the open pouch for me. "I don't dare touch them, so be careful as you place them inside."

My hands shake as I drop the orbs, one at a time, into the pouch. It takes every ounce of my strength not to snatch them back up. The Guardians push in to get a better view, and a murmur of victory rushes through the group as the orbs settle inside. But when Jung pulls the ties tight, closing the pouch, the air around me seems to cut off. I gasp, choking, needing air.

Marc grabs my body as my knees give way beneath me. The pouch flashes bright and then returns to solid black, as if nothing of consequence is inside. But I know what's in there, because the shimmering images of the Black Turtle and White Tiger have suddenly appeared on either side of Jung.

"You made the right choice," Jung says, and then he turns to Hana, who is standing at his side. "Take this to the entrance of the Spirit World and wait for Palk."

She nods, and as she does, a look passes between the two. He reaches up and touches the side of her face, which is clenched in grim determination.

I grab her shoulder. "Your vision? Has it changed?"

Her forehead knots up, and she frowns. "No, not yet." Then she turns and slips through the crowd.

The Guardians break up, many moving to protect Hana, but all I can do is watch the tiger and turtle vanish before my eyes.

"Wait!" I cry out to them. But they are gone, and their loss has carved out a hollow corner in my chest.

Did I make the right choice?

A sharp wind sails out of the lantern and into the air. The ground at my feet fills with a dark mist. It rises in a funnel until it's hard to see anything beyond Jung. The Guardians all cry out and unsheathe their weapons.

There, emerging out of the darkness, is Kud. He is cloaked in black, his ribbons of night slithering around as if searching for his first prey.

"Welcome home, my princess," Kud says. "I knew you would come and bring me my treasure. Your timing could not be more perfect. The world is changing as we speak. *I* am changing it. Together we will rule the world."

He hasn't realized yet that I don't have either orb. Maybe Jung was right. Hana can slip into the Spirit World before he realizes the truth.

"I am *not* your princess." And I lift my bow and aim an arrow at Kud's face. I know it will be pointless, but I want him to know how I feel deep down in my heart of hearts.

Then the Guardians do the unexpected. Those not guarding Hana surround me, offering protection.

"It's time to see if you really can fight against your master," Jung says to me. "Are you with us or against us?"

"I've always been with you," I say. "And I've been begging you for your help all along. South Korea can't win this war without the two final orbs. The question is, are *you* ready to fight side by side?"

It's as if a burden has lifted from Jung's shoulders. A grin flashes across his face. He draws one of the two swords strapped to his back and tosses it to Marc. Then he raises his fist into the air and lets out a vibrating battle cry. The other Guardians rally to his call.

As one, the Guardians attack with their magical swords, bows, and spears. But they are no match for Kud. He snaps into them with his thick silk cords, ripping them to pieces like string cheese.

"Help!" It's Hana, calling out from the entrance to the Spirit World.

A wave of Kud's bloodhounds is leaping out of the portal, snarling and snapping their bloodthirsty jaws. Hana wields her bident, but she's completely surrounded.

"Interesting," Kud says and then turns his silver eyes to study me. "You've hidden the orbs with her. That was stupid."

"No!" I scream just as he shoots out one of his black cords. He wraps it around her neck while the hounds leap on top of her body as one.

There are too many hounds for the Guardians. No one can reach her side in time.

I unleash arrow after arrow into the hounds' bodies. As my arrows sink into their mangy fur, they cry out and vanish into plumes of dust. Jung answers Hana's call, slicing his sword through the mass of hounds. But as the two of us race to help her, leaping over fallen bodies of Guardians, I know we're too late. Her body lies in the dirt, arms flung askew.

Kud moves in and tries to grab the pouch. I see the White Tiger and Black Turtle emerge once again. Their shimmering forms snap at Kud's hand, and he roars in pain, tumbling backward into a throng of Guardians.

Oblivious to the orbs, Jung grabs Hana's body and pulls her to him, crying out in anger. I skid to a halt and snatch up the black pouch. Without hesitation, I slip the White Tiger and Black Turtle orbs back on, and as I do, it's like I'm breathing in spring air.

"I should never have let her have these," I tell Jung. "If I'd listened to my instincts, she would still be alive. Now I have to live with knowing I could've prevented her death."

Gently he sets Hana back on the ground, and he stares at me with misty eyes. "No, Jae Hwa, her blood is mine to avenge. Kud is the monster here." Then, with a clenched jaw, he picks up his sword and sprints off toward Kud.

I'm about to join him, but I'm distracted by a light on the horizon, shining like a star at dawn. There's something about that light that draws me, but I shake my head and turn away. I need to help the Guardians. After gathering up my arrows, I lift up my bow again and aim for Kud's oncoming bloodhounds. It's ironic how suddenly Marc and I are standing side by side with those who only moments ago wanted us dead.

Kud's tentacles are everywhere, curling around the Guardians' necks and squeezing until they are dead. Then another horde of Kud's bloodhounds dive out of midair through the mist and land in the middle of the fight. Behind me I hear warriors cry out in terror. I spin around to see one hound land on the tall Nordic warrior and rip out a chunk of flesh from his back. I notch in another arrow, but as I do, the contract on my arm begins to burn.

It takes all of my willpower to let that arrow fly. I cry out in agony as the pain becomes nearly unbearable, but finally, I unleash the arrow. It sinks between the bloodhound's eyes, killing it instantly. I did it. I was able to resist the power of the contract.

There isn't time to ponder or celebrate. I let another arrow fly, aiming one after another at the bloodhounds. I've been waiting for so long to kill these horrible beasts, and if I weren't in such pain, I would laugh in glee as they fall to the ground and disappear.

"Good to be fighting on the same side again," Kumar says, coming to fight next to me. He slashes his sword at an oncoming tentacle. "I never once doubted you."

I smile at Kumar, but as he turns to give me a big grin, one of Kud's cords flies up and wraps around Kumar's neck, quicker than a flick of a whip. Kumar's eyes bulge out, and his sword clatters to the ground.

"No!" I lunge and grab the tentacle, pulling at it with all my might. It doesn't budge. Then I begin stabbing the silky material with my arrow. Behind me, Kud is laughing, and the contract on my arm flares up like it's on fire. I scream and hold my wrist. All I can see is red stars. Bending over and panting from the pain, I focus instead on Kumar. His face is turning blue.

"Hold tight," I tell Kumar. "I just need to pull harder."

I grit my teeth and put all my weight into pulling the black cords off his neck. I won't let Kud take another friend of mine from me. I won't. I can't. Tears race down my face.

"Tell Lily . . . I love . . . her." Kumar's voice sounds like tires crunching over gravel. "I'll miss . . . her . . . the most."

"No!" I scream and pull harder.

I search the crowd for Marc and his sword. Then I spot him at the far end of the courtyard, chopping at the thick cords holding down the head of the Grand Council. He is only fighting with one of the dueling dragon swords, but even alone, it doesn't disappoint. The black strings of Kud's robe snap at each slice of Marc's blades. I scream Marc's name. He lifts his head, his wild eyes searching for the source of my voice. But by the time Marc races over and reaches me, Kumar's eyes have glazed over. His head lolls back.

Seeing his friend's face, Marc lets loose an unearthly scream. His face contorts in anger and his eyes blaze. He clenches his jaw, raises his sword, and charges at Kud. It's like the same nightmare all over again: Marc and I fighting for our lives against Kud. And losing. But this time I feel Kud's anger rise, a furnace of rage ready to boil as he sees Marc. Perhaps he realizes how close Marc and I are despite the distance, despite the contract, despite being bound to two separate worlds.

The light I had noticed earlier now blazes brighter and cuts the darkness, shining down and illuminating Marc and the spectrum around him. I gape in shock.

Grandfather is flying in on a shining horse. I have seen many things, but this shocks me more than anything. I never in a million years would have thought this possible.

"Haraboji?" I say as he alights from the flying horse.

The flying horse of Korea. The Chollima. Brilliant white as the North Star, the Chollima flies on the threads of time in the Spirit World. I've only read about this horse in the old stories, and I remember the model Grandfather had in his house. Once again I realize there's a whole lot more to Grandfather than I'd ever thought possible.

"Jae Hwa!" Grandfather runs to me. "Palk sent me. You must go. Take Chollima and fly!"

"But—I can't." I gesture to the fighting around me. My eyes fall back on Marc swiping at Kud's appendages. He's been entwined by a long snaking tentacle, and I know there's no way he can win. Not against Kud and his Red Phoenix orb.

Grandfather doesn't pause to question me, but runs to join Marc, drawing a sword of his own. Knowing his collection of artifacts from ages of the past, I'm sure this weapon is no ordinary sword. He swipes at one appendage and then another, drawing closer with each blow. He twirls and swoops his sword over his head, plunging it into tentacle after tentacle. He moves like he's in a dance. A dance with death.

I should leave them all and escape on Chollima. But I can't. My chest still aches from watching Kumar's life get sucked from him, and I can't lose anyone else.

I run to join them, leaping over the snake-like cords and dodging hounds. When Grandfather reaches Marc, he frees Marc with one fell swoop. The Guardians finally spot him, and a cheer rises up within the ranks. But this doesn't please Kud. He roars like a beast that has been awakened from an ancient sleep, dreaming of treasures and power.

"How dare you face me, old one?" Kud's voice is thunder.

Marc and I flank Grandfather as the darkness swirls around us, kicking up dread and despair. I want to sag to the ground. My arm aches, the contract willing me to stab my own grandfather, to rip the sword from his hand and plunge it into his heart. Tears trickle down my face as I stand, unable to move. Unable to fight. It takes everything within me just to resist the call of the contract and the images that push me to do the unimaginable.

The darkness shifts again and Kud's robes spread open, revealing the Red Phoenix orb shimmering in a deathly fire before us. The orb swirls, around and around, spinning stronger until I feel all the anger within me and around me seeping into Kud. All around us, cries of anger shudder across the courtyard. I press my palms over my ears, desperate to drown out the screams of hatred that fill my brain. The Guardians around me fall to the ground, screaming out obscenities. Marc has his hands over his head, pressing his body against the blasting winds that threaten to send him to the ground.

But Grandfather stands strong beside me. A wall against the rage. His eyes are closed, and a slight smile crosses his mouth, as if he knows something we don't. Then his whole body springs to life.

He holds his sword before him and bows. His lips move, but I can't hear his words over the howling screams and winds. Then he charges at Kud, swinging and cutting. Kud's dark folds are sliced to ribbons. Grandfather is enveloped in a sea of crimson.

"Fly on Chollima, my Jae Hwa," Grandfather's voice sails across the winds to me. "Fly to Palk and save us all."

Hunched over, screaming in pain, my world a blur of black and red, I back away, fighting against the bronze words sizzling over my skin. If I'm going to escape, now is the time. Still, I can't leave Grandfather. I can't let him sacrifice himself for me.

Slowly, I lift my bow and let loose an arrow at a tentacle circling Grandfather. This allows Grandfather to get close enough to Kud, and he lifts his sword, aiming to pierce the orb. The blood-red rays of the orb converge together, abandoning every other inch of the courtyard. The screams halt. The wind vanishes.

It's as if Kud has given up. I hold my breath as Grandfather pulls back his sword and thrusts it at the orb. But not fast enough.

In a trembling blast, all of the orb's power and all of Kud's power hits Grandfather. Sparkles radiate from Grandfather's skin, and he cries out, his arms open wide. His sword clatters to the ground, and so does his body. The wind shudders around us all and flings me backward, sending me tumbling and rolling across the ground from the power of the hit. Red dust erupts outward, and I can't see anything. The blast is so loud, it booms and rumbles across the land.

The dust settles, revealing Grandfather lying on the ground, faceup, with Kud hovering over him. I scream. And I can't stop. Everyone else watches in silence. Their leader has been killed.

"You will be mine now," Kud says to Grandfather's fallen body. "I am always on the lookout for great warriors to enlist in my army."

"No!" I say in gasping sobs. "Don't you dare use him as one of your dead slaves."

Desperate to reach Grandfather, I start crawling across the gravelly pavement, finally free to move with ease.

"Jae!" Marc cries out my name. "Don't! You need to leave. Now!"

Marc is right. So very right. I need to get out of here and fly away. But Grandfather's body calls out for me to wrap my arms around him, to protect him. The thought of his body being used to fulfill Kud's purposes kills me.

Then a white figure stands before me. I peer up to see Bari, her white *hanbok* a sharp contrast to the darkness and blood pouring around us. Why is she here? Then it hits me. She's here to collect the dead.

"You must go," she says. "Your grandfather is gone."

I shake my head. "I can't. Kud will use his body."

I scurry around her and gather Grandfather into my arms, his face still warm against my palms. His eyes stare wide open as if gazing at the first stars peeking through the gathering darkness. My muscles freeze, and the finality of his death propels a shock of loss through me, so deep that everything inside of me aches.

Kud is reaching down to grab Grandfather up out of my arms when Bari whooshes between Kud and me. She slams her spear into the ground, splintering the pavement into jagged cracks between herself and Kud. Blinding light explodes across the area.

"You are not granted access to this departed one," Bari says in a commanding voice.

Meanwhile Marc untangles my numb arms from Grandfather and wraps his arms around me. He begins dragging me away. I stretch out my hands, my fingers clawing for Haraboji.

"No. No. No," I hear my voice say, a hoarse whisper.

"You interfere." Kud growls at Bari.

"Hardly." Bari waves her left hand in an arc, creating a banner of glistening light radiating from the spear's tip. "I'm merely following my due course of action."

The light cascades, following the path from the spear tip to Grandfather's body, and then it swirls around him. It gathers up Grandfather's body, and the two disappear.

My heart tumbles in my chest as Marc hauls me away. "Thank you, Bari," I whisper, never letting my eyes leave where Grandfather had fallen. "Thank you."

Kud now turns to me. "I warned you, my princess. Hand over the orbs, and all will be right."

Kud's voice awakens me from my stupor. The power of his hold surges back into my arm so strongly that it jerks me away from Marc and pulls me toward Kud. Marc and a group of other Guardians seize my body, gripping me from all sides, and literally drag me to Chollima.

The muzzle of a horse pushes against my back. Marc grabs me around the middle, while the other Guardians help toss me onto the horse. They hold me in place as I scream out in pain from the contract burning me. I'm vaguely aware of Marc sliding in behind me just as the horse takes off into the air. The burning sensation lessens as we pull away from Kud's presence, and I let out a long breath. Finally, I'm able to lift my head. Chollima's wings beat faster, raining stardust over the Guardians below.

Kud's roar shakes the ground. The air kicks up into a windstorm, pulling every Guardian to him. The dark funnel rises like a tornado, but Chollima pumps its wings faster, and we lift into the sky.

Higher and higher we soar. The clouds drape over me, moisture pulling at my hair and soaking my clothes. I lean in to Chollima. Its body is warm and its fur is softer than rose petals, but all I can see in my mind is Grandfather, soaked in red and lying lifeless on the ground. I clamp my eyes shut as if that will block the memory. Instead, I relive watching the Guardians being dragged to Kud, screaming their final words, and Grandfather standing alone before the god of darkness.

The most horrible part is that I know what he'll do with them. He'll create monsters from them all. I press my face into Chollima's fur, unsure if the wetness soaking my skin is tears or moisture from the air. I can't let Grandfather's death be for nothing. I must return the orbs, or all the Guardians' deaths will be for naught. Grandfather's words still beat through me: *Save us all.*

Will returning the orbs be enough, though? I've spent all this time with the monster, and I have yet to find a weakness other than unmatchable anger, fueled by an orb that takes that anger and makes him even more powerful.

"Hurry," I tell Chollima.

We are nearly there, the flying horse replies in my mind.

"How did you know my grandfather?" I ask.

We have been fast friends for a very long time. Do not worry. I know what you carry. For Korea, for the world, we must succeed.

Relief washes over me. We are almost there. All this pain and suffering can end soon. I stare down through the thicket of clouds to the ground thousands of feet below. I see buildings, highways filled with tiny dots, rice paddies, and rolling hills. And then I jerk upright.

A massive blast erupts in a city along the coast. Black plumes burst into the air.

"North Korea has struck Incheon," Marc says. "The war has advanced."

Then, directly below us, I see the black funnel we had left behind roving over the land like a tornado, decimating everything in its path. It stretches upward, higher and higher, until it has nearly reached us. Dark winds kick up in a swirling mass. Chollima neighs, rocking back and forth. Marc grabs my waist while I clutch the horse's neck to keep from falling off.

Pain sears through my arm. I lift it up and see the contract blazing in a sparkling bronze fire.

No.

Then I feel the jerk on my arm, and I'm nearly wrenched off the horse.

"Marc!" I say. "The contract is trying to pull me off."

I'm not sure what Kud is trying to do. Maybe I've finally angered him enough for him to want to kill me.

Marc tightens his hold on my waist, but my whole body is hauled left, and I slide off the horse. Marc clutches me tight, using his legs to hold himself on to the horse. Chollima neighs in resistance, pawing at the air. The darkness wells up below us, wisps of blackness trailing up like hungry vines.

I scream in agony as my arm fires out shocks that feel like bolts of electricity. My body jerks and convulses.

"Let go of me!" I have to scream at Marc over the winds. "I can't stop the pull. You can't come with me."

"I'm not letting go," Marc says. "We're in this together."

"No. He'll kill you."

Marc presses his lips together but doesn't let go of me. The pain tears through me so strongly that it takes every ounce of my energy to resist. I groan and grit my teeth as I hold on with my hand, trying to keep myself from falling into the gloom below. Chollima's wings beat frantically, but the darkness convulses around us. The horse whips its head back and forth as if lost.

My arm is literally on fire, and searing pain slams through me. I can't let Kud take me. I must reach the Heavenly Chest. But then, with an overpowering jerk, I'm yanked off the horse so quickly that Marc's hands slip from my waist.

"Tell Palk," I yell to Marc as I plummet into the void. "I won't give the orbs to Kud."

I'm falling.
Into darkness.
Into pain.
Into death.

CHAPTER 31

I awake with a jolt. Grotesque creatures leer down at me. I blink and realize they are merely paintings and that I'm lying on maroon silk sheets. Upside-down candles flicker from the sconces on the walls. Shadows flit across the mural of Kud standing on a mountain of bones.

I'm back in Kud's land. Back in my own room. I sit up, my arm still aching from being pulled off Chollima. I don't understand why Kud has kept me alive. I know it would be easier for him if he just killed me and used my dead body to do his bidding. Unless there is something more to his devious plan. The thought sends a shiver through me.

I swing my bare feet to the floor and startle. My clothes have vanished, replaced by a black *hanbok*. The material shimmers in the torchlight, and the full skirt billows out around me in an endless pile of material. My legs wobble as I stand and slide my feet into the black slippers on the floor next to me. A single lily rests on top of the slippers.

The fact that the slippers are exactly where they should be, as if someone knows I leave the bed on this side every day, makes my stomach roil. And then the memories of the fight tumble over me like a landslide. Anger boils within me at the knowledge that Grandfather and Kumar are now dead. I want to race to Kud's throne room and rip those revolting eyes out of his skull and feed them to his dogs.

Lilies represent death in Korea. This is Kud's vile way of reminding me of the deaths of those I love. I crush the lily in my fist. Tears trickle down my cheeks, and suddenly it's impossible to breathe.

But I can't lose it now. This time, more than any other, I need to focus. I take deep breaths, rubbing my palms to stop myself from digging my nails into them. I will force myself to rein in these emotions. I push aside the anger, because it does nothing other than feed Kud and make him stronger. I must prepare myself for what's ahead. For Marc's sake. For my dad's sake. For all of Korea's sake.

Slowly I walk over to my dresser and stare at myself in the shattered mirror. My hair has been brushed, and a section has been twisted into a bun. My brown eyes stare back at me. They look lost. Lonely. Angry.

My mouth is turned into a frown, and my cheeks are slightly flushed. I open my drawer, pull out Michelle's butterfly clip, and pin it into my hair. She's still alive in my heart, and I want her with me in the coming hours.

All around the mirror are Dad's origami creations, bright and colorful in this dark world of Kud's. I trace my fingers around their edges, just as I have done each morning I've lived in Kud's realm.

"I'm going to save you, Dad," I say. "I know you can't hear me. You probably don't even think I'm alive. But all of this is for you."

I bow my head and send up a prayer. I only hope God listens. Even in the shadows where I stand, I have to believe that he's been with me before and that he won't abandon me now. Not when I need him most.

Through the latticework around my door, two pairs of red eyes peer at me. Kud's bloodhounds. They've come to escort me. The carved wooden door creaks open. I turn to face the hounds. They snarl at me as usual, but this time their heads whip back and forth as if they are fighting against Kud's orders to not fling themselves at me and sink their teeth into my neck. I'm sure they are furious that I killed so many of them back at the port.

"Don't worry," I tell them in my most flippant tone. "I haven't forgotten my promise to kill you as well."

They growl and bark at me; white, frothing saliva drips from their jaws. Inside I cringe at their ferociousness, but I won't let them see how I truly feel. So I lift my chin and wave my hand for them to lead, and then I follow them into the fire-lined hallway. The heat singes my skin, and I have to tuck the folds of my dress in tightly to keep them from catching fire.

We wander through the long corridors and I take it all in once again, but this time I don't see this hole as a hopeless prison. Over the last few days I've survived one of Earth's most deadly tombs, guarded by mythological creatures I hadn't even known existed. If I can escape that, I tell myself, I can escape this. I walk out onto the winding bridge that connects my tower to the rest of the palace. There are no railings on either side, just the twisted stone walkway lined with trenches of fire. The hounds break apart, one moving before me and the other behind, since the bridge is too narrow for us to walk beside each other.

The first time I crossed this bridge, being so high up with the valley of bones probably a thousand feet below gave me vertigo. Now I'm used to it, or perhaps I don't care as much about plunging to my death. I've escaped death's grasp more times than I'd prefer to count.

The air is thick and smells like a mix of sulfur and lilies. It's a strange combination, but it's one that will be forever rooted in my memory.

We enter the main palace and head down another corridor that leads us to what I call the raindrop entryway. Drops of fire patter down from the inverted candles, and I grab the old shield I've planted by the doorway, holding it between myself and the rain of fire. I use it every time I pass this way. It's effective.

I stop at the top of the stairs leading down into the throne room. I'm not sure what I'd expected to see this time, but this was definitely not it. Long rows of soldiers line either side of the main path to the throne where Kud sits. He isn't dressed as Kud. He is Kang-dae because he knows it messes with my head.

Kud lounges on his throne, his chin propped up on his palm. His eyebrows rise when he sees me slowly tread down the marble stairs into the throne room. He's wearing black pants and a black silk tunic that's not quite buttoned to the top, as if he was too lazy to finish buttoning it. The chain of the Red Phoenix orb peeks out beneath his collar, and the thick silver ring flashes on his finger as he rubs the side of his face.

I turn away from Kud and walk toward the first soldier. Queasiness washes through my stomach as I recognize him. It's Kumar. His face is paler than death, and his eyes are dark pools. Hana is across from him. They don't move.

"Kumar?" I inch closer and peer into his face. "It's me. Jae Hwa."

He doesn't even acknowledge my existence. I snap my fingers in front of his face, and still he gives no response. I try the same with Hana. She merely cocks her head and gazes at me with those same creepy eyes that Kwan and Sang Min had. I look down the line of soldiers and see more Guardians.

This is worse than death for them. They are slaves to Kud, their spirits unable to find rest because their bodies now serve a master that they once did everything they could to stop.

I stumble backward, my chest heaving and my breath coming out in gasps. If Kud wants to hurt me, he certainly knows how.

I spin around so my back faces Kud. My hands shake as I cover my face with them, trying to block out the horrid reality before me. I know I need to pull myself together, but this is too much. It's more than anyone should be asked to bear. My wrist warms, and the Black Turtle's image flashes across my mind. A black form in a landscape of white.

Your legacy will be ours. The memory of his words echoes through me. Is this Korea's destiny? Dead soldiers following the orders of a god full of anger and chaos? No. Oh no.

Kud may know my weaknesses, but I know his, too. He's not the only one who can play mind games.

I take a deep breath and turn to face him. I give him an evil glare and point at Kumar, Hana, and the other fallen Guardians. "This is how you are trying to win me over?"

"You were planning to betray me. You gave the orbs to this worthless Guardian." He nods toward Hana.

I step closer, trying not to get creeped out by the long lines of soldiers who were once Guardians. Freshly dead. Freshly created.

"Don't act like this surprises you," I say. "You forced me to sign a contract and make my body serve you. Fine. But you will never force my heart to serve you." I wave at the men and women, silent and still as tombstones. "These are rotting bodies. They don't know what they do or why. You think that's greatness? It's not. It's cowardice."

I continue walking toward Kud. He shifts on his throne, watching me like an interested cat, not quite sure if he should strike or purr. The thought sickens me. I want him to feel. To suffer like I do now.

"You know what I hear?" I ask him, now standing at the foot of his throne. The snakes that writhe on its surface focus on me, their tongues snapping out, hungry and eager. "The dead are laughing. For you may control their bodies, but their spirits have left. They are free of you and your pain. You think you can rule this world. No. You will only destroy it. And then what? Nothing. You will rule empty corpses. You will have nothing but dust beneath your fingertips."

I step up onto the throne's platform and lean forward. "Ruler of dust. That is what you have become."

Swifter than a cat, he leaps up and grabs the front of my dress in his fist. His eyes flicker silver, a hint of his true self, and he lifts me off the ground, shoving me against the closest pillar. The wood splinters where my back smashes into it. I cry out, and my vision darkens. From the pain raging through me, I'm sure every bone in my back has been shattered. The only thing keeping me from crumpling to my knees is Kud's arm holding me up.

But we both know this is the Spirit World. I'll heal soon enough, and then he'll do it all over again. This isn't the first time we've gone through this charade.

Kud smiles, that devious smile of his. "As long as you are by my side, my most precious princess, I don't care who or what I rule."

His hand cups my chin and I fear he will kiss me, but instead he takes my hand, the one with the Black Turtle orb, and kisses my palm.

"Beautiful." He eyes my new orb. "And unexpected. Not what I imagined it to be."

"It's mine to control."

"Indeed." He steps away, still holding my hand, and pulls me with him. "I see Kwan and Sang Min didn't survive."

I make my back ramrod straight, determined not to let his watchful eyes read fear in my own. "They died fighting in the mausoleum. Or should I say they escaped?"

"And yet you survived."

"I always survive." Somehow I extricate my hand from Kud's. "I'm surprised you haven't killed me and taken control of the orbs yourself."

"Kill my beautiful princess? Never."

"Beautiful?" I laugh. "What do you know of beauty? You don't care about anything but death, power, and anger."

"True." He nods thoughtfully, as if no one has ever said such a thing to him before. "But then you have all those three things, too, do you not? I can see it in your eyes. I have heard that the eyes are the windows to the heart. Your heart is full of anger. And these hands." He recaptures my fingers and holds my palms up, tracing the lines on them. "They have hurt others. Over and over."

Then he slides one hand up my arm and fingers the chain of the orb at my chest. "And then there is the power that you hold. Yes, my princess. We are alike, the two of us. This is why I know we are meant for each other."

"No." I shake my head, but I can't deny his words. He's right. I'm all of this. And the thought of it weakens me to the core. What has become of me? I don't wish to be the girl he says I am. His words anger me.

A wry smile crosses his lips as if he has read my thoughts. He takes me in his arms, holding my hands out in a dancing pose. Then he spins me around and my skirts swoosh around me, swirling just as the despair and pain within me does. He's right. I am nothing of worth. How could I have listened to the Black Turtle or the Tiger of Shinshi and thought I was special or needed? They were wrong.

"No, I could never kill you. Such beauty must not be terminated," he says. "We are destined to live together for all of eternity."

This hardly makes me feel better. The thought of spending an eternity with Kud nearly makes my knees buckle. Living in this reeking, depressing land with a monster, pulled away from all I love—it's too much. It takes all of my power not to collapse to the floor in despair. Death seems the better option.

"You seem upset, my dearest. How about you take this"— he holds out an ancient brass key to me—"and open the door between your land and mine. And then I will release the spirits of your friends Kumar and Hana from my service."

He wants me to join Haemosu's old land, the land I now rule, to his own. I'm about to spit in his face, but then I pause. What if he's given me a way to escape? What if I can build up power there and unleash it against him? It's a risk, but I can think of no other options.

"How do I know you will keep your word?" I say. "You have a tendency to lie."

"No one understands me like you do." He chuckles and runs the key down my face and neck. "This is why I am so obsessed with you. I promise on your contract that I will release your friends if you open the door between our lands." The contract flashes and then burns on my arm. "My hounds will escort you."

Warily I study him, and then I snatch the key from his hand. Bae, the leader of the bloodhounds, and his sidekick stand by the door like sentinels.

The hounds lead me to a passageway I haven't entered since I first came into Kud's realm, bent on rescuing Marc. I hesitate at the threshold. I've always avoided this hallway because just the sight of it brings back memories of my failure to save Michelle. As if sensing my reluctance, Bae halts and glances back at me.

I clench my fists and push myself to step into the rounded hallway, focusing on Bae's mangy fur rather than the crimson engravings on the walls. Soon we come to a pile of bones littering the ground at the foot of a blazing red door. Bae motions with his head for me to enter, but when I reach out to pull on the knocker, electric sparks snap and crackle over the entrance. The door evaporates.

The ground also disappears, and I plummet through a sea of stars. The space between worlds. My arm flares into a blaze of bronze, and it hurtles me through the endless space until I find myself face-to-face with the *samjoko* symbol. I lift my hand, remembering how I once set the *samjoko* amulet into the golden plate. This time, though, I press my palm onto the plate. Golden light bursts around me, and I'm sucked through the door. The air shimmers as my feet land on solid ground.

I'm standing in Haemosu's old throne room.

Dust cakes the dragon throne and the pedestal holding the sculpture of the *samjoko*. Slowly, as if drifting in a dream, I stroll down the main pillared walkway past the dragon-tail footrest, past the long-handled fans, past the celadon pots. As my slippers touch the soiled ground, dust billows up and spirals around me, transforming into golden light. The beams in the rafters burst back into their vibrant reds, greens, and yellows. The ground rumbles. The land is waking up from a long sleep.

I take deep breaths, soaking up this world's power, and my steps become light and strong. After being in Kud's land, suppressed by his anger and the stifling air, it's like my lungs have opened up and I can finally breathe.

I emerge through the giant double doors and step into the courtyard, my *hanbok* skirts whipping around my legs. My eyes instantly seek the far end where the shattered and charred remains of the bamboo cage are scattered about. I grab the sides of my skirts and take off in a sprint to the debris pile. Once I reach it, I pick up a bamboo pole, running my palm over its smooth surface.

Remembering.

The fire. The dragon. The *samjoko*. Haemosu. But most of all, my victory. I cling to that memory, hoping it will empower me to defeat Kud.

"Oryonggeo," I whisper, calling to the five golden dragons that make up Haemosu's chariot. They are mine now, and I know I need them to complete my task.

Sure enough, the dragons answer, flying through the sky like threads of gold. One by one their sleek bodies land before me, their ruby eyes staring at me expectantly.

Master, they say as one in my mind. *Too long have you been absent.*

"I know," I say. "Kud has created a mess of things that will only get worse before it gets better."

The contract on my arm begins to burn. Kud is getting impatient.

"I need you to take me to the place where this key fits."

I hold up the key and debate whether to slip onto the back of one of the dragons. These creatures are wild, fierce, and temperamental. Before I have a chance to make up my mind, the five twist around and rise into the air, their beards swaying in the wind. I roll my eyes as they swirl above me, but instead of calling them back, I decide to test out my shape-shifting abilities and join them.

I lift my chin, studying the dragons, soaking in the warmth and sweet smell of the air. Then I close my eyes and spread out my arms, visualizing myself as one of them.

It happens, so swiftly that my legs buckle beneath me. I've barely touched the ground when my body is lifted by the transformation, and I twist around in the air, spinning like I'm being woven into a cocoon. My legs are yanked and stretched into a long, snake-like body, while my fingers curl before my eyes into four talons. Every bone snaps, and I'm reminded of the unbearable pain I felt when I morphed into a *qilin* in China. I cry out, and a stream of fire bursts from my mouth.

My vision widens, and suddenly every wooden beam, leaf, and blade of grass pops into perfect focus.

I shake my body, loving how my scales shimmer like sunlight, and then I shoot up into the air. I twist and writhe along the winds, and as I do, the other dragons soar to my side, flanking me. Joy surges through my golden body as I whip back and forth among the clouds, and I feel free . . . almost. Because the burn of the contract sears through my bloodstream, reminding me of Kud's power.

This way, the dragons tell me, and I follow.

We fly beyond the palace, past the lush fields, over the jagged mountains, and across the white-capped waves of the ocean. I remember this journey well. It's the same one that Palk took me on. The red divide looms before us, a red lava river splitting the Spirit World. The air grows hotter the closer we come to the divide, and the skies dim into a murky gray as ashes cascade like snow from dark clouds above.

You can turn back now, I tell the dragons. *What lies ahead is death and pain. I can't ask you to join me in the nightmare that I must face.*

I expect them to turn away, to abandon this mission, but they don't. Instead they continue at my side through the ash-ridden sky until a round door appears. Chinese symbols blaze from its center, ringed by a coil of snakes. This is Kud's symbol.

With my taloned claws, I slip the key into the center of the smoking keyhole. The pain from the contract rips through me so strongly that I nearly pass out.

"Who seeks the forgotten?" the smoke asks. "Who treads darkness's halls?"

"I, Jae Hwa Lee, ruler of this land."

"Yessss," the smoke hisses.

The door flings open. With a groan, a long wooden bridge shoots out from the door across the lava river and lands on top of the fiery ocean. The magma slides and bubbles against the wood, yet it doesn't burn. A heavy lump forms in the pit of my stomach as the finality of what I've just done hits me. My land is now one with Kud's.

This isn't the end, I promise myself. *It's the first step to overthrowing Kud.*

Yet, as the ashes sting my eyes and settle on my body, muting the glow of my scales, I can't help but wonder if I've finally become the pawn Kud has dreamed for me to be.

CHAPTER 32

I soar down the marble stairs into Kud's throne room. My dragons follow and then settle beside me as I shape-shift back to my human form. Kud is all smiles as he saunters to me and kisses my forehead. I touch his arm, smiling up at him, because what I'm about to do truly brings me joy.

"Beautifully done." He looks down at where my hand touches his arm, and his eyes warm. "And so you don't believe I won't keep my promises—"

He turns, and with a snap of his fingers, a black wind curls out of the eyes of Kumar and Hana. It swirls above their heads before dissipating into the air. Then their bodies crumple onto the floor.

And that's when I strike. I suck all the power from my land into my core, and then I draw out the power from the White Tiger and Black Turtle orbs. I press my palm against his chest, and his eyes widen as the realization of what I'm about to do flashes across his face. Then I unleash all the power straight at his heart. My hair flies about me, and my dress billows in the screaming wind. And for a moment it's just Kud and me, standing in a shimmering white whirlwind, in a fight for power.

My fight for life.

I'm so focused on destroying Kud that I don't notice at first when my arm with the contract begins rising on its own, blazing like the sun itself. Then I feel the pain and the shift in power. Kud shape-shifts before my eyes, morphing from his human form into the fierce Red Phoenix. Flaming beams radiate from the phoenix's eyes, and the power within me is sucked out through my contract, feeding into him. His wings stretch out and he opens his beak, releasing a haunting song. The world around me bleeds rivers of crimson.

I fall to my knees.

I have done everything I can. But it isn't enough.

And then it's over. I'm lying on the cold floor, gasping for air, while Kud looms over me in his human form. My dragons slide to my side, nuzzling me.

"Your betrayal hurts, my princess. Was my gift not enough? Did I not prove to you that I could be trusted?" Kud says, and then he draws me back into his arms and whispers into my ear. "Perhaps you will like the other gift I have for you, then."

I lift my chin, unwilling to let him believe that he could possibly please me, but my legs are jelly and I'm forced to lean on him for support.

Undaunted, he half carries me behind the row of dead warriors. And that's when my greatest fear becomes a reality. There in a titanium cage stands my dad. He's got his suit on, the tie dangling loose around his neck, the top two buttons of his shirt undone. He grabs the bars when he sees me. His mouth droops, and his eyes plead with me.

"Jae Hwa," Dad says. "I'm sorry I never believed you. I see now. I should've—" His voice breaks, and he covers his eyes with the back of his hand.

"No." I shake my head and back away, but Kud's tight grip holds me hostage. "Our contract says you will not touch my family."

"Who are you to speak of remaining loyal to a contract?" Kud clucks his tongue. "Besides, I realized how tough it must be for you to go all this time without seeing your father. So how about a little reunion, if you will."

"This isn't a gift." I spit out my words. "This is a punishment."

"It's all about perspective, my princess." Kud pushes a strand of loose hair behind my ear. "You behave, he lives. A constant visual reminder is just so much more powerful. Don't you think?"

"Absolutely not. Let him go right now."

"No. Palk has received my summons, and the time has come. But never fear, we're going to bring him along."

Kud lifts his arms, raises his face to the ceiling, and sighs. "I have waited a thousand years for this moment." Then he strides down the ranks of the soldiers lined up like the terra-cotta warriors back in China. "These last forty years have been the most difficult. I have been so close. So near. But without the other half of the orbs, the balance has always been in Palk's favor."

Kud spins around and bows slightly to me. I take a step back, not liking the look of pure thrill in his eyes. The sparkle and confidence of victory. "But then you came to me."

"You forced me."

"And brought me the seeker orb."

"You tricked me."

"And then went to a land out of my reach and brought me back the holder of time."

"To destroy you with it."

"Yes. To destroy Palk, Haechi, and all of his idiotic comrades."

A wind kicks up around us, and my hair blows about me. Darkness fills the folds of the wind, curling around me like sackcloth, rough and grinding. The warriors and my dad are sucked into the madness, funneling around Kud and myself in the windstorm. Kud strides toward me. I try to run, but my legs are pillars of stone. And then Kud stands before me, drawing me to him so that it's just the two of us in the center of the storm.

"It is time for the final battle."

CHAPTER 33

I'm standing in a wide, rocky valley. The mountains rise up into peaks around me, sharp as swords. A wisp of a cloud wafts around me, pulled by a sharp breeze that smells of summer and of things that belong in dreams. I'm drawn back to a day that feels like an eternity ago, when Marc and I hiked the Seoraksan Mountains. We raced the final leg, panting and laughing as we climbed the last peak. Thanks to Marc's smack talk, I could hardly climb the final steps, and Marc beat me to the top. He whipped off his shirt, jammed it on his walking stick, and stuck it into a crack in a rock. His shirt became his flag of victory. Despite the snow flurries that fluttered around us, he punched the air, whooping like a wild banshee.

"You're so going to get it for making me lose," I told him.

"The winner gets to choose the prize, remember?" He tugged one of my braids, and then he leaned in close and whispered into my ear, "I choose never-ending days like this. To climb every mountain peak in the world with you and only you."

The next thing I remember we were kissing, with me tucked into his arms and the heat of our passion warming us. It was heaven. The world faded and it was just the two of us standing on the mountain, snow falling over us like blossoms.

If only his wish had come true. If only everything could be so simple.

Beside me stands Kud, towering over me. He holds his scepter in one hand and the Red Phoenix orb in the other. Behind us, the dead warriors are lined up, perfect soldiers with blank eyes, slackened jaws, and matching gray clothes from head to toe. Any other day I would have rolled my eyes, but today I just feel the gnawing ache of fear.

The *gwishin* flitter around us, cackling in their ghostly glee, and on either side stand the *mool gwishin*. I shudder as I take in their empty faces. They are here for the death. They must smell it or taste it on their nonexistent lips.

Nothing good will come out of what is about to happen. I can feel it, the aching pain of sorrow that rushes from the two orbs I carry.

A streak of white light cuts across the field before us like a flying arrow. Then it explodes, filling the sky with stars and sun, all mixed into one dazzling blast. I cover my eyes, blinded by its intensity. The light rushes over the hillside until it collides with Kud's darkness. The two rise up in waves, rushing and frothing over each other, higher and higher. The ground trembles, and then the light and darkness dissipate in a rushing sound.

Standing across from us is Palk, dressed in a golden *hanbok*. His black beard is woven with streaks of golden light and stretches down to a peak on his chest. A crown sparkles on his head with glowing diamonds and gems. On his chest, light radiates from the symbol of the sun. His eyes are golden, and when they rest on me, I sense sadness.

I push against Kud's hold, desperate to join Palk. To tell him I never wanted this to happen. To ask him how to stop this madness and save us all. But I can't move. I'm locked down, the contract burning harder than it ever has before, rooting me to my spot.

Palk isn't alone. Behind him is a throng of immortals, all of them powerful in their own right. Haechi stands beside him, his horns glowing in Palk's wake. Samshin is there behind them on one side, holding a cane, a smile on her lips as she studies me.

On the peak above, the Bonghwang cocks its head to the side and aims its pointed beak at us, watching us with piercing, all-seeing eyes.

I recognize Bari standing slightly off from the others on a rockslide with King Daebyeol of the Underworld. She's wearing her usual white robes, which flutter in the breeze. She clutches her long spear, one end planted in the earth and the other pointing to the sky. Her hair is pulled back into a long braid, and her face looks harsher than I remember it ever being. She nods once, as if she's telling me that she may not be allowed to take sides, but she's with me in spirit.

And then I spot the Guardians of Shinshi, or the remnants of them. Mr. Han, the head of the Council of Shinshi, and Mrs. Byun are there, and so are Marc's dad, Dr. Grayson, and Jung. They each hold a sword and wear their brown robes. They wear no smiles. And the worry in their eyes scares me, shaking my resolve, and suddenly I wonder if Palk will come out victorious. It isn't good that they look this worried.

But all of these people aren't who I'm actually looking for. I'm searching for Marc, and I can't find him. Where is he? My heart starts beating hard, and that panic settles in. But then he comes up from behind Palk and Haechi. This time, he's holding both of the dueling dragon swords of General Yu-shin. He wears the ancient battle dress of the Koreans: leather pants and a breastplate with the Blue Dragon imprinted on it. A black band is wrapped around his brown hair. The scar on his face still stands out red along his jaw.

Then the clouds open, and a golden chest descends on two purple cords from the sky. Kud shifts beside me. Like the others, he is focused on the chest, but his eyes are filled with greed. I hear him sigh, and I wonder if this is the first time he's ever laid eyes on it.

The chest opens for Palk, and a burst of golden light radiates from it. Out soars the Samjoko. Its beak opens, and it sends out a battle cry. It flies before Palk's followers, beating its long wings. The group sends up a cheer, and the ground shakes from the power of it. Next, a burst of blue comes out, shooting into the sky like fireworks of blue stars. The Blue Dragon. I suck in a breath of awe. It too flies along the lines, reassuring the group until their faces no longer hold that worry and doubt. The Blue Dragon has huge, stag-like horns; scales that glitter like sapphires; and a jagged spike running along the top of its body.

Finally, the dragon settles in behind Palk with his wings tucked against himself, but he looks anything but calm. Unexpectedly, I hear the voice of the Blue Dragon in my head.

Jae Hwa, it tells me. *Your possession of two lost orbs cannot be chance. In every battle there is an opportunity to change everything. When that time comes, do not hesitate.*

I frown, unsure of what it means. How can I change everything? The dragon can't know that I have already tried and failed.

The last orb emerges in a burst of jade: the Chollima. The horse flies out, a twinkling glow of emeralds surrounding the snowy white creature as it beats its wings.

Hope surges through me. Perhaps Palk has a chance to succeed. If I can just make a break for it, I can reach the chest and hand over the orbs.

Behind me the dead soldiers have blank eyes, uncaring about the events before us. The ghosts continue with their laughing. I suppose that's the way of it for them. They don't care about death or loss. They have lived with it for eternity. Only the bloodhounds, frothing at the mouth, and the *kumiho*, snapping their sharp teeth and long tails, appear to care. They are hungry for the kill.

"Finally you gain the courage to face me," Kud says. "I would never have thought you had it in you."

"You hold our Guardians and Jae Hwa as prisoners," Palk says. "The orbs belong in the Heavenly Chest, not in your hands to destroy the purpose of the world."

"The purpose of the world is in the eye of the beholder," Kud says. "Is it not? Who are you to tell us how things are to be? Who are you to be keeper of the chest?"

"Hand them over!" Palk's voice booms like a thunderclap.

I try to move, but my feet are still planted to the ground. I pull back my sleeve, and the contract glows amid the swelling darkness around me. The murky mist that has been seeping out of Kud's robes has now gathered along the lines. Ravenous, it flicks out long tentacles, their ends forked like snakes' tongues.

My eyes lock with Marc's. I see no remorse in his gaze, only determination and something more. He presses his palm on his chest and bows his head ever so slightly. We are divided by lines that are beyond our powers, and yet ironically I've never felt closer to him than now. He knows my heart, and I know his. The world is about to crumble around us, but through the madness we still stand as one in our hearts.

It won't be enough, but that's okay.

I reach up and pull at the necklace hanging from my neck. The gold pendant feels smooth under my fingers.

I'LL FIND YOU IN THE DARKNESS

CHAPTER 34

Before me, Kud's tentacles clash with the light, and the two mix. Chaos erupts. The living-dead soldiers race forward, swarming all around Kud and me and then passing by us. Meanwhile, the Guardians of Shinshi and the mythological creatures race to meet the horde. I can't read Kud's expression, but I feel the gloating glee flowing off him like bands of laughter.

"Do not worry," he tells me. "Our time will come soon."

I close my eyes against Kud's voice. Its power sends a shiver through me, and I find my anger overwhelming me. Anger at him, at what he's done to my family and friends. But then I feel him pulling that anger away, like he's tugging on a thin cord wrapped around me and drawing me closer to him. My eyes pop open. The White Tiger orb hanging on my chest glows. Its white light shimmers around me. But instead of standing taller and feeling stronger as the orb's power flows through me, I find myself almost shrinking.

The light is being sucked away in a silky stream heading directly into the Red Phoenix orb in Kud's hand.

All around us, the dead ones are slaughtering the Guardians. Ancient swords clash, ringing like bells of doom. The cries of the dying join in, creating a melody of pain and suffering.

Palk has his arms lifted, light shining from his palms. Wherever the light hits, the dead ones falter and the ghosts and bloodhounds scream in agony.

King Daebyeol hasn't moved. His face is impassive, unaffected by the events unfolding. Samshin strolls among the dead tossing flowers over the fallen Guardians. At each flower's touch, a warrior is revived. The flowers must have healing power.

Marc races before us, swinging his dueling swords in perfect arcs. The dead ones are unable to match his swings, so they abandon him and attack Mr. Han with a war-cry howl. Mr. Han fights back, but they swarm him in seconds until he's buried beneath a pile of them. I fight against Kud's bonds as I watch his creatures rip Mr. Han's flesh apart. Bae shakes his head, blood flying from his jowls, and howls in victory.

Then, as one, the entire pack swivels their red eyes and faces Marc. It's as if Kud has ordered them to kill Marc.

I turn to Kud. "You promised not to hurt him," I say in a growl.

Kud laughs. "And you betrayed me."

My arm flings up to my face on its own accord, and a certain line in the contract burns red. Amazingly, I'm now able to read the ancient Chinese. It reads, "I, Lee Jae Hwa, will not engage with humans from my previous life. I, Lee Jae Hwa, will not attack my master."

The anger surges within me, and I struggle to stem the flow as more of my power seeps into Kud's orb. I clench my hands, furious that I'm playing directly into Kud's plan. He's using my anger and hatred to become more powerful.

I can't listen to his lies anymore. I must block out Kud and focus on Marc, Palk, and the light before me. It's the only way.

Somehow I take a step forward. And another. Each step is like dragging through mud spiked with knives tearing into my skin. But I can't stop. I won't let Kud control me any longer. This is my life, and I'm living it for those I love.

But it's not enough. I'm too slow, and the power that Kud has over me is too strong. The hounds break into a full sprint, loping directly at Marc, their jaws open and teeth bared, ready to tear him to shreds.

"You belong only to me," Kud says. "I will not share you."

I scream, calling out Marc's name. "Look behind you!" I shout, but it's useless. The field is too full of roars, clashing swords, and screams.

Then I see the Samjoko flying above, beating its long wings. It screeches out a battle cry, and its diamond eyes focus on me as if it's telling me to come. The anger I once held falls away, and I focus completely on the Samjoko's call.

I take another step closer, stumble, and face plant into the ground. My stupid dress tangles around my legs, but I grab on to the earth and claw myself forward across the bloodstained grass. I scream in agony as my arm burns.

The contract tells me to pull back. But my heart tells me I can't live to watch Marc be torn to shreds. I'd rather be ripped in half than witness the destruction of Palk's forces.

The glow of the White Tiger orb fades, and I'm lost in darkness. I'm not sure if I've passed out or if Kud has won. I call on the Black Turtle orb. It's ready this time, as if it's burning to be released. Once again the black surface crackles with a tempest of glacial light. It ruptures, showering the valley in an icy blue, freezing everything into place.

Time stops.

Then I hear the White Tiger and Black Turtle speaking to me, whispering in the polar light.

Just a little farther.

Reach your hand out.

I drag my body forward, but as I do so, something pulls me back. I cry out in pain. I'm losing the battle.

Then I hear Palk's voice rush over the valley, seeping into my bones, clinging to the air, racing across the ground: "What was before will be no more."

I'm not sure what those words mean, but I feel as if I've seen them or heard them somewhere before. If only I could figure it out. There's a shift in the valley, and I know we've all been intimately changed by Palk's words. The pull on me lessens, and I realize that Kud's focus is being drawn elsewhere. But my control over the Black Turtle orb is weakening, my grasp of its hold on time slipping.

Another step.

Another.

And then in the cobalt shadows emerges the dark form of the Samjoko, its diamond eyes cutting through the darkness to rest on me. It waits. I reach out through the impossible distance between the darkness and the light. And then I'm stumbling over the edge, the horizon of hope.

The Samjoko's feathers are softer than silk as I caress them, but its muscles beneath are iron. Its body is massive, larger than a full-grown man.

Help me, I speak to its mind. It's the first time I've ever been able to do that. *I must save Marc.*

Come, the Samjoko says.

I open my arms, drawing myself into the Samjoko. My skin pulls, my bones pop, and my knees buckle. Indigo-blue feathers and diamonds swirl around me in a funnel until we are one. The contract dulls to a low throb, and I release my hold on the Black Turtle orb. The air shimmers and the icy blue blanket washes away like a roaring wave. I smile. While the valley has been frozen in time, I have secretly shape-shifted into the Samjoko.

I beat my wings and rise, momentarily free of the chaos below. A red beam cuts through the darkness, roving, searching. Then Kud roars in fury from his mound. He can't find me. My laughter screeches through the air.

There isn't time for celebration, though. The Blue Dragon and the Tiger of Shinshi are battling a troupe of *imoogi,* while the Bonghwang and Chollima hold off the *gwishin* horde.

I cock my head until I find Marc, surrounded by Kud's bloodhounds. I narrow my sharp eyes until I pinpoint Bae, the leader of the Bulgae. Marc is holding him by the muzzle, fighting for his life. I cry out to the wind and sky and nose-dive straight for the group. The air shivers over my wings as I hurtle down. I reach out my talons, remembering how I ripped them through Haemosu. I will do this and more with Bae.

I plunge and dig my diamond talons into Kud's lead hound and heave him off Marc with the force of my plummet to the earth. Then I smash my beak into Bae's eyes. He runs away, howling. I continue in this way, ripping one hound after the next to shreds.

Wearily, Marc stumbles to his feet and joins me in the battle, but I feel my own body failing. I can't hold on to the Samjoko and fight any longer. These last few days have finally taken their toll on me and my body.

I can't hold on, I tell the Samjoko.

I have you, the Samjoko says.

I feel the Samjoko taking over. Its power surges through its muscles, and it calls out across the expanse. We fly up and then dive back down, even more powerful than before. Marc's sword arcs through the air while I swoop around him in a whirlwind of feathers until the Bulgae are nothing more than a mound of rotting flesh.

Once the last of the hounds lies still, its sick howls forever silenced, I flutter down to rest beside Marc, towering over him. He plunges his sword into the ground and leans on its hilt, panting. His clothes are caked in black blood, and his arms are bleeding.

"Thank you," he tells me.

I'm about to release my hold on the Samjoko when, from the corner of my eye, I spy Bae rushing at me. I had neglected to finish him off, content to let him run blind and injured. I should have remembered his insane ability to smell.

He dives at me, paws stretched out, jaws open wide. I swivel my neck around and plunge my beak into his head. But I'm not fast enough. His teeth sink into my wing.

Leave! the Samjoko screams in my mind. *His poison will kill you.*

The Samjoko kicks me out, and I fly through the air, landing with a thump on the ground next to Marc. My stomach heaves, and I barely have time to roll over before I throw up. The sky spins before me, and I can't seem to breathe as my body goes into convulsions from the rapid shape-shifting.

"Jae!" Marc hovers over me, holding my face between his palms. "How? I don't understand."

I twist my head to see a pile of feathers lying on the ground beside me, still and cold. I reach out and feel a wing.

No.

"No!"

I wail and claw for the Samjoko, but it's still as stone.

CHAPTER 35

Marc draws me to him as I sob on the battlefield. All around us, creatures battle and die. This is not how it was all supposed to happen. I was supposed to make it back to the chest and return the artifacts. It seemed a simple task.

The shadows grow, falling over the valley like death.

"Jae!" Marc yells. "The chest. We must return the orbs!"

An *imoogi* sails over and begins to circle above us. Then it opens its mouth and rains down fire. Marc and I dive away just as the air behind us ignites into a bloom of flames. I scramble to my feet, and the two of us take off running toward the chest at full speed.

Finally, I stumble up to it and throw my body over the golden box. I want to scream in joy that after all of this, every impossible moment, I can return the orbs to their rightful place. Slowly I pull off the White Tiger orb from around my neck. It's heavy in my hands. With a sense of sadness I rest it in the bottom of the chest, whispering my good-bye.

"Hurry!" Marc yells beside me.

A black horned beast with white dots crawling over its body gallops across the plain, its orange eyes glaring straight at us. I remember this beast. It showed up at my apartment, and Haechi had to fight it off.

It roars at Marc and the white dots spring to life, leaping off the beast's body and skittering toward Marc and me. Haechi comes bounding over to join us, roaring like a lion.

Quickly I rip off the Black Turtle bracelet and place it beside the white orb. The bracelet twists and curls until it is a rock once again, rugged and plain. The black and white orbs lie beside each other, reminding me of the yin and the yang, complete opposites that at the same time complete each other.

I hold my breath, waiting, expecting.

But nothing happens. If anything, the darkness seems even darker and wider, a mass of intertwining red and black, anger and endless agony.

"Why doesn't it work?" I scream my words, but no one responds. They are all fighting for their lives.

The words of the Blue Dragon fly back to me: *When the time comes, do not hesitate.*

There's just one problem: I don't understand what I've done wrong. Fear overwhelms me. Kneeling, I sag against the side of the chest, tears streaming uncontrollably down my face. Have all my efforts been for nothing?

Then a cool cord lashes my ankles, curling around them and yanking me to the ground. Two tentacles reach inside the chest and pull out the two orbs. My heart drops into the pit of my stomach, and I dive for the orbs, desperately trying to get them back. My body scrapes across the dirt as one of Kud's tentacles tows me back to him. I dig in to the ground, but it's pointless.

I'm dragged up to stand beside Kud, his tentacles woven tight around every part of my body except my hands.

"This is our moment, my princess," Kud says. His eyes shine bright silver, and his face glows in the Red Phoenix orb's light. It's the first time I can remember seeing him actually look happy. "I could not have done this without you. Once you see the full impact of our combined powers, you will never regret choosing me."

The battle rages around us. The sky is molten, a mix of crimson and black. But there's an even greater battle in my heart. I will never choose *him*. I don't want to be standing here beside him. My bindings constrict around me, but I still struggle against them, tugging and yanking. Then the two orbs, the Black Turtle and the White Tiger, are lifted up with his tentacles and thrust into my hands.

I'm confused. Why would he give me back the orbs? But then it all becomes sickeningly clear. They still belong to me, not him. And when I hold them, I am more powerful than I would be if I were dead. The orbs begin to glow, radiating their iridescent light around me. But instead of shooting their light out across the battlefield, they beam all of their brightness into Kud's Red Phoenix orb.

And just like that, the balance is tipped. Kud's power grows as all of the power of my two orbs is drawn to him. Anger bubbles within me as I watch the *gwishin* overwhelm Chollima.

Kud glances at me. A grin stretches across his face.

Weakness pulls at me, and everything is starting to grow hazy. I'm still weak from using both orbs in Kud's land, and even though this valley is drenched in the winds of the Spirit World, I'm fading. If I hadn't been bound so tightly and held up by Kud, I would surely be lying on the ground. It's then I realize that I'm still very human. I don't know how much longer I will be able to last.

As if he senses my weakening, Kud hauls Dad over, cocooned in the mummified tentacles. Dad's face is ashen, but when he sees me, it brightens. Kud expects that seeing Dad will make me angrier. That has been true in the past, but not today. Instead, an overwhelming sadness drapes over me.

"Dad!" Tears flow down my face. "I'm so sorry. I tried. I wasn't strong enough."

"No," Dad says. "You have been and even now are. You have made both your mother and me so proud. If I am to die today, I want it to be with you beside me, just as you were with your mother."

My throat tightens. I don't want to think about sitting beside her bed as her body grew cold, and I definitely don't want to live through that pain again. I've done everything, everything to keep Dad safe, and I've failed. And now I'm standing here, feeding a monster and destroying all that I believe in.

"Live a life worth dying for, right?" he says. It's another one of Dad's motivational mantras. "We all die. And in the end, it's what we've done with our life that matters."

Dad is crying now, too. He nods to the two orbs that I'm holding in my hands. "Light and darkness, the beginning and the end, life and death."

"This is not the time to falter," Kud says and spins to us. "Motivation might serve you better."

The orbs' power has lessened because I'm not angry enough, and so I'm not feeding Kud's power. There's also the fact that I'm too weak, too human.

But these things are irrelevant to Kud. Nothing will stop him from making sure I do whatever he wishes. He raises his spear over Dad. I should fight back or cry out in anger.

But I don't. Instead, all I can do is look at the pride on Dad's face. It confuses me. Here I am, the reason for his death—for all the deaths—standing before everyone with my faults exposed. But those don't matter to him, I realize. He sees and loves me for who I am, including all of my faults. Kud lifts his spear back and plunges it into Dad's arm.

"No!" I scream, realizing that Kud means for Dad to have a slow, horrible death. It's the only way to truly make me angry.

But then Dad's words vibrate through me: *Light and darkness, the beginning and the end, life and death.*

There's something in those words. They shift through me, awakening an understanding. The light from the orbs in my two palms trickles out toward Kud, weaker now. The tentacles keep the orbs tightly wrapped in my palms. What if I brought the beginning and the end together? What if I restored the balance of the two? I think about the yin yang gate in Bari's world, the two sides ripped apart. What if it's unity that must be repaired?

A whole, made complete.

And then I look over and see Palk standing across the valley from me, a bright light amid the darkness. A smile spreads across his face as if he knows exactly what I'm thinking.

"What was before will be no more," I whisper.

At my words, Kud turns his silvery eyes to stare at me in horror. Just as Palk has seen my revelation, so has Kud. He screams a bloodcurdling cry, but it's too late.

With all of my strength, I smash the two orbs into each other. An explosion erupts from their core, and they fuse into one orb. Clarity shoots through me. They *are* the yin and the yang. The first and the last. The light and the darkness.

The orbs were not meant to be separate entities. They were meant to be brought together and merged into one complete self. Now they are whole.

Kud's spear falters as my orbs draw their light back into themselves. They sparkle like a star, blinding me with their dazzling brightness. The sparkles begin spinning around the orbs, rotating faster and faster.

The Red Phoenix orb pulls away from Kud's chest, drawn like a magnet to the single star I'm still holding. With a crash, it collides with the yin yang and is absorbed into the glow.

Then the fallen bodies of Chollima, the Samjoko, and the Blue Dragon sail across the valley and merge into the orbs. Finally, all six orbs have found one another and are once again united.

This is the knowledge I had been missing, the knowledge that had been lost. The black and white orbs needed to begin the process of unification, and that could only be done when all the orbs were present.

Together, their light shines even greater. Slowly they rise, lifting above my head so that my hands are stretched out. In awe, I gaze at their beauty. The orbs are a rainbow swirling through itself, a perfect melody. I try to let go of them, but they have me gripped in their hold.

Kud screams in anger and rushes at me, but the world tilts beneath my feet. His tentacles loosen their hold on Dad and me. Dad sags to the ground, bleeding heavily, while I stagger, barely able to stand beside him.

The winds kick up, circling the orbs faster and faster above me. My *hanbok* whips in the growing whirlwind, and the rest of my hair untangles from its bun.

Kud jerks to a stop, studying me with those silver eyes beneath his black hood.

"You have destroyed the Spirit World's connection!" Kud says.

"No." Palk's voice booms across the valley. "She has reunited the Koreas physically and spiritually. The war between North Korea and South Korea is over, just as our war is complete."

Kud's robes shudder around him. Then the glittering air stretches out, weaves around him, and sucks him into the orbs. The winds expand, curling around all of the creatures and immortals, and begins sucking them into the orbs as well. It happens so quickly, I don't have time to think, question, or even say good-bye.

The entire valley swirls like a kaleidoscope of light, drawing the entire Spirit World inside. Finally everything has been sucked into the orbs except Mr. Grayson, Marc, Dad, Jung, Haechi, and Palk.

"Our work is complete for now," Palk says. "We must return to another time and another place. Haechi, you will stay as a reminder that the Spirit World is real and true. Stay vigilant and watchful to keep evil at bay."

And with those words, he is drawn into the glowing star. It lifts into the sky. I, too, am drawn up. I can't let go; the star has its hold on me.

I am also a part of the Spirit World. My silvern sheen has always been a testament to that.

"Dad!" I scream.

Dad struggles through the winds to reach me and grabs hold of my leg. The orbs waver, and I realize their hesitation: he is human. But it's not enough; the pull is too great, and I am lifted off the ground. Still, he holds on, blood streaming down his arm from his shoulder wound.

"You have to let go, Dad!" I yell at him over the winds. "Please."

He cries in pain, and his arms slip from my leg. I look down to say good-bye, and I see Marc racing across the valley, calling out my name. He leaps up and grabs me, circling his arms around my core. We are frozen there, hovering between worlds. The orbs tug at me, but Marc's grip only tightens.

"I won't let you go," he says. "I let you slip from my hands on Chollima. I won't let it happen again."

"You have to," I say, feeling my body slipping from his. "The force is too strong."

"Never." He grunts from the effort. "Not all of your humanity is gone. I can see it. You belong here. With me."

The contract in my arm burns once again. Then I see blazes of bronze light streaming up into the orbs above, pulling and tearing away from me. And as they do, my grip on the orbs loosens until finally my fingers slip from the orbs' hold.

I throw my arms around Marc, and the two of us tumble back to earth. Above, the sky explodes in a burst of fireworks, and then a hole opens, revealing stars and endless universe. The lands of the Spirit World flash before my eyes: an emerald glade where the White Tiger roams; a bamboo forest where the dragons chase one another, weaving through the golden stalks; a field of lilies where Bari stands holding her spear, a hint of a smile on her face; a wide blue sky where the Samjoko beats its wings; the Red Phoenix perched on a jagged mountaintop beside the Black Turtle, finally free of Kud's clutches; and above it all Palk rides the Blue Dragon, keeping watch over the realm.

I don't want the vision to end. I want to see all of it, but the colors stream into the gap and close it up, leaving behind an auburn sunset and clouds gilded with memories of the past.

My arms are still wrapped around Marc's as I stare into the sky, wishing Grandfather could be here in this moment. Perhaps he is as he watches from the heavens. Marc runs his hand up and down my arm where the contract once was. It tingles, and a hint of a scar lingers.

"You're free," he says.

I should be thrilled. This is what I've always wanted, isn't it? But deep within me there's an emptiness.

Marc kisses me. I cling to him, my face wet with tears, and his kiss drowns out the pain of the loss of what once was.

And then from the clouds above a single raindrop falls, landing in my palm. The water is all the colors of the rainbow. It soaks into my skin, and warmth spreads through my body. It's as if the Spirit World is reminding me it hasn't forgotten who I am or what I've done.

Slowly the two of us stand, clinging to each other. Jung, Mr. Grayson, and Dad hobble over to us. There are tears and blood, and yet we are alive. It is a miracle.

The others begin to move about the field, gathering up the bodies of the fallen Shinshi, but Marc and I can't seem to leave each other's arms for fear the spell will be broken and I'll be dragged back into the madness of what once was.

My eyes look up to the ridge of the hills where Haechi stands, outlined by the sunset. His horn glistens in the golden light, and his fur and scales blaze as if they've caught on fire. His gaze rests on me. He bows his head once before turning and bounding away.

I lean my head against Marc's chest, listening to the thud of his heartbeat. It's the sound of life and love.

I'm ready to live. To love. And to believe in the impossible.

GLOSSARY

ajumma—woman older than you

ajusshi—man older than you

annyeong kyeseyo—good-bye

appa—daddy

baozi—Chinese steamed bun filled with vegetables or meat

Black Turtle—guardian of the north and of rain

Blue Dragon—guardian of the east and of the clouds

Bonghwang—mythological bird with the beak of a rooster, face of a swallow, forehead of a fowl, neck of a snake, breast of a goose, back of a tortoise, hindquarters of a stag, and tail of a fish

Bulgae—Kud's bloodhounds

bulgogi—Korean dish with grilled meat

Chollima—winged horse

dong-gyeol—freeze

duel—two

General Yu-shin—famous Korean general during the Silla Dynasty

goong dae—quiver for arrows

Guardians of Shinshi—ancient sect of warriors dedicated to protecting Korea

guzheng—Chinese zither instrument with eighteen strings

gwishin—ghost

Haechi—legendary creature resembling a lion; fire-eating dog; guardian against disaster and prejudice

Haemosu—demigod of the sun

hana—one

hanbok—traditional Korean dress

hangul—the Korean alphabet

haraboji—grandfather

imoogi—half-dragon that must wait a thousand years to become a real dragon; some are good and others are evil

kalbi—grilled beef or pork

kamsahamnida—thank you

kim (gim)—dried seaweed sheets

kimbap—Korean dish of steamed white rice and other ingredients rolled in sheets of dried seaweed and served in bite-sized slices

King Daebyeol—ruler of the Underworld

Koguryo Kingdom—ancient Korean kingdom located in the present-day northern and central parts of the Korean Peninsula

komo—aunt on the father's side

Kud—god of darkness

Kukkiwon—the headquarters for Tae Kwon Do

kumiho—fox-tailed female shape-shifter

mool gwishin—ghost of one who drowned

no-rae-bong—room for singing karaoke songs with friends

Oryonggeo—Haemosu's chariot, drawn by five dragons

pagoda—temple or sacred building, typically a many-tiered tower

Palk—sun god and founder of the realm of light

pixiu—Chinese mythological creature that resembles a lion and wards off evil spirits

Princess Yuhwa—demigoddess of the willow trees

qilin—Chinese unicorn with antlers

Red Phoenix—guardian of the south and of fire

samjoko—three-legged crow; symbol of power and the sun

Samshin—goddess of life and childbirth

Seoraksan—national park in South Korea

set—three

sinbunjeung—identification card

taotie—Chinese mythological creature with no body; consumes the living whole

Tiger of Shinshi—protector of the Golden Thread that ties and binds the Korean people throughout time

Triads—ancient sect of warriors dedicated to protecting China

White Tiger—guardian of the west and the winds

xie xie—thank you in Chinese

yo—Korean mattress that easily rolls up

Yonsei University—one the most prestigious universities in Korea

yuan—basic monetary unit for China

zhulong—Chinese mythological creature that has a human's face and a snake's body

ACKNOWLEDGMENTS

To my Heavenly father for always being with me in the darkest of nights and in the brightest of days.

Thank you to my lovely and faithful readers of the Gilded series! I love your e-mails and notes of encouragement. You are the best.

To Cliff Nielsen for another blow-my-mind cover.

It's hard to truly show my gratitude in a few lines, but I'm incredibly thankful to the publishing team at Skyscape for their support and working so hard on *Brazen* and the entire Gilded series. A special thanks to Courtney Miller for her constant encouragement. To Andrew Keyser and Tyler Stoops for all of their marketing efforts to get my books into the hands of readers. And to Chris Henderson-Bauer, my copyeditor, for making my words shine. To my proofreaders, Mary Tod and Monique Vescia, who are masters of grammar.

A million thanks to the MiG Writers—Kate Fall, Susan Laidlaw, Andrea Mack, Debbie Ridpath Ohi, Carmella VanVleet—for always being there for me!

To my fellow ninjas! Jessie Humphries, Lori Lee, and Meredith McCardle. Here's to road trips, Google hangouts, and overall shenanigans.

Thanks, Amy Parker, Vivi Barnes, and Tara Gallina, for putting up with my crazy texts and exclamation marks. Can't wait for our next adventure—creepy mirrors, videotaping in the bushes, french-fry fights, and all.

A big shout-out to my ever-supportive critique partners, Beth Revis and Casey McCormick, who have been amazing through this entire series. Your spot-on critiques have been invaluable and I'm so thankful to you for your lightning-fast reads and pure awesomeness.

To my rock-star agent, Jeff Ourvan, for listening to all my ideas and keeping me focused. I'm grateful for your wisdom and expertise!

A heartfelt thanks to Miriam Juskowicz, my editor, who is awesome in every way. What an incredible adventure publishing this series has been and I'm so glad to have taken it with you!

I could not have written this book without the support of my family: Mom, Dad, Julianne, David, and Cassia. You guys mean everything to me.

Hugs to Caleb and Luke for being my daily inspiration. Thanks for your help with the terra-cotta warrior scene. I hope it's how you imagined it would be. I love you!

Finally to Doug for putting up with this crazy dream of mine and helping make it a reality. I love you more and more every day.

ABOUT THE AUTHOR

Christina Farley was born and raised in upstate New York. As a child, she loved to explore, which later inspired her to jump on a plane and travel the world. She taught at international schools in Asia for ten years, eight of which were in the mysterious and beautiful city of Seoul, Korea, which became the setting of the Gilded series. Currently she lives in Clermont, Florida, with her husband and two sons—that is until the travel itch whisks her off to a new unknown.